AN IRRESISTIBLE KISS

Jake caught Elizabeth's arm, halting her when she reached for the knob on the door to her room.

She stiffened at his touch.

Jake sighed. "You're mad at me."

"No. I'm not mad." Her sigh echoed his. "I'm tired and I want to go to bed."

"So do I." His low voice reflected the blue velvet quality of his eyes. "The damn thing is, Liz," he murmured, moving closer to her, "I want to go to bed with you."

Elizabeth's lips parted on a shocked gasp at his bluntness.

Jake seized the moment—and her mouth.

With an unnerving immediacy, she was caught up in the sensuous web he had spun around her that morning. His arms encircled her, drawing her trembling body to the hardening reality of his chest, his thighs, his . . .

Elizabeth's pulse danced to the drumming rhythm of her heartbeat, pounding out her need for him.

Surrendering to the erotic sensations, she raised her hands to his head, holding him to her with fingers speared through his hair.

He was devouring her with his mouth.

Tension, blatantly sexual, sang along the connecting live wires of her nervous system, bringing her to vibrant, glorious awareness . . .

Books by Joan Hohl

COMPROMISES

ANOTHER SPRING

EVER AFTER

MAYBE TOMORROW

SILVER THUNDER

NEVER SAY NEVER

SOMETHING SPECIAL

MY OWN

Published by Zebra Books

ANOTHER SPRING

JOAN HOHL

Zebra Books
Kensington Publishing Corp.

http://www.zebrabooks.com

ZEBRA BOOKS are published by

Kensington Publishing Corp.
850 Third Avenue
New York, NY 10022

Zebra and the Z logo Reg. U.S. Pat. & TM Off.

First Printing: March, 1996
10   9

Printed in the United States of America

Prologue

It was over.

Head bowed, eyes closed, her arms around the shaking shoulders of her two daughters, Elizabeth Leninger heard the solemn voice of her pastor, the Reverend Mark Hallock, as he intoned the final benediction.

Her eyes were dry; Elizabeth had done her weeping for long agonized hours in private, as she had done her silent railing, angrily condemning her husband for leaving her on her own. Even though their union had never reached the heights of passion, she had loved him, given her youth to him, borne his children, and been faithful to him—still he had left her.

Her girls, Ella and Sally, seated on either side of her, wept quietly within the protective embrace of their mother. Seated next to Ella on the row of folding chairs placed in a line before the gravesite for the convenience of the family was Elizabeth's mother, her eyes also dry; the elder Sally had also chosen to weep in privacy. Not so Elizabeth's mother-in-law. Seated to the other side of young Sally, she sobbed pitifully and loudly.

"Elizabeth, if there is anything more I can do . . ." Reverend Hallock's voice trailed away; he, better than most, knew there was nothing more anybody could do. Elizabeth's husband, Richard Leninger was dead at age forty, the victim of a massive heart attack. His survivors had little choice but to grieve for a period, then go on with their respective lives.

"Thank you, but I . . ." Elizabeth raised her head to offer him a smile of gratitude, and an invitation. "You will come back to the house?"

Mark Hallock's expression revealed his feelings of frustration and compassion, the frustration experienced by many of the cloth for the meager comfort they could give at moments like these, the deep compassion he felt for the loss suffered by this lovely, still young woman and her two teenage daughters.

"Yes, for a little while." His smile, though faint, betrayed the youthful outlook of the aging cleric. "I have to come back with you, you see. My wife is there."

"I know." Elizabeth's smile lost a little of its strain. "She's been a wonderful help." She drew a quick breath, and released it on a sigh at hearing the sobs of Sally's grandmother. "If you would," she murmured. "It might help if you were to say a few words to Richard's mother."

"Certainly." He gave her hand a reassuring squeeze, bent low to murmur something to young Sally, then moved on to the older woman who was sobbing noisily into a lacy handkerchief.

"Are you ready to leave, Elizabeth?"

Elizabeth turned to gaze over her daughter's bent head, and into the gentle, understanding eyes of her mother. "Yes, in a moment." Lowering her head to Ella's, she said, "Come, darling, you must be strong for me now. I may need your help with Sally."

Sniffing, blinking, Ella looked up. The wounded look in her soft brown eyes tore at Elizabeth's heart; Ella's eyes were so like Richard's.

"I suppose we must." Ella drew in a ragged breath. "Mustn't we?" she asked, her reluctance to approach the closed, elevated casket evident in her tone.

"Yes." Elizabeth smiled at her older daughter, before sliding her arm away from Ella's shoulders and turning to her younger child. "Come along, dear," she murmured.

Sally shook her head and pressed back against the metal chair. "I . . . I don't want to," the fifteen-year-old protested, staring in horror at the casket. "Mom . . . Mom, they're going to put Daddy in the ground!"

"No . . ." Elizabeth paused to gather her composure before going on. "Sally honey, Daddy isn't in there. You must believe that, wherever he is, Daddy is all right and is looking out for us." Elizabeth wasn't sure she herself believed in an afterlife, but she had to comfort the child, ease her burden as best she could. "Someday, hopefully a long, long time from today, you'll see him again. But for now, we have to go on. Daddy would want that."

Elizabeth was in sympathy with the trepidation evinced by her daughters in approaching the canopied casket, touching it, removing one perfect rose from the spray adorning the matte, gunmetal silver lid. And she was grateful for the assistance of Ella, who suddenly appeared mature beyond her eighteen years as, whispering encouragement, she moved around her mother to offer support to her younger sister.

Elizabeth's heart swelled with pride for her girls, for their control and demeanor under stress. She herself hated having to perform the time-honored ritual. But appearances had to be maintained, for if they weren't, she would never hear the end of it from Richard's mother. As it was, Elizabeth feared there would be something not quite up to the standards rigidly adhered to by the elder Ella Leninger.

Elizabeth knew that she would somehow endure the rituals, her mother-in-law's complaints, the shock and trauma suffered by her daughters, and the aftermath of a death in the family, picking up the pieces and getting on with life.

Suppressing a sigh, she reached forward to touch the casket, but avoided looking at it by gazing out over the beautifully manicured grounds of the cemetery.

In a deliberate escape from the pain of the

here and now—the overpowering scent of the masses of flowers, the hard reality of the gleaming casket—she ran a mental check of the chores still before her.

What Elizabeth longed to do was creep away with her girls, seclude them and herself in their darkened house, and submerge all thought in the depths of healing slumber.

Instead, she would continue to play out the rituals, returning to her home to greet and feed those who stopped by, and to accept the condolences kindly offered. A surprisingly large number of friends and of Richard's co-workers had attended the funeral, many of whom had indicated their intentions of coming to the house.

Elizabeth knew that she would somehow deal with the follow-up necessities: the legalities involved concerning Richard's will, his investments, his insurance; the chore of clearing out the business-related papers and documents in the desk in the den; and the heart-wrenching task of sorting through his clothing and personal effects.

The mere thought of facing what was to come in the days and weeks ahead left her feeling weary and drained. After three days with too many details needing her attention, and too few hours in which to attend to them, followed by three nights with only snatches of rest and sleep, she was teetering on the edge of exhaustion—and depression.

Sally gripped her hand, stifling a sob. Elizabeth refocused her mind on the present. Sufficient unto the day . . . The adage ran through her mind, calming her racing thoughts. She would do what had to be done—when it had to be done. She could do no more. A scene of peace and spring green was spread before her outwardly composed gaze.

Spring had always been Elizabeth's favorite season. But this seemingly endless spring day was tearing her apart inside.

The brilliant sunshine hurt her eyes.

The mild breeze hurt her tear-sensitized face.

But the bright yellow blossoms on the overgrown, untrimmed forsythia bushes hurt most of all.

A sigh wrenched its ragged way from her aching throat as a lost little cry whispered inside her head:

What in God's name will I do with the rest of my life?

One

His presence had an electrifying effect on the gathering. The group, male and female, young and not so young, had come to the conference room on the University of Pennsylvania campus to attend a workshop on creative writing sponsored by a local writers' organization.

The arrival of the world-famous author had been a complete and unexpected surprise. His name and face, instantly recognized by every person in attendance, caused a ripple of excited murmurs the instant he crossed the threshold into the spacious room.

Jake Ruttenburg.

In the flesh, he looked even better, more ruggedly handsome than in the photograph that appeared on the dust jackets of his hardcover novels and on the inside flap of the back covers of his mass-market paperbacks. As in that photo, his attire was casual but classy: pearl gray pants, red pinstriped white shirt, charcoal sport coat, no necktie.

He stood an inch or two over six feet, was rangy, loose and big-boned, and every inch of him was well muscled. A full crop of dark wavy hair, a little long at the nape of his neck, framed a masculine face that was arresting due to its sharp angles and smooth planes. His jaw was firm, slightly squared, his lips thin. He had a blade of a nose, and jutting cheekbones. Dark eyebrows arched naturally over intense and compelling dark eyes.

Elizabeth stared at him, her wide-eyed expression revealing the awe, admiration, and respect reflected on the faces of every other person in the room, except for the young woman standing next to Elizabeth. Her expression, while admiring and respectful, contained an odd mixture of amusement and gratitude.

Five or ten minutes earlier the pretty, fresh-faced woman had boldly walked up to where Elizabeth, feeling shy and uncertain, had been hanging back, trying to blend in with the far wall.

"Hi," she had said breezily, smiling as she extended her right hand. "I'm Dawn Davidson, but everyone calls me De De—for obvious reasons. I write romance novels." She'd grinned. "Every one unpublished. What about you?"

"Elizabeth Leninger." Elizabeth had smiled and clasped the woman's hand. "And I . . . er . . . think I would like to become a writer of mystery novels."

"No, Elizabeth," De De had said, giving a quick but sharp shake of her head that sent her smooth, bobbed dark hair swirling.

"No?" Elizabeth had echoed, feeling her small store of confidence seeping out of her.

"No, you don't *think* you want to write. None of us here"—she'd made a sweeping gesture with her hand—*"think* we want to write. We *do* write. That's what we *are*, writers. And by your just taking the time and effort, not to mention assuming the expense, to be here today, I'd say you're a writer, too."

Elizabeth had laughed, from sheer relief and because she couldn't help herself; De De's smile and confidence were so infectious. "Okay, let's start again." She had stuck out her right hand once more. "I'm Elizabeth Leninger, and I write mystery novels." She'd had to laugh again. "Even if I do sound like a member of Alcoholics Anonymous."

"The analogy isn't farfetched." De De had laughed. "Because, you see, practically every writer I know is in a way addicted to the written word. We can no more not write, or read for that matter, for any extended length of time, than we can not voluntarily breathe." She'd shrugged. "It's in our blood, or something."

"But I haven't written anything for an extended period of time," Elizabeth had confessed, once again feeling her confidence plummet.

"Hmmm . . ." De De had murmured. "Not a word?"

"No."

"Not even to yourself, inside your head?"

"Well . . ." Elizabeth had recalled the hours whiled away in secret, suspenseful plotting.

"Aha!" De De had crowed. "You're a writer."

At that moment a ripple of excited murmurs shivered through the room, drawing Elizabeth's and De De's attention to the source of the buzz.

"Ahhh . . ." De De sighed.

Though puzzled by the sound, Elizabeth was unable to wrench her gaze from the commanding figure of the author being escorted by the president of the writers' organization to the podium at the front of the room.

The president stepped up to the microphone to present the man who required no introduction. A published writer of some five or six romantic suspense novels herself, she was around forty, small, wiry, and obviously nervous.

"We have a wonderful surprise for you lucky people today," she began, pausing to turn an adoring glance on the man standing at his ease beside her. "Mr. Jake Ruttenburg, *the* Jake Ruttenburg, has agreed to address us today on the perils and pitfalls of publishing."

A muffled, choking noise drew Elizabeth's attention from the honored guest to the young woman standing next to her.

"Are you all right, De De?" she asked anxiously, frowning at the strange expression on Dawn Davidson's face.

"Y-y-yes!" Her voice sounded strangled as it came from behind the hand De De had clamped over her mouth. "But I'd bet *the* Jake Ruttenburg isn't."

It was then that Elizabeth realized De De wasn't choking but was attempting to contain her laughter. Confusion deepened her frown.

"He's probably hating this," De De explained, answering the question evident on Elizabeth's face.

"This?" Elizabeth shook her head. "What this?"

"This fuss." De De indicated the group with a flick of her hand. "This palpable display of adulation."

Elizabeth stared at her in astonishment. "Why would he hate it? He deserves it."

"Sure he does." De De nodded in agreement. "But he still hates it, just as he hates doing interviews, book signings, or making speeches to groups such as this."

"But, if that's so, why does he do them? Why did he agree to address us today?"

"Because I asked him to do it," De De said, her smile soft, affectionate.

Elizabeth started. "You know him?"

"Very well." De De's smile grew into a self-satisfied grin. "He's my uncle."

"You're kidding."

"Nope." De De's grin got even wider. "He's my mother's younger brother."

Recalling what the girl had said about not as yet being published, Elizabeth gave her a quizzical look. "With a famous author for an uncle, how come you're still un—"

"Shhh . . ." De De murmured, directing her gaze to the podium. "The great one speaks."

And so he did, the rich, dark sound of his voice sending shocking tingles of awareness skittering over Elizabeth's skin.

Amazed and appalled by the intensity of her reaction to the mere sound of his deep voice, she stood immobile, hearing intonations in his speech, while utterly oblivious to the substance of his words.

Jake Ruttenburg must have ended with an amusing remark, for the sudden burst of laughter from the group jerked Elizabeth out of her daze and into the realization that, to a round of appreciative applause, he was weaving his way through the chattering crowd, on a frequently interrupted but determined path toward where she and De De had remained standing against the far wall.

To her consternation, as he drew ever nearer, an odd, almost panicky sensation tightened Elizabeth's throat. Her chest seemed compressed, her breathing constricted. Incomprehensibly, her spine stiffened, her fingers curled into her palms, crescent nails digging into her flesh.

On closer inspection, he looked older and tired. Shadows pooled in the hollows beneath his eyes. She could see the tracks of time fanning from the corners of his eyes, the trenches bracketing his nose and mouth. And yet, he was even better looking with the indelible stamp of maturity than he had appeared to be from a distance.

Drawing nearer, Elizabeth noted that his eyes were not the dark brown she had imagined, but were the darkest blue she had ever seen.

"Where's Beau?" De De asked when he finally managed to get to them.

"You know he hates these things," he murmured, pulling her into his arms in a bear hug of an embrace. "And hello to you, too, brat."

All five foot six and a half inches of Elizabeth trembled; the man's voice was as dark blue as his eyes—a warm, crushed-velvet dark blue.

Laughing, De De freed herself from his arms and stepped back to stare at him from excessively widened eyes. "Are you really *the* Jake Ruttenburg?" she asked in a tone of breathless wonder and admiration.

"Can it, kid," he snarled, softening the nasty note with a flashing grin. "And introduce me to your friend."

Elizabeth didn't even make the simple connection between herself and the word friend. She was too distracted by the confusing riot of sensations attacking her nervous system due to the blatant sexiness of his grin.

This man is positively lethal, she thought, automatically withdrawing into herself. While Elizabeth had had a safe and protected life, she had never been either unconscious or dense. She was fully aware that there were men who, by their very existence, possessed an uncanny allure for the female population. And she very much feared this man was one of them.

She had met his type before; yet strangely she had always been immune to their charm. The very fact that she felt the impact of this man activated her natural reserve.

"Oh, sorry," De De said, her lips slanting into a rueful smile. "Elizabeth, my favorite uncle, *the* Jake Ruttenburg," she was unrepentant about the emphasis. "Uncle Jake, I'd like you to meet my new friend, Elizabeth Leninger."

"Elizabeth." He extended his hand.

The sound of her name murmured by that blue velvet voice raised the short hairs at Elizabeth's nape. The lazy perusal he gave her stiff form, from her face to the toes of her low-heeled suede shoes, sparked an unfamiliar— and uncomfortable—humming awareness in her of him as a man and herself as a woman.

Instantly, Elizabeth questioned her choice of the severely cut chocolate brown skirt suit and the plain white silk shirt she had recently purchased to wear to this meeting. At the time, she had wanted to project an image of businesslike professionalism. Yet, beneath his deceptively casual gaze, she didn't feel at all professional. Instead she felt underdressed, inadequately dressed—undressed.

Instinctively withdrawing deeper into herself, she clung to her composure, responding coolly "Mr. Ruttenburg," and put her hand in his.

The friction of palm on palm was minimal, but the electric shock wave from the touch of his warm flesh shot directly from her hand to the base of her skull.

Coming right after her reaction to his disrobing glance, it scared the hell out of Elizabeth.

"All De De's friends call me Jake." His tone

held a hint of mockery; his smile held a tinge of mischief.

The effect of that gently teasing smile played havoc with her equilibrium. Frightened by her unusual and unwilling response to his appeal, Elizabeth mentally dived behind a protective shield of composure.

"But I'm a very new friend," she pointed out in a tone finely coated with frost. "I don't feel I know De De well enough, as yet, to address her uncle so informally."

"Whoa . . ." Jake Ruttenburg arched his dark brows. "It's suddenly freezing in here. Did someone open the door and let in a blast of frigid autumn air?"

"I'm sorry . . ." Elizabeth began, flustered and growing colder and more remote by the second.

De De chastised her uncle. "Oh, give her a break. She's nervous about meeting you."

"Really?" His eyes took on what appeared to Elizabeth to be a predatory sheen. "How interesting."

Thanks a heap, De De, Elizabeth railed, doing a bit of silent chastising herself. Hanging on to her composure for all she was worth, she managed a creditable laugh.

"Of course, I am," she admitted, looking him straight in the eyes. "I greatly admire your work. You're one of my favorite authors."

"You write?" he probed.

"Er . . ." she hesitated.

"She does," De De answered.

"Romance novels?"

"No." Elizabeth gave a quick, negative shake of her head, grateful, for De De's sake, that his tone hadn't been condescending, as had been the case with some other authors she had heard interviewed on TV talk shows.

For some reason that she was at a loss to comprehend, many writers, both male and female, working in other genres were openly disdainful of romance writers and of the genre.

Although Elizabeth preferred mystery and suspense novels, she occasionally dipped into other genres; science fiction, fantasy, historical—and contemporary—romance. In her personal opinion, in the romance genre, as in all others, including mystery and suspense, a lot of the writing was excellent, some not so good, and some plain awful. To her way of thinking, a writer was a writer was a writer, regardless of the genre.

"She's into mysteries."

Until De De tossed out the information, Elizabeth hadn't been aware of the pall of silence. Feeling foolish merely added to her discomfort concerning her odd, almost violent reaction to Jake Ruttenburg, as it did to her sense of inadequacy.

"Published?" asked Jake, immediately raising a silencing hand to his niece, while fixing a direct and probing stare on Elizabeth.

"No." She again shook her head, and dredged up a self-deprecating smile. "In fact,

I have never submitted anything to a publishing house."

"Why?"

Persistent son of a—

"Give it a rest, Uncle Jake!" De De's exclaimed protest cut across Elizabeth's less than complimentary silent evaluation of this tenacious man.

"It's all right, De De. I don't mind," Elizabeth lied through gritted teeth. She leveled a saccharine smile at him and forced her teeth apart. "I haven't submitted because I haven't finished working on the manuscript as yet." Even as she said this, she experienced pangs of guilt for being less than truthful. Finished? Ha! She had barely begun.

"Hmmm." He frowned in disapproval.

She bristled. Her normally passive temper flared. Who did he think he was? God? Her agitation must have escaped her control of facial expression, because De De stepped in to save Elizabeth from exploding all over him.

"Ah! Will you look at the time!" De De raised her wrist to brandish her watch in front of his eyes. "Aren't you due somewhere for an interview?"

"Yes." He heaved a sigh, and shot a glance at the doorway. "And there's Beau, giving me the look that says 'get your ass in gear, Ruttenburg.'"

Naturally, Elizabeth had to look. The man standing just outside the room literally stole the breath from her.

He was a veritable giant, measuring at least six foot six inches, and his physique rivaled the classic form of the famous *David*. His hair lay in burnished gold curls sculpted against a perfectly shaped head and framing a masculine face that could only be described as beautiful. The sight of him instilled a feeling of near reverence, much as viewing an exquisite work of art.

"Who . . . ?" Elizabeth turned to De De. "Who is that beautiful person?"

"My assistant," Jake Ruttenburg answered for his niece. "And you had better not ever let him hear you call him 'that beautiful person.'"

Elizabeth opened her mouth to inform him that she highly doubted she would ever see the man again, but he didn't give her time to utter one word.

"Gotta go," he said, pulling De De into his arms for a goodbye hug. "See you, brat. Be good. You, too," he added, slanting an intense, narrow-eyed look at Elizabeth over his niece's shoulder.

And then he was gone, weaving his way through the chattering crowd to the man at the door and leaving Elizabeth standing there, wide-eyed and quivering from the intensity of his stare.

Disgusted with herself for her physical response to him, she turned to De De, firm in her intention to dismiss him from her thoughts.

"De De, I think we should—" Elizabeth

broke off, struck by the look on the younger woman's face.

De De stood still, staring at the now-closed door. Her expression was one of aching longing. She blinked at the sound of Elizabeth's voice, then shrugged and turned to her.

"I'm crazy about the guy," she said.

"Well, I can't fault you for that." Elizabeth understood, even though she didn't share the feeling. "After all, he is your uncle, and he's obviously fond of you."

De De grinned and shook her head. Her grin was so similar to her uncle's, it caused a reflexive thrill of unease inside Elizabeth.

"Did I say something wrong?"

De De again shook her head. "No, but you made a wrong assumption. I wasn't referring to my uncle. Although I am crazy about him, in a different way. I meant I'm crazy about his assistant."

Elizabeth's eyebrows shot up. "That beautiful man who was at the door!"

"The very same." De De heaved an exaggerated, dramatic-sounding sigh. "I'm crazy in love with him, have been since I was a teenager." She heaved another heartfelt sigh. "But, other than as Jake's favorite—and only—niece, he doesn't know I'm alive."

If it hadn't been for the girl's dejected look, Elizabeth might have laughed at De De's reference to being in love since she was a teenager; at present she didn't appear to be too far removed from her teens.

However, Elizabeth, being a mother to two girls not much younger than De De, felt a surge of compassion.

"Oh, dear, I'm sorry," she softly commiserated. "But even from way back here I noticed that he looked to be a great deal older than you."

"Not a great deal older!" De De protested. "He and Jake are the same age. They'll both be forty this year."

"And how old are you?" Elizabeth asked, digesting the fact that the man was three years older than she was herself. "Twenty? Twenty-one?"

"I'll be twenty-six," De De said indignantly, but then grimaced. "Well, I turned twenty-five a couple of months ago, but what difference does that make?"

"None, to me," Elizabeth soothed. "But, I can understand why almost fifteen years might matter to him."

"Yeah, and not only to him," De De acknowledged. "Although my parents like Beau, I just know they'd probably freak out if I became involved with him."

Knowing full well that she would freak out should either of her girls become involved with a man fifteen years their senior, Elizabeth chose not to comment. Instead, she decided to change the subject.

"Look. The workshop is going on and we're missing it." She indicated the speaker now at the podium. "Since we paid to hear this, perhaps we'd better find seats and pay attention."

"Oh, right," De De agreed, smiling in apology. "Take your pick." She waved at the few remaining empty chairs close by. "I'm right behind you."

Other than an occasional remark in regard to information provided by the speaker, there was little conversation between Elizabeth and De De throughout the rest of the workshop.

When the speaker finished, the president of the organization announced that there would be a break for the buffet lunch included in the registration fee for the daylong session.

During the meal period, De De introduced Elizabeth to several members of the active group, and all of them urged her to join the organization.

When the workshop reconvened, the speaker, an attractive and articulate, multipublished young woman, addressed the nuts and bolts of writing in general. Her presentation was so basic and interesting, further conversation between Elizabeth and De De was limited to murmurs exchanged on points of mutual concern. And so it went throughout the rest of the afternoon. They both took copious notes; Elizabeth hoping she'd be able to decipher her quickly scribbled words when she went over them later in the privacy of her home.

It was some thirty-five minutes after the originally scheduled time of four P.M. when the session ended, to the obvious dismay of everyone, including Elizabeth.

There ensued the usual lingering, those remaining clustered in little groups and discussing the pros and cons of the workshop.

De De joined in the chatter, but excused herself from the group she was with when she noticed Elizabeth gathering up her notebook, purse, and jacket.

"Are you expected home for dinner?" she asked, coming to a stop at the chair next to Elizabeth's to scoop up her own things.

"Well, no." Elizabeth shrugged. "As a matter of fact, I'll be going home to an empty house." She had to suppress a shudder at the thought, and went on quickly to explain. "My daughter has a free day tomorrow—from school—so she's spending the night with my mother-in-law."

"I'm alone, too." De De hesitated, then smiled. "Would you care to join me somewhere for dinner?"

"I'd love to," Elizabeth smiled in relief. "Thank you, De De."

"Thank you," the girl returned, her own smile widening. "I hate to go off alone after one of these sessions—when I'm all revved up and primed to talk for hours."

Elizabeth laughed. "I've been feeling the same way. I hope you won't mind too much if I bombard you with questions over the dinner table?"

"Mind?" De De exclaimed. "I'd love it!"

"Wonderful." Elizabeth felt excited, eager as a young girl. "Where should we meet? Do you have a place in mind?"

"Well . . ." De De frowned. "Where are you located?"

Elizabeth told her the name and location of her development, then waited while De De gave the information some thought. It didn't take her long.

"I've got it," she said, grinning. "There's a tavern I know of, about halfway between your place and mine. It's nothing fancy, but it's quiet, conducive to conversation, and the food is plain but good."

"Fine," Elizabeth grinned back at her. "Give me directions and I'm off."

De De immediately dropped onto a chair, flipped open her notebook, and jotted down some instructions. Tearing the sheet from the book, she handed it to Elizabeth, along with a verbal admonition.

"First one there grabs a table."

"Right," Elizabeth agreed.

"And orders drinks. I'm parched."

"Wine?" Elizabeth arched her eyebrows.

De De nodded. "White."

"Same here." Elizabeth smiled, waved, and turned away. "See you soon."

On exiting the building, Elizabeth paused to draw in a deep breath of crisp October air. Halloween would soon be upon her, and after that Thanksgiving and then Christmas and New Year's . . . the first holidays without Richard.

The optimism began draining from Elizabeth. Facing the holidays without their father would be hard on the girls. A gust of sharp-edged wind sliced through her suit jacket. Elizabeth shuddered, not only from the chill in the air. A sigh of despair slipped past her guard before she caught herself up short.

She'd handle it. Whatever came her way, she could deal with it. Hadn't she always dealt with any and all crises, in the immediate family and otherwise?

Reminding herself of all the times she had coped alone, because Richard was too busy or was away from home, gave Elizabeth the strength needed to shore up her confidence and renew her optimism.

She'd cope again, with the coming holidays and anything else that might occur. She had become an expert on coping alone, she mused wryly.

It was now her time to enjoy the moment, the here and the now, the expectation and the hope.

You, too.

Elizabeth went still, hearing Jake Ruttenburg's voice in her head, cautioning De De to be good and then her. With her mind's eye, she could see the intensity in the depths of his fathomless blue eyes. An expectation of a different kind raised the fine hair at her nape and sent a thrill skipping along her spine, an unfamiliar warmth spreading through her insides.

But I am good, Elizabeth thought. She had

always been good . . . a good daughter, a good wife, a good mother. She didn't know any other way to be.

Banishing her memory of the man and of her involuntary response to him from her mind, she defiantly raised her chin and promised herself that she would work with dedication to be damn good at her chosen craft.

Walking briskly to where she had parked her car, her hazel eyes once again bright with anticipation, she distracted herself by admiring the blaze of autumnal colors on the splendid variety of quivering trees sparkling in the mellow golden glow of the late afternoon sunlight.

Maybe life wasn't too bad, after all.

The sudden thought elicited a soft burst of laughter from her as Elizabeth joined the line of Sunday traffic streaming along the Schuylkill Expressway.

She had made a new friend.

It was odd in a way, Elizabeth reflected. De De was nearly eleven years her junior; yet something had clicked between them, almost as if there had been an immediate recognition.

Serendipity?

Or perhaps a meeting of like minds?

Elizabeth didn't know the answer. She simply knew that she was looking forward to continuing the discussion activated by the afternoon workshops.

With her enthusiasm firmly restored, she decided she felt good. No, Elizabeth corrected herself, smiling into the golden glow of sunset, more than good; she felt expectant, hopeful for the future—her personal future.

How had she arrived at this point, when she had experienced such a dearth of optimism less than two months ago, at the beginning of September?

Elizabeth knew the answer to that query, of course, knew precisely when she had decided to take a step in the direction of self-fulfillment.

While certain of her ability to keep a careful eye on her driving, and the thinning late afternoon traffic, Elizabeth let memory swirl, mentally replaying the events preceding her fateful decision.

Two

She was alone. The endless summer had finally ended. She had driven Ella, a chattering bundle of nervous anticipation, to Easton a week ago to begin her freshman year of college. Sally had dashed from the house, running late as usual, a few minutes ago to catch the bus for high school.

Could she be suffering the fabled empty-nest syndrome?

Elizabeth sighed. She had wanted more children, at least one more, possibly two. But after the difficult time she had had with Sally's birth, her doctor had advised her and Richard against another pregnancy, warning them it could cost her her health, possibly her life.

Feeling the silence close in on her, Elizabeth sighed again as she wandered aimlessly from room to room in the spacious house that had been her home for almost six years.

It was the second house she and Richard had purchased during their nineteen years of marriage. The first mortgage they had assumed had been on a small dwelling they had found a few months after Ella was born. It was located in one of the new bedroom communities of town-houses that had just begun to spring up in the environs around Philadelphia.

Elizabeth smiled wryly, recalling how spacious that tiny house had seemed at first—spacious in comparison to the confining constraints of living, primarily in one bedroom, with Richard's parents.

She had been happy in that small house. They had outgrown it with Sally's birth, but had been financially unable to consider a bigger place while Richard was in the process of moving up through the ranks of his employer, a major petroleum company located in Philadelphia, at which he had been employed since graduating from college with a business degree.

Drifting into the kitchen, Elizabeth started a pot of coffee she didn't want, just to have something to do. A sad, reminiscent smile tugged at her lips as she watched the water trickle into the glass coffee carafe.

Ella had been twelve and Sally nine when Richard, soaring on a much deserved high induced by his promotion at long last to the position of assistant vice president of one of the divisions of his firm, declared proudly that they were to begin the exciting process of house hunting.

Sally had danced exuberantly around her father, chanting in a singsong voice "We're going house hunting, we're going house hunting," while Ella, always more self-contained than her sister, contented herself with bombarding Richard with rapid-fire questions, demanding to know when they would begin, where they would look, what kind of house was wanted, and how much he was prepared to pay.

Richard endured all with good humor, laughing with Sally, then patiently answering every one of Ella's questions. When it came to how much he planned to pay for a house, the figure he blithely tossed out sent a shock wave of alarm through Elizabeth.

"Richard, are you sure we'll be able to afford a house that costs that much?" she had asked him later that night, after the girls had finally settled down and were in bed.

"With the raise I've just been given, why not?" He had answered her with a question of his own, appearing affronted at having his judgment challenged.

"But . . . for how many years?" Elizabeth had persisted in the face of his obvious displeasure.

"Twenty." He had shrugged. "Maybe twenty-five." He had then bestowed a chiding smile on her. "You know we need a bigger, more . . . suitable house now, a place to better reflect my success." His tone took on not only a tinge of self-confidence but a blatant cockiness. "The sky's the limit, Liz. You always did worry too much."

Elizabeth disliked the nickname, and Richard knew it. His deliberate use of it effectively silenced her. She did not remind him that her budgeting was what had kept them solvent and relatively free of debt. Hurt by his attitude, she closed her mouth and kept it closed, even when the price of the house he and the girls eventually fell in love with sent her into a state of shock.

They could not afford it. Elizabeth had paled at the very thought of making such high monthly payments for twenty-five years; still she held her peace.

Richard bought the place.

A two-story Colonial, it was located in a new, select, upscale development even farther removed from Philadelphia. The house was beautifully designed, set like a newly cut gem in the center of over a half-acre of artfully landscaped grounds.

Elizabeth also fell in love with it. But after living in a narrow building that was in fact little more than a tract house, it was predictable that she fall in love with a home containing four bedrooms, a den, and three full bathrooms on the second floor, and a large kitchen, laundry room, powder room, formal dining room and living room, as well as a family room, on the first floor. The place had a large basement plus an attached two-car garage. Of course, she reveled in it.

It was the thought of paying for it that gave Elizabeth stomach-churning fits. She had suggested that, although she was untrained, perhaps she could find some sort of employment, if only on a part-time basis.

Richard had immediately and strongly rejected the idea, as he had when Elizabeth had made a similar suggestion when they had taken on their first mortgage. His adamantly stated reason was the same as it had been; Elizabeth had more than a full-time job in the performance of her roles of wife, mother, and homemaker.

In truth, Richard's assertions had proved correct. With Elizabeth's careful money management, in addition to the yearly raises he received, they had succeeded in making the payments and in stretching their funds enough to occasionally entertain Richard's business associates, to indulge in family vacations, and to continue to contribute to the college funds they had started for the girls. In fact, she had managed their funds so well that two years ago, Richard had insisted she employ someone to help with the cleaning.

And now the mortgage was paid.

Elizabeth shuddered at the thought, the realization that the costly premiums on the mortgage insurance Richard had insisted upon taking, and she had had to struggle to meet, had spared her the worry of attempting to continue making the payments for another nineteen years or the hassle of selling the house and looking for something less expensive.

Further, unbeknownst to her, Richard had somehow found the extra funds to pay premiums on a large life insurance policy, which, along with the generous benefits provided by his firm, guaranteed her the capital to maintain the house and her lifestyle.

The sickening fact that she was free of debt and financial worry due to Richard's death was unnerving. Her fingers trembled, rattling the cups when she reached into the cabinet mounted above the countertop. Composing herself, she managed to retrieve one without causing any breakage.

Pouring out the coffee, Elizabeth cradled the delicate, flower-strewn cup in her hands and walked from the kitchen to the sliding glass doors giving access from the dining room to the brick patio and the backyard.

In real terms, since it was still early September, the summer wasn't over. But, for most parents of school-age children, for all intents and purposes the summer ended around Labor Day when the children returned to classes.

Having heard the weather forecast earlier, Elizabeth knew the temperature outside her centrally air-conditioned house was in the mid eighties. But signs of approaching autumn were evident in the droopy, tired look of bushes and of the leaves on trees, in the subtle, deepening blue of the sky.

The kids were back in school. It was quiet outside, even more quiet inside. The stillness pressed down on Elizabeth like a smothering substance. The autumn and winter months loomed before her like an endless and frightening black tunnel.

Now . . . what?

It was not the first time the question had plagued Elizabeth. She had avoided answering it on each previous occasion by concentrating on her girls, keeping them mentally and physically occupied as a means of helping them accept their loss, the absence of their adored father in the house and in their lives.

And she had succeeded beyond her expectations, possibly because Richard had been at home so seldom, due to the time he spent traveling to further his career.

Stifling a groan, Elizabeth turned away from the glass doors. Richard's career. There was a job waiting for her, the last one in the awful business of separating and dealing with his personal possessions.

Richard had not only put in long hours at the office and gone on frequent business trips, he'd worked at home. Other than retrieving insurance documents from a drawer in his orderly desk, Elizabeth had yet to venture into the den, Richard's office away from his company.

Someday—soon—she knew she would have to attend to the chore of sorting through his desk and files, as well as see to the personal effects brought from his firm. His secretary had gathered them together and had had them delivered to Elizabeth right after Richard's death.

At the time, still in shock from the suddenness of his demise, and the subsequent necessity of making arrangements concerning the viewing and interment, Elizabeth had shoved the carton into a corner of the den, out of the way—and her sight.

Nevertheless, out of sight or not, she knew the carton was there and that she would have to attend to it and to Richard's desk at some point in time.

Why not today?

The doorbell rang, its shrill summons echoing through the too quiet house. Grateful for the distraction from the inner probe to get to work in the den, Elizabeth set her cup on the dining-room table and rushed to the door. Her mother stood patiently on the front step.

"Well, hello there." Elizabeth laughed in surprise at the unexpected visit. She peered around her mother and asked, "Where's Dad?"

"On the golf course." Sally smiled. "Where else?"

Elizabeth arched her brows as she pulled the door open wide. "Without you?"

"I thought you might like some company today," she said, smiling as she stepped into the flag-stoned foyer. "So I'm offering my voice to drown out the silence."

"Thanks, Mother." Elizabeth grimaced as she shut the door. "At the moment, I appreciate all the noise I can get."

"Well, there's always the soaps, you know?" Sally Graham chuckled, fully aware of her daughter's aversion to most television.

Elizabeth's grimace curved into a responsive smile. "I'm appreciative of a distraction, not desperate. I made a pot of coffee a few minutes ago. Would you like a cup?"

"Yes . . ." Sally's voice faded as her critical

glance ran over her daughter's ultraslim frame. "Actually, I came to invite you to lunch." Her concerned gaze returned to Elizabeth's face. "You've lost a great deal of weight since . . . over the summer. Haven't you?"

"Don't fuss, Mother," Elizabeth said, a note of pleading in her voice, moving around the older woman to lead the way to the kitchen. "I'm fine."

"But a lot thinner," Sally persisted. "I'm amazed you can still wear any of your clothes." A frown creased her brow as she sent another probing look at the knee-length denim shorts hugging Elizabeth's narrow hips. "New?"

"No." Elizabeth shot a grin over her shoulder. "I borrowed the shorts from Ella."

"Size seven?" Sally asked wryly.

"Eight," Elizabeth answered.

"Uh-huh." Sally accepted the cup of steaming coffee Elizabeth handed her. "And, if I recall correctly, you bought a pair of size twelve shorts for yourself while we were shopping together when you visited your father and me in Florida just last January," she went on, raising her voice so it carried to the dining room, where her daughter had gone to collect her own half-full, cup.

"Yes," Elizabeth readily agreed upon reentering the kitchen, but then she nudged her mother's memory, "But, if you'll recall, I said at that time I wanted to lose some of the pounds I'd taken on over the past several years." Her smile was strained and overbright. "Shall we go into the living room?"

"Are you changing the subject?"

"I'm trying."

"Yes, you are lately," Sally observed. "And at the moment, you're trying my patience."

"Mother, please . . ."

"No," Sally interrupted, giving a quick shake of her head. "I didn't come here today simply to keep you company, Elizabeth." Sliding a chair away from the glass-topped kitchen table, she sat down and settled in. "I think we need to have a heart-to-heart talk."

Recognizing the determination in her mother's voice, and in the expression on Sally's well-cared-for, still very attractive face, Elizabeth accepted the inevitable and seated herself opposite her at the table. She didn't need to prompt her mother to begin.

"Your father and I had planned to return to Florida at the end of this month, as usual, but now . . ." Sally broke off, sighed, then shrugged.

"But now . . . ?" Elizabeth repeated, frowning, at a loss to interpret her mother's vagueness. Ever since her parents had taken early retirement from their respective teaching posts, five years ago, they had spent the fall and winter months in Florida, and the spring and summer months in their home near Valley Forge. Why should this particular autumn be any different?

A twinge of alarm flared inside her: was one

of her parents ill? Her mother looked fine—slender, vibrant, healthy. Her father? The twinge inside expanded into the beginnings of real fear. Was something wrong with him?

"Mother, what are you trying to say?" she asked when Sally failed to elaborate and the silence stretched out ominously between them. "Why would you and Dad consider changing your schedule?"

"Why?" Sally appeared astounded by the question. "Why, because we're worried about you, Elizabeth."

"Worried?" Elizabeth blinked in confusion. "I don't understand. Why should you be worried about me?"

"Why indeed!" Sally exclaimed. "Elizabeth, just look at yourself, then ask yourself why we're concerned." She indicated Elizabeth's entire person with a flick of her hand. "You're every bit as slim now as you were at seventeen. You must have lost thirty pounds over the summer."

"Twenty-four, actually, and I'm still five pounds heavier than I was the summer I was seventeen." Elizabeth said, arching her eyebrows. "So?"

"So, your father and I are naturally concerned about why you have lost so much weight so quickly. You look so drawn, so tired. Have you seen a doctor?"

"Doctor? No." Elizabeth gave a quick negative shake of her head, and stifled a burst of incredulous laughter. Here she had been sick over the speculation that one of them was ill, while they were worried about her health. If the situation wasn't so sad, it might have been funny. "Mother, I assure you there's nothing wrong with my health."

"Then what's wrong?" Sally persisted.

"Mother." Elizabeth sighed. "It's not even five full months since . . ." her voice faded. "You know."

"Yes, and I understand how difficult it has been for you." Sally's tone softened as she reached across the table to grasp Elizabeth's hand. "But you can't continue like this, losing weight, looking so drawn and tired." Her fingers gently squeezed Elizabeth's hand. "I don't mean to sound cold and unfeeling, but . . . Richard is gone. Continuing to grieve will not bring him back. You have got to think of your girls, as well as yourself."

Elizabeth felt a sharp prick to her conscience. Her mother believed she had let herself go because of grief, when in fact, she had set grief aside at some point during the summer. The explanation for her loss of weight, and for her appearance, was simple; she had run herself ragged during one of the hottest summers on record, distracting and entertaining her girls. If the price she had had to pay was weight loss—which she didn't mind—and looking beat—which she did mind—it was worth it, because it had worked.

Fleetingly, Elizabeth acknowledged that sooner or later she would have to deal with the relative ease with which she had overcome her grief—just as surely as she would have to face Richard's desk and the carton in the corner of the den.

But not now, and certainly not aloud, to her mother.

"I have devoted the entire summer to the girls," she said. "But today"—she grimaced—"it suddenly struck me that I was thinking of myself."

Sally frowned. "In what way?"

Elizabeth shrugged. "Lately, since the girls returned to school, I find myself wondering, What now? What do I do, how do I fill the hours in each and every day? To continue on as before—the social work, the bridge club, gardening, shopping—just doesn't seem enough, not challenging or satisfying." She gave her mother an apologetic smile. "I want to do something for me, something . . . Oh, I don't know how to explain it, but I want to do something self-fulfilling. Is that utterly selfish?"

"No, of course not," Sally assured her, again squeezing the hand she still held. "I'd say it was self-preservation. You are only thirty-six—"

"Almost thirty-seven," Elizabeth interjected, honest, if not yet resolved to the idea of facing forty.

"You're telling me?" asked Sally in a tone dry as dust. "I was there, an active participant, remember?"

It was just the right note to ease the guilt coiling through Elizabeth. She laughed, then picked up on her mother's light banter. "Well, no, I actually don't remember. I was too young at the time."

Sally shared her daughter's laughter, and appeared to be sharing the release of tension, as well. Raising her cup to smiling lips, she finished her coffee, then set the cup gently but decisively on the table.

"So, what have you come up with?" Her expression one of interest, she arched her brows. "Any ideas?"

"Yes . . . and no." Elizabeth laughed again, self-consciously this time. "Despite my lack of qualifications, I considered the possibility of finding employment, if only on a part-time basis."

"You could always flip hamburgers," Sally suggested, a twinkle lighting her soft blue eyes.

"It's honest work," Elizabeth said in a tone of mild reproof, afraid the light in her mother's eyes had been sparked by ridicule.

Sally sobered at once, her expression revealing affrontery. "Of course it is!" she retorted sharply. "And, from my own observations, I'm convinced it is hard work." Her lips curved in a small, knowing smile. "Dealing with the public quite often is very difficult."

"I'm sorry, Mother." Elizabeth felt foolish and contrite. "I misunderstood."

"Yes, you did." Sally sternly reprimanded her, then immediately relented. "But I forgive you."

"Thank you." Elizabeth's expression eased into a smile. "You always do, don't you?" she murmured, recalling with aching clarity the long-past time when she had most sorely tested the depths of her mother's forbearance.

In one encapsulated flash of memory, Elizabeth experienced the shame she had felt during the early days of her freshman year at college, when she had had to go to her mother to confess to being pregnant with Richard's baby. Sally had not so much as attempted to conceal her pain and disappointment in her only child, but she had valiantly surmounted both emotions . . . after her demand for Elizabeth and Richard to marry was met. And, six months later, both she and Elizabeth's father had greeted their newly born granddaughter with open and loving arms. Sadly, the same could not be said of Richard's parents, most especially his mother, Ella. She only accepted the situation—and not very graciously, at that—after her name had been bestowed on the innocent infant.

"And always will." Sally's soft voice scattered the piercing memory. "Just as I'm certain you will always forgive Ella and Sally."

"More than likely," Elizabeth agreed, sharing an understanding smile with her mother.

"So, are you actively looking for a job?" Sally's voice was now brisk, interested.

"Well . . . no." Elizabeth sighed. "I really don't need to work, since Richard left me well provided for, and after thinking it over, I wouldn't feel right about the very real possibility of taking a job away from someone who probably does need the money."

"You always did have a well-developed social consciousness," Sally observed, obviously pleased.

"Instilled by two caring parents," Elizabeth deflected the compliment.

Sally accepted with a smile and a quick nod, then as quickly returned to the original topic. "It would appear to me that, if you feel your usual pursuits are not fulfilling enough, but you hesitate about taking a job, you've got something of a dilemma on your hands."

"Yeah." Elizabeth nodded. "But it's certainly not anything for you worry about. You and Dad can return to Florida as planned. I'll work something out."

Three

The flash of an oncoming car's headlights brought Elizabeth out of her mental wanderings. The last of the sun's rays had deserted the highway. Noting the thinning late afternoon traffic with a sense of relief, she flicked on her own lights, shifted position on the contoured seat, then allowed the reel of memory to again unwind.

She had hit upon the *something* that same afternoon, something she had always wanted to do, something that, since becoming a mother, she had lacked the time and the nerve to pursue. But that something beckoned again, after she had hit upon another—upsetting, demoralizing, and angering—something.

She had readily agreed to her mother's suggestion of going out for lunch. But later, after Sally dropped her off at home, Elizabeth had once again found time hanging heavily on her hands. Changing from the summer dress she'd donned to accompany Sally into the borrowed shorts her mother had remarked upon, she resolutely went to Richard's den, determined to complete the last and final task thrust upon her by his sudden demise.

Less than an hour was required to clean out Richard's desk. Chiding herself for putting off the chore for months, she retrieved the carton from his office from the corner and started sorting through the contents.

There were the usual items: pens, notebooks, his leather-bound appointment calendar, the obligatory family photo he had kept on display on his desk. There was also a manila envelope, in which his secretary had deposited his memos and correspondence.

Elizabeth was halfway through the pile of mail she had dumped onto the desk, rifling swiftly through the business letters, when she got to the first envelope marked private and personal. Curious as to why any business correspondence should be so designated, she removed the letter and read it.

In total, there were fourteen Love letters. Love letters so explicit in sexual content, Elizabeth had gasped aloud. The dates on them spanned a period of three years. All were penned and signed by the same hand. Elizabeth recognized and identified the signature of a female associate of Richard's, Valerie Marks, who was based in the San Francisco office he had so frequently visited.

Cringing inside, she faced the devastating fact that, while she had dutifully and faithfully played out the role of unassuming helpmate,

Richard had betrayed his vows, his children, and his wife by indulging in an affair.

The effect of his betrayal was more than devastating, it was defeminizing.

Elizabeth was wounded in the deepest, most vulnerable part of her psyche—her sense of her own womanhood.

How could Richard have done this?

The cry was silent, an inner scream of pain and rage. On surrendering her body to Richard at the tender age of seventeen, she had in effect not only surrendered her youth and innocence but her individuality, as well.

With the life-changing realization that she was pregnant, Elizabeth had placed herself and her future in Richard's hands. Since that day, it hadn't mattered that the relationship they had shared, their love for one another, had not been the earth-shattering stuff of fiction. Nor had it mattered that she was virtually living in his shadow. She had felt safe, secure, comfortable in her assigned place.

Now, to learn that her place had been violated, by the very man who had designated that place for her, undermined Elizabeth's sense of value and self-worth.

Who was she if she was not the woman she believed herself to be? Wife? Mother? Person?

Damn your soul, Richard.

Elizabeth felt not a shred of guilt or remorse for her condemnation of the man whose life, whose bed she had shared for nineteen years.

The only thing she felt was an emptiness of spirit.

Deathly still, she sat at the desk, the revealing letters clutched in her hand, staring sightlessly out the tastefully curtained den window.

Three years. *Three years.*

Cringing inside, Elizabeth reviewed those years during which Richard had indulged in infidelity, walking the precarious tightrope of a double life.

Her mental inspection cast the light of understanding on the context of her own life during that three-year period. She and Richard had made love with less and less frequency, hardly at all in the previous thirteen to fourteen months.

Elizabeth had attributed Richard's lack of attention and ardor to overwork. Hadn't she read somewhere that physical and mental stress were the primary causes of decreasing libido? She had. She had even believed it.

A sob was wrenched from Elizabeth's constricted throat. While she had been making excuses for Richard, he had been . . .

It didn't matter now that she herself had never possessed a strong sex drive, or that she had rarely enjoyed or found satisfaction in the physical act of lovemaking.

She had never denied Richard, never refused his advances.

Even so, he had betrayed her.

Had he planned to leave her for this other woman, this Valerie Marks, who had to have known he was married and the father of two? Had he been planning not only to betray her but to rob her of her position, her security, her sense of herself as a woman?

Elizabeth's stomach lurched.

Damn you, Richard.

Time meant nothing, everything meant nothing, until the slamming of the front door broke the silence, turning nothing into something.

"Mom, I'm home. Where are you?"

Sally.

Elizabeth blinked, only then becoming aware of the mist clouding her eyes. Startled, she raised a hand to her face. Her fingers came away wet.

She had to pull herself together, she realized, brushing at her tears with impatient fingers. If nothing else, she was a mother, with her fair share of protective instincts. She could not allow Sally to witness her despair.

Composing herself, she shoved the letters to the back of the bottom desk drawer. Then, her calm exterior masking turmoil, she rose and went to the door.

"I'm up here, Sal, in the den."

Quick, light footsteps bounded up the stairs. Sally came to a halt before her mother.

She frowned. "Have you been crying?"

"Yes." Elizabeth moved her shoulders in a shrug. "I've been sorting through your Dad's desk."

"Oh." Sally's eyes shadowed with residual pain. Her soft lips curved down at the corners.

"It had to be done. I'd put it off long enough."

"I suppose." Sally gazed into the den over Elizabeth's shoulder; then her glance skittered away.

Elizabeth stepped into the central hallway and closed the door behind her. She experienced a sharp sensation of having closed her past behind her.

"Hungry?" Her voice was too bright; fortunately, Sally didn't appear to notice.

"No." Her gaze touched the door and skittered away again. "I . . . er . . . some of the kids are going to the multiplex at the mall for the early movie. May I go?"

Elizabeth frowned; Sally knew her rule against going out in the evening without supervision.

"Janice's mom's going along," Sally quickly clarified, before Elizabeth could voice an objection. "Mrs. Carmichael said she wanted to do some shopping while we're at the movie. It's that romantic adventure film I've been wanting to see. May I go? Please?" she pleaded.

Elizabeth was well acquainted with Angie Carmichael. Not only was Angie a member of the bridge club, she was as diligent in her dedication to her children as Elizabeth. Angie's daughter Janice and Sally had been best friends since the Carmichaels moved into the development, when the girls were in the third grade.

"What about dinner?" Elizabeth asked, inwardly cringing at the idea of spending the evening alone.

"Mrs. Carmichael said we can grab something to eat at the food court in the mall. May I go?"

"Yes," Elizabeth said, always a sucker for mournful expressions and sad-eyed looks from her girls.

"Thanks, Mom." Sally's hangdog expression dissolved into a beaming smile. "I gotta call Janice," she said, spinning around and dashing for her bedroom.

It was later, while Elizabeth picked at the salad she'd tossed together for her solitary meal, that her disinterested glance touched on a small, boxed notice in the evening paper she'd been leafing through, not in search of news, but for distraction from the too quiet house and the unwelcome, self-destructive thoughts crowding the edges of her consciousness.

The notice imparted information about a writers' workshop being given a week from that coming Sunday. All interested persons were invited, for a nominal fee, to attend. A buffet lunch would be provided. A registration form took up the lower portion of the notice.

A seminar on writing.

Elizabeth's thoughts flew to the department-store shirt box secreted in the attic. Inside the long box, probably yellowed by time—nineteen years of time—were six loose-leaf notebooks containing rough drafts of mystery stories Elizabeth had laboriously penned in longhand the summer before she'd met Richard.

A sad smile flickered over Elizabeth's lips. A

smile for the reverence she had had for the
written word and for the hopes and dreams she
had harbored of someday joining the ranks of
the published.

Laying the paper aside, she rose and carried
her barely tasted salad to the sink. Dumping
the vegetables into the disposal, she rinsed the
plate and stashed it in the dishwasher. Her
glance fell on the notice again while she wiped
the table and replaced the floral centerpiece.

Could she?

The thought halted Elizabeth midstep between the table and the sink.

What was she thinking? Surely she wouldn't
so much as consider filling out that registration
form, never mind writing out a check for the
amount posted?

Elizabeth shook her head, telling herself to
get real. She had no formal education. Everything she knew about writing—which wasn't
much—she had garnered from reading. Hardly
the credentials for becoming a writer.

But, on the other hand . . .

This time, the sharp blare of a car horn
jerked Elizabeth out of her memories and into
the very immediate danger of the present. Lost
in her thoughts, she had drifted perilously close
to another car.

Exhaling a deep breath of relief, Elizabeth
focused on her surroundings. She groaned
aloud at the realization that she had driven past

the exit ramp that would take her to the tavern where she was meeting De De.

Taking the next exit, she doubled back, upbraiding herself for woolgathering while she should have been concentrating, thereby keeping De De waiting, not to mention endangering herself as well as another motorist.

De De.

Visualizing the other woman reactivated the feeling of excitement and anticipation inside Elizabeth.

She had immediately felt an affinity with De De, and she was looking forward to dinner and conversation with her.

Another image formed in Elizabeth's mind. She dismissed it with a quick shake of her head.

She didn't want to recall Jake Ruttenburg. While she admired his work, in person he was too volatile, too unnerving . . . too sensuously compelling. And, if the articles she had read in several national magazines could be believed, he was much too active sexually. Divorced for some years, he apparently took his pleasure wherever and whenever he chose to do so.

Certainly no affinity there.

Elizabeth firmly reminded herself that she was searching for something meaningful, not the sort of sensuality Jake Ruttenburg had a reputation for indulging in to appease his oft-reported insatiable appetite.

And, Elizabeth mused, it appeared that De De just might be the one person to assist her along the scary path to self-enlightenment.

Four

"I saw on 'on-line' the other day that the house had lowered its entry level advance by two thousand dollars."

The statement issued with such conviction by the obviously worried, unpublished woman drew groans and gasps of shock from those around her, and it drew De De's attention from her goodbyes.

"Where did you say you heard this?" she asked, unable to credit this action by a publishing house with a track record for buying and grooming romance writers with potential.

"I saw it on-line." The young woman grimaced. "I don't recall who posted it; I'm so bad with names."

"Do you think it's true?" The quavering voice came from another, even younger woman. "I have a manuscript in that house that the editor appears interested in." She seemed stricken. "It took me over a year to write it, and if they've really lowered the advance . . ."

Her voice trailed away, but none of the seven women in the group needed to hear the words; they understood, perfectly. If the house had lowered its advance, it would mean over a year's worth of work for a few thousand dollars. They knew as well, if one house lowered its advances, other houses publishing romance novels would soon fall into line.

"In other words, don't give up your day job," clarified an older woman.

De De's snort of laughter held little amusement. She had recently submitted a proposal to the house under discussion. "I wasn't planning on doing that anytime soon, anyway."

"Why isn't my husband rich?" the older woman groused. "Like our guest speaker, Jake Ruttenburg."

Mention of the extremely well-paid author elicited a barrage of comments from the other women. Except De De. Reminded of Jake, her mind went wandering again, straight to the cause of her personal frustration.

Beau.

De De heaved a heartfelt sigh. She saw the bone-headed giant so rarely, in mere glimpses, like today, or in a group, usually at family gatherings. How was she ever going to get him to take notice of her as a woman instead of as her uncle's young, impetuous niece? And why oh why couldn't she simply put the man out of her mind, concentrate all her effort on her writing so it might prove successful?

How did one stop loving?

Where was the cool, elusive Beau now? Still with Jake for the dreaded interview or on the plane to Arizona?

De De knew her uncle's schedule, had committed it to memory. She glanced at her watch.

Yikes! She nearly squealed the word aloud. She had to get moving; Elizabeth had probably arrived at the restaurant already.

Calling out her goodbyes, she scooped up her things and literally ran from the building to her car.

"Bitch."

Beauregard Kantner cast an amused, sidelong glance at the disgruntled expression on Jake's face.

"You expected Mary Poppins?"

Jake scowled at the taller man. "Cute," he snarled, striding to the black limousine that glided to a stop alongside the curb. "Are you looking to get fired?"

Keeping pace effortlessly with his boss, Beau laughed; the sound was every bit as attractive as the rest of him. "Boy, oh man, that lady reporter really got to you, didn't she?" he observed, wryly.

"That lady reporter was no lady," Jake retorted, his lips curling in disgust.

"She's only trying to make a living," Beau said in the woman's defense, nodding to the chauffeur as he followed Jake into the car.

"No, my fair-minded friend." Jake shook his head in despair at his gentle giant of an assistant. "That female had set out to make a name for herself with that interview."

"How so?" Beau arched his toasty-gold eyebrows. As was his custom, he had politely not listened in on the interview. While Jake and the race horse-sleek freelance reporter had lunch at one side of the tony restaurant, Beau had occupied, at his request, a single table on the opposite side of the large dining room in the midtown hotel. "Did she get personal?"

"Personal?" Jake snorted. "She slipped her hand under the table and squeezed my knee, then trailed her fingers up my thigh."

"How intriguing." Beau's lips twitched with amusement. "And did she reach her goal?"

"Hell no." Jake curled his lip. "I caught her hand and gently placed it on top of the table."

"Spoilsport."

Though Jake cast his assistant a quelling look, his dark eyes took on the sheen of humor. "If I want to be fondled, I'll choose the time, the place, and the female fingers, thank you." He shrugged. "She was not well pleased . . . to say the least. She got down and dirty, and decided to play hardball." A smile flitted over his tight lips. "Pardon the pun."

"Sure." Beau was nothing if not accommodating. "Hardball, in what way?"

"In all the ways guaranteed to seriously irritate me." Jake glanced through the window, noting the passing scene with disinterest. The route to Philadelphia International was too familiar to him to take notice.

"Ahhh . . . I see." Beau's tone was wry, and

knowing. "She asked about how much money you earn."

"Of course." Jake managed to sound both angry and bored. "Don't they always?"

"Invariably." Beau chuckled. "But that's never thrown you before. You've always responded politely, but succinctly, that the information was not for publication."

"I let her know up front that the figure would not become a part of her private knowledge, either." Jake's voice was hard, adamant. A tight smile flattened his lips. "Our charming interviewer took umbrage at what she considered my unwillingness to cooperate."

"And that's when she got down and dirty?"

"Hmmm." Jake nodded, and shifted on the cushy, butter-soft leather seat, revealing his agitation. "She plunged into a rash of questions about my sex life."

"Of course, you are reputed to be more active than the much-hyped Don Juan," Beau dryly inserted.

"Yeah." Jake favored him with a cynical look. "If I were the womanizer I'm reputed to be, I'd be too damned exhausted to get out of my bed of debauchery, never mind accomplish any serious writing."

Beau contrived an expression of innocent astonishment. "You mean you haven't seduced hundreds of lovely ladies?"

"Not even dozens."

"I'll never tell."

"Thanks a lot." Jake frowned at Beau's fatuous grin. "When I dodged her barbed probe concerning all those lovely ladies, she dug deeper, and I quote: 'Tell me all about your relationship with that gorgeous hunk of an assistant of yours.' " He had assumed a breathy voice, and had effectively wiped the grin from Beau's face.

Beau grimaced and groaned. "Not again?"

"What do you mean, again?" Jake gave him a weary smile. "When did it ever stop?"

"I had hopes that the attempts to cop a coup by *outing* us were over." Beau shrugged. "The last couple of interviewers merely skirted the subject."

"But skirt they did." Jake grinned. "The uncertainty about our sexual preferences sure does drive 'em up the old wall, doesn't it?"

"Which is precisely why you deliberately keep them guessing," Beau drawled. "You're having too much fun needling them to admit that we are both straight as the proverbial arrow and fornicate only with females."

"Fornicate." Jake drew the word out, as if savoring the sound of it. "Good word, fornicate. Definitive."

Beau's laughter shimmered on the temperature-controlled air in the limo. "So's another one starting with F, more common and even more definitive."

Jake assumed a look of superiority. "But crude, my friend. Not too crude for the ears and lips of gossipmongers, you understand"—

he flashed a devilish smile—"but much too crude for you."

The beautiful giant actually blushed.

Jake roared with laughter. "No fornicating kidding, Beauregard, you are not to be believed."

"So I was raised by a devoutly religious mother." Beau defended his prudish ways, and not for the first time. "So what?"

"So I wouldn't have you any different," Jake avowed, still laughing. "Ah, we've arrived at the airport, and not a moment too soon from the look of your fiery cheeks."

"Get bent, Ruttenburg."

Laughter erupting from him once more, Jake stepped from the car before the driver could circle it and open the door. "There just might be hope for you yet, Beau." He sent a teasing look at the taller man. "After all these prim and proper years, you're finally loosening up a bit."

"And that's about as loose as I'm probably ever going to get," Beau muttered, moving to the back of the car to take four soft-sided suitcases and two nylon carry-ons from the driver. "I'll do that," he offered, giving the man an angelic smile. "Mr. Ruttenburg is rather particular about his luggage."

With a slight shrug, the driver stepped aside—not a moment too soon. In quick succession, one after the other, Beau unerringly tossed the four cases from the trunk to within inches of the skycap standing on the walkway.

His face blanching in alarm, the driver shot a worried glance at Jake.

He responded with a what-can-I-tell-you shrug. "Mr. Kantner has his moments of retaliation for insults, both real and imagined," Jake explained in droll tones, eyeing the expensive luggage with wry acceptance.

"I see . . ." The driver's blank expression revealed bafflement, rather than understanding.

I seriously doubt it.

Keeping the assessment to himself, Jake nodded and proffered his right hand to the confused man. "Thanks for the ride," he said straight-faced, grateful the man's handshake wasn't as limp as his sense of humor. He raised an eyebrow at Beau, who immediately stepped forward to hand over an envelope containing a gratuity.

"I'll request your services again," Jake promised as the envelope disappeared into the man's pocket, adding dryly, "If I do another promotional tour in Philadelphia."

Which will be never, if I have any say in the matter, he vowed in silent determination.

Smiling his satisfaction, the driver slid behind the wheel and drove the stretch black limousine away.

Jake leveled a benevolent glance on his assistant.

Beau laughed. "Feeling pretty good . . . now that the dreaded ten-city marathon tour is over, are you?"

"God, I hate doing that shit."

"No fornicating kidding?" Beau pulled an innocent, wide-eyed expression. "I'd never have guessed."

"Get bent, Kantner," Jake returned the phrase to its origin. His smile smug, he strolled to the electronically controlled doors into the terminal. "But first, take care of the bags, will you? And tip the skycap, please."

His smile bemused, shaking his head, Beau proceeded to do his employer's bidding.

"I'm almost afraid to ask, but is our flight to Phoenix on schedule?" Jake asked when Beau came up beside him, looming like an elongated shadow. Their friends had made arrangements to have a car meet them, and he hated to keep anyone waiting. Besides, he thought with wry self-amusement, now that the damned tour was over, and his research completed, he was looking forward to a brief vacation before diving into the first book of his trilogy.

"Yes," Beau answered solemnly. "Amazing, ain't it?"

"More like miraculous." Jake grinned and checked his wristwatch. "I see the sun's over my forearm. Time for a fortifying drink before we depart." He grimaced. "Linked with the term terminal, the word 'departure' conjures up some rather unpleasant images."

Beau chuckled. "You are tired, aren't you?" he drawled, pacing beside Jake into the cocktail lounge nearest their departure gate.

"Yes." Jake nodded, leading the way to a small table removed from the other, mostly dejected-looking patrons. "Tired and frustrated."

"Mentally frustrated? Emotionally frustrated. Or physically frustrated?" Beau raised his eyebrows as he set down the two carry-ons before folding his considerable length onto the narrow chair.

"All of the aforementioned." Jake gave their drink orders to the bored-looking young waiter. Then he brought his hooded gaze to Beau. "You happen to notice the woman standing beside De De earlier when you arrived at the U of P?"

Beau's frown answered before he did. "No. Why? Is it important?"

"Could be." Jake shrugged and held his silence until the waiter served their drinks and walked away. "She's an aspiring mystery writer. De De met her today at the seminar."

"Serious or a wide-eyed wannabe?"

"Hard to tell." Jake shrugged again. The smile tugging at his lips was derisive. "But that woman, more than that damned tour, is the cause of my frustration."

Eyeing Jake speculatively, Beau picked up his accustomed seltzer and lime and took a deep swallow. "You felt physically attracted to her?" he asked with the bluntness of long familiarity and friendship.

"Strong as hell." Jake followed the acknowledgment with a long pull from his bottle of light beer.

"She come on to you?" Though still solemn, Beau's voice was laced with strands of amusement.

"No. Just the opposite, in fact. That's the bitchy part." Jake raised his bottle in a silent salute to his friend. "She was cool, distant, and repressive." He expelled a short, self-mocking laugh. "And, weird as it sounds, the colder she got, the stronger the attraction got. I wanted her, on the spot, and the wanting's still running hot, even after several hours." He scowled. "Uncomfortable feeling."

"I can imagine. And you're right."

"Right?"

"It's weird."

"Yeah. That's what I said." Jake looked long suffering. "I knew I heard it somewhere."

The infectious peal of laughter from Beau drew reciprocal smiles from patrons sitting close by. "Well, since we are about to depart the city of brotherly love—if you'll excuse the expression—and your chances of seeing the woman again in the near future are just about nil, I'd venture a guess that you're somewhere between a rock and a hard place."

"You've got it wrong, Sherlock," Jake murmured quite seriously. "I *am* a rock and a hard place."

Beau's lips twitched with renewed laughter. "In that case, since you rejected the overtures of the lady reporter, I'd suggest you find another woman—soonest."

Jake contrived to look shocked. "Here in the airport? Are you indicating I initiate a ground-level club to compete with the sky-high society?"

"It has merit," Beau intoned judiciously. "It's a lot less farther to fall."

"And the landing's a helluva lot softer," Jake observed, relieved at the lessening tension in his body, while continuing to marvel at his unusual and unexpected response to the woman under discussion.

For the life of him, he couldn't figure out what had happened to him earlier. Although he had experienced immediate attraction to other women, never in his adult life had it been such a strong and intense physical desire on first sight. And then, to have to endure the aching discomfort of such an encounter—and turn down an offer to have the ache appeased—was altogether beyond his comprehension.

Weird barely defined the bizarre experience.

Of course, there was no way he'd have taken on the reporter; that would have been like bedding a barracuda.

He'd do well to forget the whole episode, the immediate response of his body, the unpleasant free-lance reporter . . . and most especially, Elizabeth Leninger.

"Feeling better?"

"Yeah." Jake finished off his beer, set the bottle on the table next to Beau's empty glass, and shoved his chair back, grateful for the necessity to move. "I suppose we'd better amble on over to our designated area." He stood and glanced at the large clock on the wall. "If the flight is indeed on schedule, they should be boarding pretty soon."

"One can but hope," Beau muttered, falling into step with Jake as he exited the bar. "But I wouldn't wager the homestead on it."

Five

The flight was on time.

Feeling uncomfortably like a sheep being herded as he went through the boarding process, Jake shuffled along, marveling at the girth of the man in front of him, and figuring the odds against the man fitting into a single seat, even one of the roomier seats in first class.

But the moment they were ushered into the plane, Jake forgot about the man and his potential seating problem. Sinking with a silent sigh into the plush window seat, he absently watched Beau stash their carry-on bags in the overhead compartment.

"I wonder how soon they'll serve dinner?"

Beau settled into the seat next to Jake before responding, "You just had lunch."

"I hardly touched it." Jake grimaced. "I was too busy keeping *her* from touching me."

"And now you're hungry?"

"No." Jake rested his head against the back of the seat and closed his eyes. "Sleepy."

"So sleep." Beau's voice held amusement. "I'll hold the flight attendant at bay until you wake up."

"My hero." Jake smiled and opened his eyes. "But I think I'll wait till we're airborne."

"You know, it's remarks like 'My hero' that keep speculation about us alive," Beau observed.

Jake grinned. "Yeah, I know. Ain't it fun?"

Beau shook his head in despair. "You have a twisted sense of humor, Ruttenburg."

"You should know," Jake retorted. "How often, do you think, I have heard similar remarks you made that were deliberately intended for the ears of others?"

Beau laughed, eliciting a quick but comprehensive and appreciative look from the pretty flight attendant moving along the aisle, securing the overhead compartments in preparation for takeoff.

"I see a possible conquest there," Jake murmured, indicating the attendant. "If you're interested?"

"I'm not." Beau didn't bother to take a closer look at the woman. "Layover quickies don't turn me on."

"What does?" The teasing note had vanished from Jake's tone, leaving it dead serious. "On reflection, I can't remember the last time you showed any interest in a woman. How long has it been for you, anyway?"

Beau's good-humored expression changed, becoming austere yet strangely even more attractive. "In all due respect, sir," he said, very softly, "that is none of your frigging business."

Hearing the next thing to the absolute no-no

word coming from the mouth of his oh-so-proper assistant triggered Jake's amusement. His laughter filled the first-class section, causing a few reciprocal smiles and an equal number of frowns. He ignored both.

"Touché, friend," he said, chuckling at the flush creeping from Beau's neck to his cheeks.

Beau responded with a scowl and an accusation, "Every bad word I speak, I learned from you. If my mother knew . . ." He shook his head. "Well, I don't think she'd adore you quite so much as she does."

"So, are you going to tell her how reprehensible I am?" Jake asked soberly, laughter dancing in his eyes.

"And shatter her illusions after all these years?" Beau grimaced. "I haven't the heart."

"Thanks . . . I . . ."

The whining of the jet engines cut across Jake's quiet voice, drowning it out. Offering Beau a shrug, he settled back for taxiing and takeoff.

His smile serene, Beau followed his employer's example.

"You can go to sleep, now," Beau said when the large craft attained cruising level. "I'll stand—sit—guard to insure you are not disturbed."

"Hmmm," Jake murmured by way of a response. He smiled at Beau; then, releasing the seat, he tilted it back as far as it would go, settled in, and closed his eyes.

With the drone of the engines and the soft

conversation of his fellow passengers receding into the background, Jake drowsily reflected on the cause of his excessive weariness.

He loved writing. Period. His love affair with the written word had begun with the first book he had ever read; it was still on-going. He had scribbled his first stories in longhand while in grade school. He still had those barely legible stories, carefully wrapped in blue paper, stored in the bottom drawer of a water- and fireproof filing cabinet. He had continued to write throughout middle school, high school, and college. In retrospect, Jake couldn't recall a time when he had given so much as a passing thought to doing any other kind of work.

Of course, he had done other work. One had to eat. So, while waiting, hoping, and praying for some editor at some publishing house to *discover* him, Jake had held numerous and varied jobs.

While still in college, he had waited tables—which he didn't mind, since the tips were good—and had clerked in a men's shoe store—which he hated, since a sizable number of his customers were flat-out difficult. After college, he had worked for a spell in a small advertising agency, writing inane prose to promote equally inane products.

He had been two years into the advertising work with a larger agency, and beginning to feel desperate, when he'd made his first sale to a small but prestigious publishing house. The female editor who had contacted him had lavishly praised his work and had offered him the princely sum of seven thousand dollars in advance against royalties in exchange for the right of the house to publish his work.

Jake knew that, should he live to be seven thousand years old, he would never forget the heady thrill he had experienced from that very first sale.

Naturally, he had tripped all over his tongue in accepting the offer. He still published with the same house, and the same complimentary female was still his editor.

There was one significant difference, however. Now, after over a dozen and a half novels in print, Jake's hardcover, softcover mass-market, multibook contract advances ran into several millions of dollars.

But, as in just about everything else in life, there was a downside to success. Jake first experienced it in the guise of a beautiful and ambitious young assistant editor. Her name was Allison, and she was blond, slim, and elegant. She had advanced on him at first meeting. Flattered, then besotted, he had surrendered without a whimper.

They had married in heated haste; Jake had lived to slowly regret it.

He had neither objected to nor even minded the way she had spent his money; by then he was earning plenty. He could afford to indulge his bride. Nor had he uttered a questioning word when, despite her earlier claim of being professionally ambitious, Allison had turned her back on her career soon after their wedding. He could afford to keep her.

Jake had even persevered when she'd revealed an extravagant, self-indulgent streak and often turned cruel when thwarted. He himself possessed traits that were less than perfect. He tended to get grouchy and growly when under deadline pressure, and he could be a cold bastard when riled.

But Jake's perseverance ended, and whatever feelings he had left for Allison died, on the day he discovered that his wife had willfully and secretly destroyed their child in the first trimester of pregnancy.

"I don't care how you do it, or how much it costs, get her out of my life!"

Jake had been in his cold bastard mode when he had issued those instructions to his lawyer on the day he had walked away from his marriage. In the eleven years since, he had never looked back, nor had he ever again entrusted his emotions to a woman. The major bane of his existence became promotional tours. To say he didn't enjoy doing tours would have been to greatly underestimate the case.

Jake cringed at the mere suggestion of a tour.

It wasn't that he was uncomfortable with meeting and conversing with readers and fans of his work. In truth, he enjoyed the discourse and communication. But he definitely did not like doing interviews, whether for TV, radio, or print. His major resistance to the tours, though, was to the brutal scheduling.

Invariably, the drill was: hop a plane, fly to a city, be whisked from one place to another; the hours of each day filled from early morning to late at night with a never-ending round of autographing sessions and interviews. And then it was back to the airport, to fly to another city, to start the process all over again.

Jake always came home from a tour exhausted and hungry, since it seemed the persons in charge of scheduling often forgot that the human body required nutritional sustenance to function and to survive.

So it was that Jake rarely conceded to his publisher's pleas to agree to a tour, and under no circumstances would he agree to one during a period of work in progress. He had only relented for this last tour because his publisher had caught him in a mellow mood, while he was between books and doing research for a newly conceived trilogy.

And if Jake was averse to doing promotional tours, he was adamant against doing writing workshops. It was his firmly held belief that writers—good writers—weren't taught, they were born. To his way of thinking, one, almost anyone, could be taught the correct mechanicals of writing, but the spark of creativity was either there to begin with, or it wasn't, and no amount of lecturing would instill it.

Only for his niece, De De, would Jake so much as consider breaking his own rule against doing a workshop. In truth, he hadn't consented to conduct a session; he had agreed to speak to the assemblage for a few moments.

And he had fulfilled his agreement. He had addressed the group for less than fifteen minutes, and even then he had been cutting it too close to his appointment time with the freelance barracuda disguised as a reporter.

That was why he had made a beeline for his niece after finishing his little speech. Jake didn't get to see De De all that often, and he had wanted to give her a quick hug and say hello before rushing off to the interview.

The attraction to the woman next to De De had slammed into him when he was still several feet away from them. The sensation had been so strong, it had nearly stopped him in his determined passage through the chattering group.

Who was she? Jake had wondered, slightly shocked at the heat shimmering through his body, as he forged ahead, toward the cause of that heat.

Jake judged the woman to be some nine or ten years older than his niece—and a lot more mature.

She certainly wasn't beautiful at any rate, not in the currently accepted definition of beauty. But her features were finely delineated, almost patrician, and there was a reserved serenity about her that he found compelling.

She stood a good five or six inches taller than his niece, was slender and long limbed. Her apparel and makeup were conservative, her hair style severe.

Jake had been overtaken by a nearly compulsive desire to stride up to her, yank the pins from her neatly folded French plait, then spear his fingers into the loosed strands of her gleaming auburn hair.

Naturally, he had taken no such liberties, nor had he taken her mouth with his own—a desire that had quickly overridden the one to feel her hair curl around his hands.

Weird barely described these impulses.

Tearing himself away from the meeting room, from the woman De De introduced to him as Elizabeth Leninger, had been one of the most difficult feats Jake had ever accomplished.

Had he been without a woman too long, or what?

Laughing to himself, at himself, he gave a fleeting thought to the predator posing as a female reporter who had blatantly if silently offered a means of release to him. Then, he just as fleetingly shoved the thought aside. Hell, before he'd allow himself to get that desperate for appeasement, he'd take himself in hand.

The idea of the necessity of taking such a drastic measure struck a sober note in Jake's mind.

Pull it together, he advised himself. He'd do well to take Beau's advice and find another woman—soonest.

Settling into a more comfortable position, Jake yawned, banished all thought, and fell asleep.

* * *

Seated next to Jake, Beau heard the even cadence of his employer's breathing and knew Jake had drifted off. Silently he settled his long frame as comfortably as possible in the confining seat and closed his eyes.

But sleep did not embrace him. Jake's words held slumber at bay.

How long has it been for you, anyway?

The answer that Beau refused to voice rang loud and clear in his head.

I haven't touched a woman, or even been tempted to do so, for almost ten years . . . ever since De De celebrated her eighteenth birthday.

De De.

Beau sighed, hoping to relieve the sudden pressure in his chest. Merely thinking of her set him on fire. His arms ached to hold her, his hands itched to touch her soft, fair skin, his lips burned to explore her sweet mouth.

She had been such a cute, adorable child, he recalled, a gentle smile easing the tightness of his lips. He had loved her then, too, but in an avuncular, uncomplicated way.

Now he merely loved her.

Merely?

Beau swallowed a burst of deprecating laughter. "Merely" barely touched on the depth of his love for her.

Why did she have to grow up?

He fought back another burst of laughter. Of course, she had to . . . but did she have to grow up into the only woman he had ever felt he couldn't live without . . . and the only woman he knew he couldn't have?

The urge to laugh dissolved in the face of hard reality. Opening his eyes, Beau gazed at his best friend, and employer. Sleep smoothed the sharp angles and taut planes of Jake's face, revealing a vulnerability he worked diligently at concealing. Beau knew it was there, deeply buried and hidden from the world.

And Beau knew as well that Jake's beloved niece was a part of his vulnerability. Anything, or anyone, that even appeared to be harmful to De De would be harmful to her uncle. And Beau would forfeit his own happiness, even his own life, to protect Jake.

He loved Jake like a brother, no, more than a brother, for not all brothers would rush to the defense of another without a thought for their own safety, as Jake had done.

Jake hadn't even known Beau at the time of the incident.

Over twenty years had passed since then, and still Beau's stomach muscles clenched at the memory.

At twenty-one, Beauregard Kantner had been a golden-haired, smooth-cheeked, absolutely beautiful young man. That he was also soft-spoken, gentle, and sensitive to the feelings of others made him not only suspect so far as his masculinity was concerned, but a target for certain types of young men who had a need to prove their own masculinity.

On one crisp fall evening it had been Beau's misfortune to be crossing a deserted section of the college campus just when a group of such young men happened to be on the prowl, their course intersecting with his at a dark and isolated spot.

"Well, if it isn't the pretty girlie-man," sneered one, elbowing the man next to him. "Doesn't he have the prettiest mouth?" he went on, suggestively.

The harassment was immediately taken up by the others. Making lewd and obscene remarks, they encircled Beau, then moved as one, closing the circle.

Devoutly religious and a pacifist, greatly outnumbered into the bargain, Beau remained absolutely still, eyeing his tormentors. Preparing to defend himself, yet certain he could not prevail, he knew he faced the possibility of losing not only his innocence and pride but his very life.

Though Beau got in a few good shots, the outcome, with odds of eight to one, was a foregone conclusion. He was on hands and knees, blood trickling from the split in his lower lip, bruises beginning to purple the fair skin of his chest and back, exposed because of the rents in his shirt. His pants and briefs had been yanked down over his behind. Revulsion churned in his stomach, terror clouded his mind.

The eight rape-intent toughs were closing in

on him, one had gripped his hips and another had grasped his hair, jerking his head up, when a savior appeared, seemingly out of nowhere.

Beau learned later that his savior's name was Jake Ruttenburg, all-American college quarterback, and that Jake had decided to take a short-cut back to his dorm after football practice and a follow-up lecture from the coach.

Even with the dim illumination cast by the streetlights, some distance away, Jake had instantly perceived the situation. Without hesitation, he'd rushed forward, plowing into the eight with the same ferocity and intent with which he himself had so often been sacked, leveling the playing-field odds to four to one.

No real contest.

And, although Beau's fighting spirit was renewed, he proved a rank amateur in comparison to his defender; Jake dispatched six of the would-be bullies, while Beau struggled with the other two.

Now, after all those years, Beau's stomach muscles relaxed and he could even smile at the horrific memory. For, as terrifying as the encounter had been, there had been one positive result. That was his friendship with the now-famous man who slept on the seat next to him.

Without question, Beau would do anything to retain the friendship of that peacefully sleeping man, even denying himself the only woman he had ever loved.

Six

Even with having to backtrack, Elizabeth arrived at the tavern before De De. The hostess escorted her to a table along the side of the room, next to a bank of uncurtained windows. Through the windows, she could see a summer dining patio, now deserted, and a garden with narrow pathways beyond, illuminated by strings of tiny lights festooning the trees and shrubs. She had given the waitress the bar order when the hostess returned to the table, a breathless De De in tow.

"Sorry I took so long, but I got sidetracked before I left," she said, after thanking the hostess. Heaving a sigh, she settled onto the chair opposite Elizabeth, and indicated the room with a flick of her hand. "So, what do you think of the place? Not fancy, but nice, isn't it?"

"Yes, and I like it," Elizabeth answered both questions. "It has . . . ambience."

"Exactly," De De agreed. "Did you order our—" She broke off as the waitress came up to the table, two glasses of white wine balanced on the tray on her palm. "I see you did." She smiled at the waitress, then at Elizabeth. "Thanks, now I'm doubly parched."

Elizabeth felt a surge of anticipatory excitement. De De was a new experience for her. Unlike Elizabeth's other female friends, all of whom were more sedate and reserved, the younger woman was a breath of invigorating air, bubbly and brimming over with enthusiasm.

And there was no sense of newly met awkwardness between them. They chatted throughout dinner as if they had known one another for years. De De did most of the talking, in response to Elizabeth's questions concerning the business of writing. And the girl proved a fount of information.

"Have you written anything?" she asked bluntly over the piled-high plate of nachos they shared.

"Ummm," Elizabeth murmured, chewing the corn chip in her mouth before elaborating. "I wrote some stuff longhand the summer between high school and college, and some more the following winter while—" She broke off, reticent about confiding in the younger woman when she had never done so before. Then, determined to match De De's candor, she continued, "I was pregnant with my first child."

"You had to leave school?" De De's voice was warm with understanding and sympathy.

"Yes." Elizabeth gave her a faint smile. "My parents insisted on marriage." Her shrug was even fainter, and said volumes. "His parents, or more precisely, his mother, insisted I leave school." From a distance of nineteen years, she could now see the idiocy of it all. "So as not to advertise my fall from grace, if you get my drift?"

De De groaned. "Your mother-in-law was the old-fashioned, appearances-matter, prudish sort?"

"Not was, is."

"Gee, some gals have all the luck," De De said wryly. "Don't tell me, let me guess. She won't approve of your writing either, will she?"

"Oh, probably not."

"Then don't tell her."

Elizabeth grinned at De De's bulldog expression. "I wasn't planning on telling her."

"Good for you." De De grinned back.

All consideration for Richard's mother dispatched, the conversation continued.

Somewhat to her amazement, over the main course, Elizabeth found herself giving De De a synopsis of the three stories she had packed away in a shirt box. She refrained from mentioning that De De was the first person she had ever taken into her confidence.

"I'm sure the stories would now read like the work of an immature teenager, which of course they are," she finished, sparing a smile for the waitress who was clearing away the dishes. "No dessert, I'll just have coffee, please."

"Just coffee for me, too," De De said, also declining the dessert menu. "You haven't read them since you packed them away?" she asked in surprise when the waitress left to get their coffees.

Elizabeth shook her head and let out a short laugh. "I was going to . . . after I mailed the registration form for the seminar, but"—she decided to confess—"I guess I was afraid to see how bad they are—to be appalled at my own audacity."

"Audacious, smacious." De De snorted, dismissing the very idea. "When did you decide you wanted to write fiction?" She raised her eyebrows.

Elizabeth noted that they were as dark as her uncle's, and was jolted when his image loomed in her mind. The sensation was unfamiliar, and rather scary. Rejecting it, she rushed to reply.

"I don't remember, exactly." She frowned. "When I was in the third or fourth grade, I suppose."

"And you are how old now?" De De persisted.

"Thirty-six." Elizabeth grimaced. "I'll be thirty-seven in a few months."

"You don't look it," De De opined, narrowing her eyes as she minutely examined Elizabeth's face.

Elizabeth laughed. "Thank you, and may I return your generous compliment?"

"No." De De set her dark hair swirling with a sharp shake of her head. "The bane of my life is forever being told I look younger than my years."

"You'll change your mind about that before too long," Elizabeth predicted.

"I doubt it."

The grim certainty in the girl's voice jogged

Elizabeth into recalling that De De had declared herself hopelessly in love with her uncle's assistant.

De De's uncle . . . Once again an image of Jake Ruttenburg formed in Elizabeth's mind, playing havoc with her pulses, twanging her nerves. And once again, with firm determination, she rejected that vision.

"If you say so," she murmured, knowing better.

"I do." De De looked belligerent for a moment, then her fierce expression softened. "I don't want to look like a dewy-eyed kid, Elizabeth."

"Beau?" Elizabeth asked, recollecting the name of the incredibly handsome man who had arrived at the conference room to collect Jake.

"Yes. Beauregard Kantner." De De sighed. "I long for him to stop seeing me as a youngster, his employer's kid niece." A devilish light sparked to life in her eyes. "Although it would probably shock the socks off his big feet, what I really long for is to crawl all over that tree-tall man."

Elizabeth didn't respond. She couldn't, for in truth she was a little shocked herself, not exactly at De De's desire for the man, that was understandable. Beau was the most gorgeous man she had ever seen. What startled and shocked Elizabeth was the forthright way in which the young woman had declared her intentions and desires.

"Now I've shocked you," De De said, reading Elizabeth like a book. "Haven't I?"

"Well . . . a little," Elizabeth admitted. "I'm not accustomed to such . . . plain talk from a woman."

De De's eyes grew wide, and she stared at Elizabeth in stark disbelief. "Are you serious?"

"Yes."

"Where have you been hiding all these years, in a cave removed from the real world?"

Elizabeth shrugged, unfazed by the girl's bluntness. "I guess I've led a sheltered existence until now."

"Until me, you mean?" De De grinned. "Hadn't you heard that women had been liberated from repression?"

"I never felt repressed," Elizabeth objected. "And, so far as I know, none of my friends did, either."

"Hmmm." De De eyed her over the rim of the coffee cup she had raised to her lips. "How did you feel?"

"Me, personally?"

"Uh-huh." She took a tentative sip of the steaming coffee. "That's hot," she warned, as Elizabeth brought her own cup to her lips.

"Thanks." Elizabeth gently blew on the brew, contemplating her answer to the girl's question. How had she felt all these years?

"I suppose I felt comfortable, secure, and protected," she finally replied.

"Protected from what?" De De lifted her cup for another test taste. "From life?"

"Not at all," Elizabeth said at once in protest,

while secretly beginning to doubt. Were she
and her kind as outdated as the poodle skirt?

The thought was unpalatable, so, of course,
she defended her position. "I've experienced
life; I've raised two daughters, you know. And
I've experienced death." She paused, then said
quietly, "I lost my husband this past spring."

"Oh, Elizabeth, I'm sorry." De De's bright,
challenging gaze softened. "How did it happen? An accident?"

Elizabeth shook her head. "No. Richard suffered a massive heart attack, brought on, I feel
sure, by overwork and stress." And trying to
maintain two separate and different lives, she
added in anguished silence.

"Yes, stress is a killer." De De sighed. "We
lost my grandfather, my mother's father, to a
stress-induced coronary almost four years ago."

"I'm sorry to hear that," Elizabeth murmured, feeling the sentiment inadequate.

The shadows fled from De De's eyes before
a teasing gleam, causing a catch in Elizabeth's
breath because of their similarity to her uncle's
flashing blue eyes.

"Fortunately his son, my uncle Jake, though
as much of an achiever as his father, handles it
better."

"How does he handle it?" Elizabeth asked
almost against her will, yet too curious to hold
it in.

"He walks away from it."

Elizabeth frowned. Somehow the statement
didn't fit with the dynamic-looking man she

had briefly met, but had been so unsettlingly affected by.

"Seriously," De De said, smiling into Elizabeth's frown. "I know for a fact that he has walked away from his computer and missed contract deadlines that were, supposedly, chiseled in stone."

"But however does he explain the lapse to his publisher?" Elizabeth asked, from a position of ignorance.

"We're talking about fiction here, friends, not brain surgery," De De intoned in a theatrically deepened voice, in a very bad imitation of her uncle. "No one is going to die on the table of lateness."

"Incredible."

De De grinned, once again reminding Elizabeth of the man under discussion. "I call it ballsy."

Though again shocked by the girl's frankness, Elizabeth couldn't contain a burst of laughter.

"You're incorrigible," she said.

"Not at all." De De's superior tone vied with her mischievous expression. "I'm honest."

"Yes." Elizabeth agreed, nodding. "Refreshingly so. And, for my part, I hope we are going to be friends."

De De's eyes grew round with feigned surprise. "Oh, didn't you know? We're already friends."

A warm feeling of acceptance spread through Elizabeth. A spontaneous smile curved her lips and brightened her usually somber hazel eyes. "Thank you, De De."

"You might not be thanking me before too long," De De cautioned, her blue eyes dancing with merriment. "I have this tendency to shake up my friends' preconceptions."

"That's okay." Elizabeth gave a careless shrug that felt good. "I'm beginning to think my preconceptions need a little shaking up."

"You're on, and we'll start with your cock-eyed idea of being audacious in wanting to write." De De shot a glance at the delicate, expensive watch encircling her equally delicate wrist. "But not tonight. I still have some things I must do at home, and I have to work tomorrow."

"Yes . . . ahh . . . of course." Elizabeth was crushed by a ridiculous sense of disappointment and rejection.

"Do you have anything on for Wednesday evening?"

"No, nothing," she quickly assured De De, her spirits lifting. "What did you have in mind?"

"We could get together somewhere." De De's brow creased in a thoughtful frown. "Your daughters are still at home?"

"The younger one, Sally, is. Ella is away at college. Why?"

"Well, I'm sure you wouldn't want to leave your daughter home alone while you came into the city to my place—even though, naturally, she'd be more than welcome to come with you, if she'd want to," she explained. "But I could come to your place . . . if you'd like?"

"I'd like that very much," Elizabeth said. "You could come for dinner . . . If you wish?"

De De laughed. "Love it. I go bonkers over home cooking. Just give me the time and directions, and I'll be there." She pulled a stern expression. "And have some of your work ready for me to look at."

"On the condition that you'll bring a sample of yours for me," Elizabeth countered, asking herself how in the world she could get a sample of her writing together in three days' time.

"Okay." De De shrugged. "Who knows, maybe you'll notice something I've been missing."

"But I don't know much about romance novels," Elizabeth said in mild protest.

"Do you know what you like?"

"Well, of course."

"Then that's all you have to know." De De gave her a satisfied smile.

In turn, Elizabeth gave De De directions to her house, and specified her usual time for dinner.

They parted with mutual and obvious reluctance on the restaurant parking lot a few minutes later.

Elizabeth was not distracted by the flow of memories during the drive home; she was too busy planning the menu for what she hoped would be only the first of many of De De's visits to her home.

Seven

The plane was not only on time, it was early.
It was hot in Phoenix.

Exiting the terminal after collecting the luggage, Jake felt as if he had walked into a blast furnace, and was more than happy to see the limo—this one white—which was late, glide to a halt along the curb.

The driver stepped out of the car and frowned as he scanned the faces of the people exiting the terminal. He reached into the car to retrieve a sign, but before he could straighten and hold the placard aloft, Jake called out to him.

"Ruttenburg?"

"Yes, sir." The man flashed a quick smile of relief as he again reached into the car to pop the trunk. "Am I late, or was the plane early?" he asked, circling around the back of the car to collect the luggage.

"It was early." Jake shrugged and, leaving Beau to help the man stash the bags, got into the car.

After the dry heat outside, the interior felt frigid, not to mention welcome.

"If it's still this hot in October, what must it

be like in the middle of July?" Beau wondered aloud, folding himself onto the plush seat next to Jake.

"The bowels of hell?" Jake responded in a tone of voice every bit as dry as the outside air.

Beau chuckled.

Jake grinned.

The long car pulled smoothly into traffic, and was soon on the highway, heading away from the city.

"Lord, I'd forgotten how dry everything looks out here, after the greenness of Pennsylvania," Beau muttered, staring through the side window at the arid landscape.

"Yeah," Jake agreed, staring at the passing scenery from the other side of the highway. "But, in a strange way, the desert is as mesmerizing as the ocean."

"Hmmm," Beau murmured, nodding. He turned in his seat to delve into the drinks compartment. "Makes me thirsty," he said, grunting in appreciation for their host and hostess's forethought in providing several bottles of seltzer water, as well as beer, wine, and harder stuff. "You want a beer?" he asked before serving himself.

"Why not? I'm on vacation." Jake turned to smile at Beau. "I'm also thirsty."

"Natural reaction," Beau drawled, passing the opened bottle to him. "See the desert, get thirsty."

Jake grunted agreement, then took a deep swallow of the beer. "Mmmm, that's good.

Cold." He raised the bottle. "Thank you, Patsy and Bryan." He was saluting the couple who had arranged for the vacation, the car, and the liquid refreshment. "May your union long survive."

"Hear, hear," Beau seconded the toast, gulping back the last of his seltzer. Twisting off the cap on another small bottle, he poured, sipped, then slanted a bemused look at Jake. "You know, it's still hard for me to believe that Patsy and Bryan have been together almost ten years."

"I know." Jake chuckled. "It's even harder to believe that scruffy, brainy little girl we met in the political science lecture hall at the very beginning of our senior year turned out to be the sleek, savvy, knock-'em-dead campaign manager she is today."

"Or that the same scruffy kid managed to snare Bryan Connigan, who ten years ago was a handsome, suave, rich, and eligible bachelor doing his political thing in and around the Arizona capital."

"Yet Patsy hasn't changed all that much."

Beau looked surprised.

"Inside," Jake clarified. "She's still the gutsy, sincere, genuinely nice gal we took under our collective wings all those years ago."

"Yes, she is." Beau's voice and smile were soft.

"You know, friend," Jake murmured, his dark gaze steady on Beau's face. "At the time, I thought you had a 'thing,' strong feelings for her."

"I did," Beau was quick to admit. "But the

'thing' and the strong feelings were of the big brother variety." He grinned. "They're still in me. Much as I like and respect him, if Bryan should ever hurt her in any way . . ." He drew a deep breath, and his voice took on a hard, serrated edge, "I think I'd pound him into the ground."

"You'd have help," Jake said, unfazed by the threat of violence from his pacifist friend.

"I figured I would," Beau drawled, the perfection of his white teeth revealed by a flashing grin.

"Hopefully it will never come to that," Jake said sardonically. "Bryan has influence and friends in high—and some low—places."

"Yeah." Beau's smile was serene, unaffected. "We could turn up missing."

Jake gave a mock shudder. "Perish the thought."

"Patsy would miss us."

Jake erupted in strangled laughter, choking on the swallow of beer he'd taken into his mouth—and on Beau's dryly voiced observation.

"You okay, sir?" Beau widened his eyes in a patently false show of concern.

"Get laid," Jake muttered, swiping at the tears stinging his eyes.

Beau laughed in his face. "If I'm not mistaken, you are the one claiming frustration. Aren't you?"

Jake growled an expletive.

"Tsk, tsk." Beau sorrowfully shook his head.

"Take heart—or something—oh profane one, perhaps a fair damsel will appear to alleviate your . . . condition in the near future."

"You're close to the edge, Kantner," Jake said in soft warning.

"Who knows?" Beau went on, supremely unconcerned. "She might show up at Patsy and Bryan's anniversary party at the end of next week."

Though Jake scowled, Beau's mention of the party distracted him from thoughts of vengeance. "Only Patsy would plan a combined anniversary and Halloween party," he said, shaking his head in wonder at the idea.

"Yes, but then, only Patsy would plan a Halloween wedding and wear black instead of white," Beau observed.

"Too true." Jake laughed, then glanced through the window as he continued, "And speaking of that witchy woman, I do believe we will soon be arriving at her plush den."

The driver turned the long car off the highway and through two stone pillars standing sentinel on either side of a private road. A mile or so later, he turned onto a curving drive and brought the car to a purring stop before the open gates of a walled, sprawling Spanish-style hacienda.

Before the driver had stepped from the car, one of the two large, carved, and heavy doors of the ranch house opened, and a small, slender woman came running along the short path to the parted wrought-iron gates. Behind her, strolling at a more leisurely pace, was a tall, dark, and handsome man.

"Jake! Beau!" she cried in obvious excitement and delight, launching herself into the arms of the first man to exit the vehicle—which happened to be Beau.

Laughing, the gentle giant swept her diminutive form into a close embrace.

"Hey, what about me?" Jake groused, slanting a hello grin at Bryan, who stood back, an indulgent smile curving his classically masculine lips.

"What about you?" Patsy chided, disentangling herself from Beau's arms to fling herself into Jake's.

While Jake exchanged hugs and kisses with Patsy, Bryan exchanged greetings and handshakes with Beau.

"Shall we go inside, out of this heat?" Bryan asked, transferring his hand to the one Jake held out to him, while keeping his one arm draped around Patsy's shoulders.

Meanwhile, Beau turned to assist the driver with the unloading of the luggage.

"I thought you'd never ask," Jake replied, planting a last kiss on Patsy's cheek before releasing her to hoist one of the bags. "After the autumnal crispness of the air back home, this heat feels brutal."

"You get used to it." Patsy blithely dismissed the high temperature. "Low humidity, you know."

"Sure." Jake tossed her a skeptical look.

Bryan laughed, and led the parade into the house.

Jake and Beau groaned with relief upon entering the cool and spacious foyer.

"You're in your usual rooms," Bryan said, loping along the hallway leading into the east wing of the sprawling ranch house. "Come along, and we'll dump the bags."

Patsy started off along the central hallway. "I hope you guys are hungry," she called after the men. "I have a cold snack prepared for you."

"As long as you have a cold drink to go with it," Jake called back to her, trailing after Bryan.

"But of course," her fading voice wafted to them. "A full pitcher of frozen margaritas for us and some chilled bottles of seltzer for Beau."

The evening was easy, relaxed; the conversation general, at times nonsensical; the food excellent; and the liquid refreshment ever flowing, setting the pattern for the lazy days that followed.

Unencumbered by work or any kind of pressure, Jake felt the tension slowly drain from him. He did not venture outside, into the dry heat, other than for a quick and refreshing plunge into the olympic-size pool located by the patio a short distance from the house.

However, despite his unwinding, a niggling sense of frustration lingered, prodding him at odd moments of the day and night—primarily at night, and most noticeably whenever Bryan and Patsy touched lightly or cast intimate glances at one another.

Even at such a lazy pace, the days inevitably drifted by. Too soon, by Jake's reckoning, the evening of the anniversary/Halloween party arrived.

Thinking of everything, as she always did, Patsy had provided costumes for Jake and Beau.

"Oh, swell," Jake muttered when she produced two large boxes, emblazoned with the name of a Phoenix costume shop. "I do adore playing dress-up," he lied sarcastically, grimacing when she laughed at him.

"You're going to like it," she promised, sharing a secret smile with Bryan. "It's definitely you."

"I doubt it," he retorted suspiciously.

Jake's suspicions proved correct.

Whereas Beau's monk costume, consisting of a long robe, braided rope sash, and sandals, perfectly fit his personality, the getup of a Roman gladiator—a diaperlike hip swathing, mesh-metal breastplate, and short sword—provided for Jake, he found just shy of obscene. Feeling ridiculous, as well as embarrassed in the skimpy rig, he strode along the hallway and into the living room where Patsy, Bryan, and Beau waited. Beau received a quelling glance for having the temerity to grin.

"You can't be serious about this," he said, leveling a glare at his host and hostess.

"But it is you," Beau said.

"A gladiator?" Jake demanded. "Get real."

"I think it's a perfect match," Bryan opined.

Jake scowled at him.

"Honestly, Jake," Patsy insisted, "the only difference is, you fight the lions with sharp, pointed words, and not a sword. And you do have a great body."

"Yeah?" Jake snorted, pleased by the double compliment in spite of feeling not only foolish but overexposed. "Well, I think you're all nuts."

After the dozen or so guests arrived, and as the evening progressed, Jake was forced to concede that the costume did have appeal—that of the sexual variety.

Several of the female guests cast hungry looks over his physique, their glances lingering on the section with the most covering, but one woman in particular caught Jake's attention, and his fancy. Her costume, if that was what it could be called, was even skimpier than his.

Jake supposed she was disguised as a California beach bunny. Since her costume consisted of the two wispy pieces of a string bikini, it couldn't be called a disguise.

She was about his own age, and her height was the only thing average about her. Sunbronzed skin stretched taut and firm over abundant, ripe curves. Her breasts were high, firm—too high and firm for her age, suggesting the possibility of cosmetic enhancement.

The possibility didn't concern Jake. In his opinion, whatever artifice—makeup, clothing, cosmetic surgery—made a woman happy with herself, had to be good for the man, or men, in her life. Besides, at that moment her breasts looked pretty damned exciting.

Her hair was blond, with a little help from a bottle and a professional. Jake didn't care about that, either. He was too caught up in the snare of her eyes. They were hot, the smoldering blue found in the heart of a flame. And they were boldly devouring his body.

She had a lot of appeal, the strongest being that she was the complete opposite of Elizabeth Leninger . . . whom he refused to think about.

Jake recognized opportunity when it knocked against his libido. Feeling the heat from the blond's searing gaze, he ambled across the room to her.

"Dance?" His gaze prowled over her suntanned form. "Surf?"

Her smile put the much-touted canary-munching cat to shame. "I'll ride the curl of any wave you care to make."

"Name's Jake," he said, sliding his arms around her waist and flattening his palms against her slippery warm flesh. The feel of her shot heat to his loins.

"I know. The author." Her eyes smoky, she moved in step with him to the sultry beat of the music. "I'm Cassie, Cassie Metcalf, and I've never had an author."

Although he thought her remark a bit odd, Jake was feeling too hot to ponder it.

"Well, Cassie Metcalf, you've got one now," he drawled, suppressing a shivering response to the play of her fingers in the hair at the nape of his neck. "What are you going to do with him?"

Though Jake wouldn't have believed it possible, her smile became even more sensuous, her man-eating eyes hotter. Moving even closer, she rubbed her jutting breasts against the mesh covering his chest. The friction jolted through him like the touch of a live electric wire.

"Careful," he murmured in warning, experiencing a near painful heaviness between his thighs. "Do you want me to embarrass myself right here, in front of all Patsy and Bryan's nice guests?"

"And waste all that exciting power I feel thrusting against my belly?" The tip of her tongue snaked out to circle her lipstick-shimmered lips. "I can suggest a much better place for that action."

Whoa boy. Jake's imagination, and pulse rate, kicked into overdrive. Understandable, he told himself. He hadn't been with a woman since long before he began the research for the trilogy, and that was over three months ago.

"Your bed or mine?" he asked, trying to sound blasé, certain he had failed.

"Wherever." Leaning into him, she arched her lower body into the heat of his. "Whenever."

Jake swallowed . . . at least he tried to; his mouth was so dry, there was nothing to swallow. Even through the mesh covering his chest and the thin material covering her breasts, he could feel her hard nipples jabbing into his flesh.

Visualizing the metal mesh abrading her nipples into hard arousal nearly did Jake in. He had never met a woman quite so blatantly sexual. Hell, he thought, for all he knew she was into the game of pleasure/pain.

But that was her problem, Jake reasoned. At the moment, he had to deal with his own burgeoning discomfort, and the evidence of it that was probing her belly with growing insistence.

"My room," he muttered, dancing her toward the archway into the foyer. "Unless . . ." He let his voice trail away, before asking, "Do you have a room?"

Cassie smiled and nodded. "The first one off the hallway to the east wing."

"Yours is closer." He danced her over the cool tiles of the foyer, through the archway into the east wing, then paused an instant while she flung open the door to her room, pulling her into a bone-crunching embrace before the door slammed shut behind them.

Her mouth was open and ready for his; crushing his lips against hers, he thrust his tongue deep into that hot, wet orifice.

Cassie's reaction was immediate and devastating. Sliding her hands down his sides, she gripped the swathing around his hips and tugged it down. When she had lowered the material as far as she could, she tore her lips from his and slid down his body, her tongue teasing a tight, flat nipple under the mesh before gliding lower, lower. Her lips found his navel, her tongue probed the depths, her fingernails raked his muscle-bunched thighs . . . and then her hands found him.

Jake went rigid in pleasurable shock. The blood surged through his veins, his heartbeats thumped in his chest and against his eardrums.

Her fingertips danced along the throbbing length of him, wrenching a groan from his parched throat. His body clenched, then arched, thrusting deeper into the hands she enclosed around him. While her tongue stabbed evocatively into his navel, her hands moved in time to the ancient rhythm.

She was killing him with sensation. Mindless with pleasure, he was loving every agonizing minute of it, teetering on the jagged edge of release.

A protest screamed inside his head when she suddenly pulled her hands and mouth away.

"I think you're ready now, and I know I am," she said, sprawling nude and spread-eagled onto the carpet.

Stunned, shuddering in reaction to the abrupt cessation of the action, Jake stared down at her in bewilderment, absently wondering when she had removed the bikini.

But she lay there bare, oil and sweat glistening on her lush, ripe body, a feral smile baring her teeth, her arms raised to him, her fingers curled as if to grasp, her hips arched high and undulating suggestively; a shocking picture of carnal abandonment.

Through his mind flashed a vision of another woman, tall, slender, coolly composed, auburn highlights streaking her dark hair, her eyes clear and alert.

A chill invaded Jake, cooling the sweat on his flushed skin, freezing the heat of desire torturing his body, instilling a roiling sensation in his stomach, and bringing on a feeling of revulsion.

What in hell did he think he was doing?

"Hurry."

Cassie's rough-voiced command jarred Jake out of his stupor and into uneasy awareness. In actual time, mere seconds had elapsed since she had released her mind-fogging sexual hold on his senses, but in that time he had fully recovered his control.

Grasping the material encircling his legs, Jake yanked the diaper up and over his hips.

"Hey! What are you doing?"

"I'm sorry," he muttered, turning away. "I feel sick. Musta had too much to drink." It was a lie; he'd had only two beers, and hadn't finished the second. Still, his throat burned with the acid sting of aftertaste.

"But what about me?" she called after him, halting him at the door. "Damn you." Her voice was petulant. "I've had a famous actor, a senator, and a famous C and W star—but I've never had an author."

"I'm sorry," Jake repeated, gulping back the stinging bile rushing into his mouth. "I . . . can't . . ." Twisting the knob, he pulled the door open and made his escape.

"You'll be even sorrier," she called after him. "I'm good. Ask anybody important. You'll see, Mr. Hotshot author. You'll be sorry."

Dammit. A celebrity banger. Shutting the door on her rising voice, Jake grunted in disgust—with her, but even more with himself. But how could he have known she was an aging groupie, for Christ's sake?

From the end of the hallway and across the foyer, he could hear the clatter and chatter of the party still in full swing. Turning away, he padded along the hall to his room. For him, both the party and the vacation were over.

Fortunately, Jake and Beau had scheduled an early afternoon flight, so Jake was required to be friendly with the remaining guests for only breakfast and lunch. To his relief, Cassie chose not to put in an appearance.

Still, he had to tamp down on his growing impatience to be gone. Finally the moment of leave-taking arrived.

While Beau carted their bags out to the hired car, Jake drew Patsy into an embrace.

"Thanks for the use of the hall," he said, skimming a kiss over her cheek. "And happy anniversary," he raised his gaze to Bryan, "to both of you."

"I won't tell you to come back soon, because I know you won't." Patsy disentangled herself from his arms. "Where do we send your Christmas card, Pennsylvania or New Jersey?" she asked, referring to the two houses he owned, one in the Pocono Mountains, the other along the South Jersey coast.

"Pennsylvania," he answered, just as Beau strolled back into the house.

More hugs, kisses, handshakes, and goodbyes were exchanged. Then Patsy and Bryan escorted them to the gate, and stood arm in arm while Jake and Beau crawled into the limousine.

"You've been kinda quiet all day," Beau said, probing Jake's expression for a hint of his feelings. "You hung over or something?"

"Or something." Jake grimaced as a vision of carnality incarnate seeped into his mind. "Beau, old friend, I think I'm getting old." He reflected uneasily on his aborted and monumentally stupid encounter with the hot-eyed, hot-mouthed Cassie.

"You?" Beau laughed. "Nah. You're just still bummed out from that tour."

"Maybe," Jake muttered.

Beau slanted a knowing look at him. "What you need, my friend, is to get back to work."

"Yeah, I know." Jake sighed in acceptance; Beau knew him so well, knew when the writing itch was on him. "And that is precisely what I intend to do."

"So, it's back to Pennsylvania, is it? I heard you tell Patsy to send your Christmas greetings there."

"Yes, to the mountains." Jake nodded. "At this time of year, it'll be quieter there, peaceful. So prepare yourself for some heavy-duty stuff." He tossed a wicked grin at the other man. "Dust off the fax machine, and don't be surprised if the work comes flying fast and furious from my desk to yours."

"Plan to keep me busy, do you?"

"I fully intend to complete the first three—maybe four—chapters of this new manuscript before I take a break to join the family for the Christmas gathering in New England."

Cassie Metcalf stood at the arched window in the cool living room, her lips tight, her eyes narrowed, watching as the limousine glided past the wide iron gates.

Selfish bastard. Her eyes glittered at the thought. But the bastard would learn . . . Oh, yes. He'd learn the hard way that a man, no man, no matter how successful or rich he might be, walked away from Cassie Metcalf, leaving her hungry and wanting.

What she needed was a plan, she mused, her agile, some might say devious, mind already beginning to spin sticky webs. But there was no hurry; Cassie had as much time as she desired to concoct a suitably self-satisfying way to get back at Jake Ruttenburg.

She didn't have the distracting bother of having to appear on time every day at a place of employment, thanks to a very talented divorce lawyer who had managed to wring extremely generous financial settlements—and nice fat fees for himself—from her three former husbands.

Oh, yes, she had all the time required to formulate a plan for retaliation.

Faintly the voices of her host and hostess, returning to the house, filtered through Cassie's bemusement. Like a practiced actress, she smoothed her expression into one of disappointment and regret.

"Did I miss them?" she said anxiously as they strolled into the room. "Jake and his assistant?"

"Yes," Patsy answered, crossing the room to Cassie. "And we missed you all morning."

Cassie's expression melted into embarrassment. "I . . . I'm afraid I enjoyed your party a little too much last night, and had to pay the price today." She lowered her eyelashes, and her voice. "I didn't want to inflict my misery on either of you, or the rest of your guests."

Bryan chuckled in indulgent understanding. "You should have said something. I have a cure for a hangover."

"Which is almost as bad as the hangover," Patsy inserted wryly. "I much prefer sleeping it off."

"And that's exactly what I did do." Cassie smiled faintly, then sighed dejectedly. "The problem is, well . . ." She hesitated, bit her lip, and finally confessed haltingly, "You see, Jake and I . . ah . . . had a little party of our own in my bedroom, and well . . ."

"You don't have to apologize to us," Bryan was quick to assure her when she again hesitated.

"Oh, I'm not apologizing," Cassie assured

him. She again lowered her lashes. "It was . . . Jake was . . . wonderful. I wanted to say good-bye and . . . well, thank him for the thrill of it all."

Patsy and Bryan exchanged amused glances. Cassie smiled—to herself.

"I'd drop him a little note but"—her voice faded away on a sad note, then rose again—"I don't know where to send it."

Patsy and Bryan again exchanged glances, this time in silent communication. Then Patsy nodded.

"We rarely if ever divulge Jake's address to anyone," she said.

"Of course, I understand," Cassie hastened to respond. "The man is entitled to his privacy."

"But this is a rare occasion," Patsy went on as if she hadn't been interrupted. "Wouldn't you agree, Bryan?"

"Yes." Bryan smiled benevolently at Cassie. "An exception can be made in this instance."

"I'll write his address down and give it to you before you leave," Patsy promised.

"Thank you." Moving to her, Cassie leaned forward to brush her lips over Patsy's cheek. From Patsy, she went to Bryan to do the same. "I'd say Jake and I are both lucky to have you two for friends."

Eight

Seasonal music filled the room.

Where had the time gone?

Elizabeth contemplated the swift passage of the days as she taped the neatly folded end of the gold-foil wrapping paper. Shaking her head in wonder, she fastened a large shiny green bow to the package.

Setting the gift atop the mounting pile of presents, she eyed the dwindling, yet still daunting, mound of unwrapped gifts on the end of the dining-room table.

She sighed. She had overdone it. She knew why, of course. This would be their first Christmas without Richard, and judging by the way his absence had affected Sally and Ella at Thanksgiving, she had hoped to compensate for their loss by distracting them with gifts.

It was not only expensive, but probably a futile effort. Recalling the amount of money she had spent on frivolous things, she stared at the boxes, small and large, and shook her head in disbelief; as if mere things could possibly compensate for a father.

Coffee break, Elizabeth advised herself, shifting her despairing gaze away from the pile of gifts.

Turning from the table littered with rolls and odd-size bits of wrapping paper, scissors, tape, pen, name tags, and ribbon, bows in assorted sizes and holiday colors, and the two tall stacks of presents, she straightened her back and walked into the kitchen.

While waiting for the coffee to trickle from the automatic maker into the glass carafe, Elizabeth stared out the window above the sink. The day was overcast, moody gray, and threatening. Rain? Snow, perhaps?

It was a little early for snow, she decided, gazing at the few brown and curled leaves on the mostly bare branches of the trees in the backyard. The barren look of the land and the stark bareness of the forsythia bushes were proof enough of the closing days of autumn.

Winter had not yet officially begun, and though it was early for snow, it might fall. She could remember years when there had been a light, but measurable, coating on the ground weeks before Christmas.

Christmas.

Caught up by the sudden fullness of her life since she'd met De De, and her shopping indulgences, the holidays had come upon her like a rushing train.

De De.

Reminded of her friend, and that she would be arriving at the house in a few hours for dinner, Elizabeth deserted the dreary outdoor scene to go to the stove. Pulling down the oven door, she inhaled the aroma of pot roast, which De De had said was one of her favorite meals.

A smile curved Elizabeth's lips as she spooned the juice from the meat over the pot roast and vegetables. Of course, she recalled, her smile widening, De De had professed that she had enjoyed every meal in Elizabeth's home. There had been many such meals since that first one, now nearly two months ago, which was one of her favorites.

Having learned that De De ate most of her meals out, since she openly confessed to being a lousy cook, Elizabeth accepted the younger woman's praise of her culinary skill with grateful thanks—and a grain of salt.

Laughing to herself, Elizabeth now closed the oven door and poured herself a cup of coffee.

Sipping the rich French-roast brew, she allowed herself a short break from the gift-wrapping chore, while reflecting upon the changes in herself and in her life since the irrepressible De De had spun into her orbit.

Her days no longer dragged as they had when she was marking time, counting the hours between Sally's exit from the house in the morning until she returned after school.

Dragged? Elizabeth mused, smiling. Now the hours flew by, thanks primarily to De De.

If nothing more, De De was a fantastic motivator.

And she's a lot more, Elizabeth thought, sipping coffee she didn't taste while reminiscing about the weeks that had flown by since the end of October.

In addition to being a great motivator, De De had proven herself to be intelligent, compassionate, fully aware of the current styles and mores, and at times impatient with them. She was up to speed on the publishing world, and the reader market. And, as a bonus, she had a wonderful sense of humor, if at times a bit dry and acerbic, a trait, Elizabeth couldn't help but notice, that she appeared to share with her famous uncle.

Elizabeth didn't want to think about De De's famous uncle just then—although she often did, too often for her emotional peace of mind. Dragging her thoughts away from Jake Ruttenburg, she refocused on her expected guest.

Because of De De's easy, outgoing manner, Sally had taken to her the first time she had come to the house. Ella had joined the ranks of De De's Leninger admirers when she'd come home for the Thanksgiving break.

Elizabeth had immediately invited De De to dinner when the younger woman had mentioned in passing that she would be alone for the holiday. Because of the demands of what De De referred to as her "day job" in an upscale women's dress shop, there was not enough time for her to make the long drive to her parents' home in New England.

Moreover, along with the laughter and the information De De always provided, she both coaxed and bullied Elizabeth in regard to her writing.

Due primarily to De De's ceaseless nagging, Elizabeth had completed three entire chapters of a mystery, a novel that she herself considered not half bad, even in rough draft.

And now, the swiftly approaching Christmas holiday was less than two weeks away.

Oh, gosh!

Startled out of her introspection, Elizabeth shot a glance at the kitchen wall clock. Telling herself to get it together, she rinsed her cup and set it in the sink, then went back into the dining room to tackle the mound of gifts waiting to be wrapped.

Fortunately, it was Sally's weekend to spend with her grandmother Ella, so she would not be coming home after school. If that weren't the case, since school had already let out, Elizabeth would have been caught with her presents, wrapped and unwrapped, still scattered all over the table, a terrible temptation for any fifteen-year-old.

She was putting the finishing touches on the last gift—a shockingly expensive Coach handbag for her older daughter—when De De arrived.

The young woman swept into the house like a refreshing breeze.

"I want to tell you, it is cold out there." Her cheeks and the tip of her nose were red; her eyes sparkled. "It feels like snow to me."

"I was thinking earlier that it might snow,"

Elizabeth said, taking De De's coat and hanging it in the entry closet.

"It's cold, crisp . . ." De De grinned. "Skiing weather."

"Wonderful." Elizabeth's tone indicated the opposite.

"You don't like to ski?"

"Not particularly."

De De laughed. "That's funny. That's exactly what my uncle always says."

"What?" Elizabeth frowned—at De De and the odd shivery sensation attacking her spine. "Who?" she asked, as if she didn't know.

"Jake, silly." De De shook her head, as if in despair of the man. "He's always said he finds nothing particularly appealing about tearing down the side of a mountain on two narrow pieces of wood, or whatever."

"My sentiments exactly," Elizabeth murmured, turning away from the closet—and the subject. She didn't want to be reminded of De De's disturbing uncle. "Dinner's ready, we can eat as soon as I clear the dining-room table."

"We're eating in the dining room?" De De asked, falling in step beside Elizabeth.

It was a perfectly logical question, since they usually ate at the smaller kitchen table when Sally wasn't home.

"No." Elizabeth shook her head. "But I want to get this clutter put away." Walking into the room, she flicked a hand to indicate the mess.

"Wow, you have been busy," De De murmured.

With her usual good humor, she made a few teasing observations concerning the exhaustion factor inherent in accumulating such a large number of gifts, but immediately pitched in, helping Elizabeth collect the wrappings and gather the booty.

"Boy, Ella and Sally are making out like bandits this year," De De said, groaning to exaggerate the heaviness of the load she was bearing up the stairs.

"Yes." Elizabeth sighed, leading the way to the third-floor storage closet. "I'm afraid I overdid it."

"Just a tad," De De agreed, exhaling in relief on attaining the top of the second flight of stairs. "But completely understandable, under the circumstances."

"I suppose." Elizabeth gave her a faint smile. "But I dread to think of the lecture I'll get about the danger of spoiling the girls—and financial prudence—from my mother-in-law." Her smile went wry. "Never mind that she has been spending lavishly and spoiling them rotten since the day they were born."

"Grandmother's privilege?" De De drawled, having taken the elder Ella's measure on Thanksgiving Day, the one occasion she had been in the woman's company.

"So I gather, from her superior attitude." Frowning, Elizabeth stowed the last of the packages and locked the door.

De De shrugged and grinned. "So, this year,

if the old drag— er, dear complains, you claim your privilege as their mother."

Elizabeth laughed. "Okay, I will."

"And speaking about mothers," De De went on, trailing Elizabeth back down the stairs, "I have an invitation to relay to you from mine."

"Really?" Elizabeth gave her a quizzical look. "What sort of invitation?"

"For you and the girls, to spend the Christmas holidays with the family in New England."

Elizabeth's expression went from quizzical to astonished. "But I—"

"I know, I know," De De interrupted, beginning to set the table while Elizabeth opened the oven door to remove the pot roast. "You wouldn't dream of celebrating Christmas away from home, especially this year. I explained that to Mother, and of course, she understood." She smiled and inhaled in appreciation of the aroma wafting on the steam rising from the roast pan. "That smells so good."

"Thank you." Elizabeth ladled the beef and vegetables into a large oval serving dish. "Will you pour the wine?"

"Sure. Anyway," De De went on, pouring cabernet into stemmed glasses, "although Mother understood, she still wanted me to relay the invitation."

Touched by the unexpected consideration, Elizabeth had to swallow against a tightness in her throat before she could speak. "That was very kind of your mother, considering she

doesn't know me and hasn't even met me. Will
you convey my thanks and my regrets."

"Yes, of course. But, even though she hasn't
met you, Mother does know you . . . or she
knows about you." De De grinned. "I'm a blab-
bermouth."

Elizabeth shook her head in mock despair.
"Well, I can only hope what you told her about
me was good."

"How could it have been anything else?"
De De's tone and expression were dead serious. "Other than my mother herself, you are
the most genuinely good person I know."

"Oh, De De," Elizabeth murmured, blinking
at a rush of moisture to her eyes. "Thank you.
You can't possibly know how fortunate I feel at
having you for a friend."

Her words caused De De to blink. Obviously
touched, she said, "I think we'd better eat this
delicious food, before we ruin it by diluting it
with tears."

"You're right."

The emotional moment over, they spent a
lovely evening, lingering over their after-dinner
coffee, talking and laughing together.

Nine

Elizabeth was up early on Sunday morning. After a quick breakfast of juice and toast, she carried a second cup of coffee to Richard's office, which she had made her own.

The furniture remained, but his personal files, papers, and decorations were gone. With a determination she had not known she was capable of, Elizabeth had packed everything of his into cartons and had stashed them all in the attic storage room.

At first, being computer illiterate, Elizabeth had hesitated to touch Richard's personal computer. She knew it had a built-in word-processing program, because he had told her it did.

But . . . where to begin?

Fortunately, while cleaning out the desk drawers, she had discovered the computer manual. Surprisingly, it was presented in language she could both read and understand. By the tried-and-true method of trial and error—many errors—she eventually learned to run and use the program.

That Elizabeth could now work on the machine with relative ease was a testament to her tenacity.

Still perking along on a De De-induced shot of adrenaline, Elizabeth had lost track of time and was working smoothly on her story when the intrusive sound of the doorbell pierced the silence, and her concentration.

Damn, she thought in irritation, who could that be? The bell sounded again. Muttering imprecations, she darkened the screen, pushed her chair back, and hurried from the room and down the stairs to the door.

"Hi, Mom, what kept you?" Sally asked, grinning as she breezed by Elizabeth.

Confused and slightly disoriented, because she was still "inside" her story and hadn't been expecting her daughter until after dinner, Elizabeth frowned at the glow of excitement in Sally's eyes. "I . . . er . . ." she began, only to be impatiently interrupted by her mother-in-law.

"Were you sleeping in the middle of the day?" the elder Ella demanded, her expression stern and disapproving as she swept past Elizabeth.

Old bitch, Elizabeth thought, shocking herself. "No, of course not." She gave a quick shake of her head in denial of the accusation. "I was upstairs. In the office. With the door closed."

"Richard's office?"

The short hairs at Elizabeth's nape tingled at

the sharp note of condemnation in the older woman's voice.

No, *my* office, she said to herself resentfully. Aloud, she simply murmured assent, nodded and gently shut the front door.

"I thought you said you would bring Sally home after dinner," she said, smothering a sigh as she accepted the job of hanging away the coats the two held out to her.

"I did, but—"

"But I couldn't wait," Sally gushed, bravely cutting off her grandmother.

Ella merely smiled with sweet indulgence at the girl's rudeness. Elizabeth didn't.

"You interrupted your grandmother, Sally," she scolded, though gently.

"Oh, that's all right." Ella waved away the unintended slight. "She's bursting with the news."

"News?" Elizabeth glanced from one to the other, settling on Sally. "What news?"

"Oh, Mom, wait'll you hear!" Sally was practically dancing in place. "It's great!"

Elizabeth pulled her patient parent expression. "Well . . . ?"

"You'll never guess what Grandmother is giving me and Ella for Christmas." The girl's voice was high with excitement, her eyes were bright with anticipation.

"In that case, I won't even try," Elizabeth said, her warm voice reflecting the pleasure she took in her daughter's exuberance.

Sally hung on to the secret, savoring it for

an instant; then she blurted out, "Grandmother's taking us on a skiing trip to Colorado!"

Elizabeth went still for a moment, questions swirling in her mind. Colorado? For Christmas? Surely not for Christmas Day? Needing answers, she shifted her gaze to the smugly smiling older woman.

"For Christmas?"

"Yes." The elder Ella's voice was as smug as her smile. "It will be a thrill for them; that's when all the celebrities are there, you know."

"All the really big names," Sally confirmed, actually quivering. "Movie stars, music stars . . ." Her voice took on an awed, breathy sound. "Maybe even the Boss!"

"The boss?" Elizabeth frowned. "What boss?"

"What boss?" Sally looked shocked. "There is only one 'Boss' . . . Bruce Springsteen, of course."

Ahhh, yes. The New Jersey troubador . . . lately of California, Elizabeth recalled. How could she have forgotten, after hearing first Ella and then Sally rhapsodize over repeated playings of "Dancing in the Dark"?

"Didn't I tell you it was great?" Sally said, seeking a response when her mother remained mute.

"Yes . . . great," Elizabeth replied, infusing unfelt enthusiasm into her voice. "Wonderful."

"Ella was so excited, she said she doesn't know how she's going to stand it till school closes!" Sally exclaimed, dancing to her grand-mother to give her a hug and an accolade. "You're the absolute best!"

The elder Ella laughed, then slanted a sly, superior look at Elizabeth.

The woman's sneaky game of one-upmanship was wearing very thin, Elizabeth decided, gritting her teeth while working her lips into a weak smile.

"I can't wait, either," Sally sang, pirouetting into the living room, thus reminding Elizabeth that they were still standing in the foyer.

"Have you had dinner?" she asked her mother-in-law as pleasantly as she could.

"Yes." Smugness was evident in the woman's voice. "We ate early. But I would like a cup of tea . . . if you don't mind?"

"Not at all," Elizabeth lied, leading the way to the kitchen. "Would you like something, Sal?" she called to the girl rifling through the stack of CDs in the corner rack. "Milk, tea, hot chocolate?"

"Hot chocolate sounds great."

Thinking wryly that "great" appeared to be the word of the day, Elizabeth entered the kitchen and went to the cabinets to get teabags and chocolate mix. Not at all thrilled with the idea of spending the holiday away from home, especially this year, and after not having been consulted on the matter, she had to impose control to keep from banging containers and cups onto the countertop.

When the drinks were ready, and served,

along with a plate of packaged cookies, she cradled her own warm cup in her cold hands and calmly faced her mother-in-law.

"When are we leaving? What day?"

"Oh, dear!" the elder Ella exclaimed, with patently false chagrin. "Elizabeth, I am sorry, but . . . well, knowing how you dislike skiing"—she hesitated, then rushed on, as if flustered—"I'm afraid I only made reservations for three, the girls and me."

Elizabeth froze. Her hands gripped the cup as hot anger surged through her, thawing her mind and her tongue. "I see," she said, her voiced tight and strained. "And when—on what day—are the reservations for?"

"Both the flight and the resort reservations are for the twenty-fourth."

"The day before Christmas?" Elizabeth stared at the woman in astonishment, unable to believe that even she, unpleasant as she had always been, would stoop so low.

"Mother's not going?" Sally cried, turning confusion-clouded eyes to her grandmother.

"I'm sorry, darling." The elder Ella expressed genuine concern—not for her daughter-in-law, Elizabeth knew, but for her own standing in Sally's eyes. "But I just assumed your mother would prefer to stay home, since she has so often mentioned her dislike of the sport."

"But . . ." Sally swiveled her head back and forth, to her mother and then her grandmother. "Mother will be alone on Christmas!"

"Oh, my." Her grandmother fell back on fluttering her hands, her eyelashes. "But it is merely a day of the week, dear," she said, with sweet reason. "We could celebrate the holiday here, the day before we leave." Her lips quivered, and she dabbed at her eyes with her fingertips. "Couldn't we?" she asked, in a pitiable whisper.

Elizabeth held her breath, waiting for Sally's response, hoping she would . . .

Her daughter's face brightened, and she became bubbly and animated again. "Yeah, we can do that." She turned pleading eyes to Elizabeth. "Can't we, Mom?"

Concealing the pain that lanced through her was one of the hardest things Elizabeth had ever had to do. Forcing herself to agree damn near choked her.

"Yes, we can do that," she murmured, now clinging to the hope that her daughter Ella would adamantly refuse.

That hope was dashed the very next day, when Elizabeth spoke to Ella on the phone. Although her eldest daughter displayed genuine dismay at learning her mother would not be going to Colorado—there not being a seat on any flight to be bought or begged, because Elizabeth had tried both—she finally accepted her grandmother's plan to celebrate the holiday on the twenty-third instead of the twenty-fifth.

Hiding her lacerated feelings behind a serene facade, Elizabeth somehow managed to

get through the days that followed. While Sally
was in school, she tried to work on her story,
but with little success. Suddenly, the mystery
seemed to lack suspense, and the characters
had become flat and one dimensional, the entire process not worth the effort.

Filled with dread of spending Christmas
alone in an empty house, Elizabeth couldn't fo-
cus her mind on the complex tale of a woman
in terror of losing her life.

She felt betrayed, yet guilty for such a feeling.
Christmas *was* just another day. Wasn't it?

But it was the first Christmas Day without
Richard. Perhaps, if he were here, she wouldn't
mind so much, wouldn't be so crushed. But no.
Elizabeth knew without doubt that, if he were
here, his mother would never have thought of
taking the girls away over the holiday, let alone
have made the arrangements before consulting
her son.

Elizabeth hadn't seen or heard from De De
since the evening her friend had pitched in to
help stash the presents. In one way, it was a
good thing. She had a nearly overwhelming
need to unburden herself to a friend.

But De De had enough to contend with,
working all day, writing in the evenings. Besides, it wasn't Elizabeth's style to confide personal problems to anyone, not even her
mother. She knew it wouldn't be fair to dump
on her friend.

De De called on the twenty-second.

"Hi, how's it going?" She sounded both tired

and upbeat. "Earlobe deep in last-minute preparations for the big day?"

"Not really." Elizabeth kept her voice care-free. "Everything's under control," she said. Everything's falling apart, she thought.

"Here, too." De De laughed. "Even though I know it's hard to believe, I've not only done my shopping and wrapping, I have all the stuff packed in my car—including my suitcase. And the shop's been a zoo; I feel more like a keeper than a clerk. How are the kids?"

Elizabeth had to laugh; De De did have a penchant for changing a subject in mid ramble.

"They're fine. Anxious for the . . . big day to come," she said. "They've both asked about you." She veered from the subject, copying her friend. "Wondered why you haven't stopped by."

"I was planning to," De De said. "But we've been swamped at the shop with the last-minute frantic." She chuckled. "Mostly men, of course. I'll probably have to be at the shop all day on Christmas Eve, and then I'll jump in my car and take off for Connecticut." She paused to draw breath. "In addition to everything else, the writing's been zipping along; I can barely keep up, and—"

"You don't need to explain. I understand, and so will the girls," Elizabeth reassured her. "We can get together after you get back in the New Year."

"Thanks, you're a real pal." Relief was evident in De De's voice. "I've got to run, I've got a hot love scene simmering on the machine. Merry Christmas to all. Give my love to the kids . . . and, oh, yeah, tell them I found super gifts for them. They're gonna freak."

"Drive carefully." Elizabeth grimaced as soon as she'd given the warning, and swiftly added, mimicking Sally, "Duh, like you're deliberately going to drive carelessly."

De De roared with laughter at the out-of-character remark. "Way to go, Elizabeth," she commended. "Welcome to the world of reality."

"Thanks for inviting me in," Elizabeth said, not altogether in jest. "Merry Christmas, De De, and please convey my best to your family."

"Will do. 'Bye, love."

A soft smile curved Elizabeth's lips as she hung up the phone. For a few moments, she basked in the warm glow of De De's friendship. It occurred to her that perhaps she should have confided in her friend, asked if the invitation to go to New England was still open.

Elizabeth's smile faded. Christmas Day loomed before her, desolate and lonely.

Maybe she'd just spend it in bed, she thought. But first she had to get through the "make-believe" day.

The twenty-third turned out to be exactly as Elizabeth had feared it would—make-believe. She put forth an effort. All of them, Ella, Sally, and even the elder Ella tried. Of the four, Elizabeth suspected her mother-in-law of being the only one actually enjoying the farce; but that . . . dear lady . . . had instigated it.

Spicy holiday scents permeated the house. The large blue spruce tree and the windows were decked with dark red velvet bows, yards of frosted white garlands, and tiny twinkling lights. Presents of all sizes were arranged around the base of the tree with calculated abandon.

It smelled like Christmas. It looked like Christmas. Problem was, it was not Christmas. And, no matter how hard Elizabeth worked at believing it was, that fact remained.

Ella and Sally squealed in delight at the abundance of gifts. They said thank you with an abundance of hugs and kisses.

Elizabeth prepared the traditional holiday meal of turkey and dressing, too many vegetables, and far too many desserts. She herself ate little and tasted less.

Then, all too soon, her girls were gone, whisked away by their grandmother, whose benign smile was not reflected in her glittering eyes.

Elizabeth was alone. Again. All that remained of the holiday was a refrigerator stuffed with leftovers; a trash container overflowing with discarded shreds of colorful wrapping paper, ribbons, and bows; sun-shimmered decorations; and a mound of unwrapped gifts stacked neatly beneath the darkened tree. To one side, looking gaudy and out of place, lay three still brightly wrapped presents, gifts for De De from Elizabeth, Ella, and Sally.

She was vacuuming the carpet in the living room shortly after noon on Christmas Eve when the doorbell sounded above the low growl of the cleaner.

"Hi!" De De stood on the stoop, an oversize shopping bag in hand, a broad smile on her pixie face. "Merry Christmas Eve to one and all." Her smile melted into a frown at the somber expression Elizabeth was wearing. "Isn't it?" she asked, stepping into the foyer.

"Afraid not." Elizabeth shrugged, and changed the subject. "I thought you had to work all day."

"I thought so, too." De De grinned. "As I believe I told you, I loaded everything into my car days ago, so I could take off as soon as the store closed this afternoon. And, boy, am I glad I did."

Setting down the shopping bag, she slipped out of her jacket and put it into the hand Elizabeth extended. "To the amazement of everyone, after the crush in the store yesterday," she continued, trailing Elizabeth into the living room, "there were so few customers this morning, my manager told me I could take off a little while ago and . . ." She came to an abrupt halt, her eyebrows drawing together at sight of the unwrapped gifts. Her puzzled gaze shot to Elizabeth. "What's going on? Where are the kids?"

"On a skiing trip with their grandmother. They left early this morning."

"Without you?" she asked in astonishment.

Nodding, Elizabeth briefly, and as unemotionally as possible, explained the situation.

Flabbergasted, De De stared at her friend in stunned silence.

Elizabeth managed to meet her gaze with a modicum of composure.

"And they went?" De De demanded when she finally found her voice. "Leaving you alone for Christmas?"

Elizabeth lifted her shoulders in a slight shrug. "As I said, we celebrated Christmas yesterday."

"Big deal. That miserable old bi—"

"It's all right, De De," Elizabeth interrupted, still feeling small for thinking what De De had begun to say. "I'll be fine."

"Right." The younger woman made a rude noise, and flicked a hand at the shopping bag. "I came today full of holiday cheer, bearing gifts for you and the kids."

"We can exchange gifts when they get back," Elizabeth said in a soothing tone.

"And when will that be?"

"The second of January."

De De shook her head. "So, you will not only be alone for Christmas but New Year's Eve, as well."

"It doesn't matter." Elizabeth wasn't sure whether she was trying to convince De De or herself.

"It matters to me." De De drew a deep, harsh breath. "Go," she ordered. "Throw some things in a bag. You're coming with me."

"No. Really, I couldn't." Elizabeth shook her head. "They're not expecting me. I won't intrude."

"Oh, stuff it, Elizabeth." De De actually snorted. "Get your fanny in gear. I want to hit the road." She shifted a glance to the shopping bag. "I'll leave this stuff here until we get back."

"De De, I—"

Her friend leveled a fierce, narrowed gaze on Elizabeth, stifling argument. "Move," she ordered, her voice as commanding as her eyes. "Intrude, indeed."

Elizabeth moved.

Ten

"Do we have very far to go?" Elizabeth asked once they were on the road.

Over an hour had passed since De De had appeared at the house. Although she had given in to the younger woman's demand that she accompany her, Elizabeth had determined that she would not go empty-handed. To De De's amusement, she had dumped several gifts out of their boxes, then had filled the boxes with cookies and the other untouched desserts she had prepared for the holiday. The deep box that had held the Coach handbag proved the perfect receptacle for a mound of traditional Christmas cookies. Finally, dashing into the dining room, Elizabeth had swept up the carefully arranged basket of fruits, nuts, and candies—over which she had labored mightily—had wrapped the entire thing in plastic, and had stuck a large gold bow on it. Sparing a second to eye the finished product critically, she had decided it made a presentable gift for a hostess, then slid it into a wide department-store shopping bag.

The last thing Elizabeth did before leaving

and securing the house was place a call to Denver. Neither the girls nor their grandmother were available. She left a message for them with the desk clerk, detailing where she was going and providing a number at which she could be reached.

"Their place is located on the fringes of a small town, about halfway between New Haven and Waterbury." De De explained. "Actually, calling it a town is stretching it. It's really little more than a village."

"You were born there?"

"Heck, no." She flashed a grin. "I was born smack-dab in the Pennsylvania Dutch country, near Lancaster. Both my parents were, too. My maternal grandmother still lives there, in the same house."

The information jogged Elizabeth's memory. "Now that you mention it, I recall reading somewhere that your uncle was from the Lancaster area."

"Hmmm." De De nodded, while accelerating to pass the car in front of her. Passing completed, she elaborated. "Uncle Jake hasn't lived there since he left home for college. He loves the mountains and the ocean, and divides his time between the two houses he owns. One in the Poconos, the other in New Jersey, south of Ocean City."

"I see." What Elizabeth saw was that she and the famous author had at least one thing in common: Elizabeth also loved the mountains and the seashore. But she didn't want to talk about Jake Ruttenburg; truth to tell, she didn't want to think about him, so she casually steered the conversation in another direction.

"Does your father work in Connecticut?"

"Yes." De De gave a quick nod of her head, and kept her gaze steady on the highway. "My father was an executive for an electronics firm in Philadelphia. A couple years ago he was offered—and accepted—a lateral transfer to a subsidiary company in New Haven."

"Didn't your mother mind pulling up roots?" Elizabeth asked, knowing she would have.

"She was delighted." De De laughed. "They had been planning to retire to Connecticut ever since I was a kid. They fell in love with that state during a vacation on which they drove through New England. I think I was about eight or so. I don't remember much about it."

"That explains it, then."

De De slanted a look at her. "Explains what?"

"Why you have no New England accent."

"Mystery solved." De De grimaced teasingly.

"Will your brother and his family be there?" Elizabeth had been told that De De had one sibling, an older brother who was married, had two children—boys—and was an English literature professor at a Midwest university.

"Not this year." De De sounded disappointed. "They switch years, one with our parents and the next at home, with his in-laws. His wife, Helen, was born and raised in Nebraska,

you see." She glanced at Elizabeth. "My grandmother will be there, though. She flew out of
Philadelphia yesterday. Spent the night before
at my place."

"Really?" Elizabeth raised her brows. "I'm
surprised she just didn't wait and drive up with
you today."

"The trip's too long for her. She gets stiff."
She lifted her shoulders and glanced at Elizabeth. "Arthritis."

"Oh. Too bad." Elizabeth frowned. "It
sounds like your parents will have a full house.
Are you sure—"

"E-liz-a-beth," De De interrupted. "Will you
stop! They invited you. Remember?"

"Yes. But they're not expecting me. Remember?" Her frown deepened.

"Sure they are." De De shot her a compla-
cent look. "I called Mother while you were
packing."

"Oh." Elizabeth waited a moment, then
nudged her, "And?"

"Mom told me I wasn't even to consider
coming without you, under the circumstances."

Elizabeth's spirits took a dive. "The circumstances?" she prompted.

"Well . . ." De De shifted in her seat. "I had
to explain the situation, about the girls and
all."

"Yes, of course." Elizabeth swallowed a sigh,
along with her pride, and produced a faint
smile.

De De was quick to fill the sudden silence.

"Elizabeth, my folks know you have two daughters. I had to tell them, otherwise, they'd have thought it strange if you arrived without Ella and Sally."

"I suppose so." Elizabeth loosened the fingers she hadn't been aware were gripping her handbag. "It's just . . ." A sigh escaped her. "I hate being the object of pity."

"I know." De De risked a compassionate look at her. "You are so damned self-contained."

"That's bad?"

"Not bad, but"—now De De sighed—"I sometimes feel as if I'm tiptoeing through a minefield. I keep waiting, half expecting I'll make a serious misstep and set off a long-suppressed explosion."

Elizabeth laughed, spontaneously and freely. "Stride on, friend," she said, when her laughter subsided. "I can assure you, there will be no explosions from me."

"Glad to hear it." De De dropped her shoulders in an exaggerated gesture of relief. "I wasn't looking forward to the blast."

"And you're sure your parents have room for me?" Elizabeth was back to worrying the issue. "I can always stay at a nearby motel, if there is one."

"Jesus, give it a rest," De De pleaded in exasperation. "They have a big house, for heaven's sake. Four bedrooms on the second floor and two on the third."

"That is a big house."

"That's what I said."

"I wouldn't want to clean it."

"My Mother doesn't, at least not by herself," De De clarified. "She has a woman come in to help her. Okay? Can we change the subject now?"

"Yes." Elizabeth relaxed for the first time in over a week. "What would you like to talk about?"

De De grinned. "Writing, of course. What else?"

As the day progressed, the traffic became more and more congested. Last-minute shoppers, people leaving work, and folks like Elizabeth and De De, on their way to visit relatives and friends, added to the crush.

The duo stopped late in the afternoon for a break and a snack. They were back on the road in less than an hour. It was easier going in the early evening, as folks were gathered in homes and churches to celebrate this night.

The last miles of their journey were made along a winding back road. Fortunately, by then few cars were on the road. It was after eight when they finally turned into the driveway of De De's parents' home.

Even in the darkness, Elizabeth could see how large the place was, warm-looking, welcoming. Every window held one candle—the symbolic invitation to the Christ child or the Magi.

The night was cold, raw. Frost rimed the grass on the front lawn and made billowing clouds of their breaths. Quickly collecting as much as they could carry in one trip, Elizabeth followed De De along the walkway and up the three steps to the deep porch which ran around two sides of the house. Talk, laughter, and music spilled out when De De opened the door, making Elizabeth wonder exactly how many people were inside.

"Hey!" De De shouted above the noise. "How about a little help here?"

There was a moment's pause, then the racket resumed, intensified. From her position behind the girl, Elizabeth heard greetings ring out, at least a dozen, she thought. And despite that din, one voice struck a chord of familiarity inside her, an unsettling chord.

Jake Ruttenburg?

Although De De hadn't mentioned that he'd be among the guests, the author's distinctive tone was immediately recognizable.

A sinking sensation quashed Elizabeth's warm, fuzzy holiday feeling.

Reluctantly trailing De De into the pine-scented interior, Elizabeth saw him immediately.

"Well, hello." His voice, soft and warm, held the promise and the kick of spicy mulled wine.

Elizabeth didn't understand, or appreciate, her sudden difficulty in breathing. "Hello." She stole a quick breath. "How, uh, are you?"

"Compared to whom?" Amusement laced his words; a teasing light flickered in his dark eyes.

Spontaneous laughter tickled her throat before escaping through her lips. Jake's laughter blended with hers and brought back the warm fuzzies.

"You don't have to answer that. It was a rhetorical question. Designed to make you smile." Though the light still gleamed in his eyes, they probed hers with intent. "You looked so . . . uncertain there for a moment."

He saw too much. Much too much. Of course, his remark made her even more uncertain. How to answer? Elizabeth tried to come up with a brilliant reply. She came up dry. "I . . . ummm . . . I do feel a bit—"

"Well, don't just stand there, Uncle Jake," De De interjected, saving Elizabeth the effort. "My car's jammed with stuff to be hauled inside."

With good grace, and a wry smile, he trooped after De De's father to the car.

Despite the wall of sound De De and Elizabeth had walked into, there were actually only eight people in the house. Since two of them were children, the offspring of the Davidsons' nearest neighbors, aged four and six, the noise level was understandable.

The first few minutes were nothing but a confused blur for Elizabeth.

While their coats were whipped away to be thrust inside a closet, De De rattled off names so rapidly Elizabeth caught and retained only a couple, those of her friend's parents, Mary-

anne and George Davidson, and her grandmother—Jake's mother—Margaret Ruttenburg.

Elizabeth was relieved when her hostess interrupted the confusing babble.

"We waited to have Christmas Eve supper
with you, and everybody's starved, especially
the children." Maryanne spared a soft smile for
the eager-eyed boy and girl. "We can chatter
away all we want later, after you've settled in."
She smiled at Elizabeth. "Welcome. De De will
show you to your room. It's on the third floor."
A tiny crease scored her smooth brow. "I hope
you don't mind?"

"Not at all," Elizabeth assured her. "Thank
you for inviting me. And I would like to freshen
up."

"I know a cue when I hear it." Chuckling,
De De scooped up her suitcase and headed for
the stairs. "Which room, Mother?" she asked,
pausing at the bottom of a wide and curving
staircase.

"Why the room on the left, of course," Maryanne replied.

"Of course." Giving her mother a look and
a shrug, De De started up the stairs, Elizabeth
at her heels. "I must be tired. I suddenly went
stupid for a minute."

For all of the exchange Elizabeth understood
it could have been made in a foreign language.
"What was that all about?" she asked curiously
when they had reached the broad landing, off
of which ran two hallways leading in opposite
directions.

A spark lit the younger woman's eyes, lending to her the look of an excited young girl. "There's another guest room on this floor, and for a second, I wondered why Mother hadn't put you in there," she explained, the spark in her eyes beginning to glow. "I forgot that that's where she usually keeps all the Christmas presents."

"Are you tempted to peek?" Elizabeth teased, following her to a door opposite the stairs.

"Sure." De De tossed the word back as she opened the door and started climbing another, narrower staircase. "Can't though. Mom keeps the door locked."

At the top of the stairs was another, shorter hallway, two doors to either side. De De turned to the first door on the left. "I'm afraid you'll have to share a bath," she said, motioning to the second door on the right.

"I don't mind," Elizabeth assured her. "Are you in the other room?" She indicated the door opposite, feeling certain Maryanne would not have allocated the third-floor room to her arthritic mother.

"No. I'm on the second level." De De opened the door and switched on the lights. "That room's reserved for Uncle Jake. He staked a claim to it when they moved in."

The room was lovely, spacious even with the sloping ceiling at the far side. In a state of shock-induced agitation, Elizabeth could barely absorb the decor—the cherry furniture, violet-sprigged cream wallpaper and bedspread, and the cream lace curtains at the room's one window which overlooked the front lawn.

"It's charming," she said, working her lips into a smile for De De.

"Yeah." De De nodded her agreement. "The whole house is. Mom and Dad love it."

"I can understand why." Maintaining the smile put a strain on Elizabeth's mouth. Walking to the bed, she slung her suitcase onto the pretty spread and set the shopping bag containing the fruit basket on the floor. "It will take only a few minutes for me to freshen up." She lost the battle with her facial muscles; the smile vanished. "I'll leave the unpacking until after supper."

"Right. I'm outta here." De De started out the door, then called back, "Meet you downstairs."

Downstairs. Elizabeth sighed. Jake Ruttenburg was downstairs. Flipping open the case, she removed her makeup pouch, turned, and headed for the bathroom across the hall—the bathroom she would be sharing with Jake Ruttenburg.

A shiver zigzagged down Elizabeth's spine as she stepped into the green, black, and white tiled room. The tangy scent of men's aftershave permeated the air.

It had been over six months since she had smelled a man's fragrance in a bathroom. Not that the scent in this room was reminiscent of the one Richard had splashed on his body. Richard's preference had run to a heavier, muskier, unsubtle variety.

The aroma now assailing Elizabeth's nostrils and senses had a sharper, more astringent quality, conjuring images of wind-tossed waves and frigid mountain air.

Elizabeth liked it.

Even as she drew the lingering scent deep into her lungs, she resisted.

She didn't want to like it.

Her stomach did a free-fall when her exploring glance collided with the contents of a man's shaving kit that littered the vanity.

Elizabeth hesitated at setting her very feminine-looking pouch next to the masculine toiletries, feeling it would appear too intimate and personal.

But the minutes were ticking by. De De's parents and their guests were waiting to have their Christmas Eve dinner.

Telling herself to grow up, she strode to the vanity and dropped the pouch on the smooth marble surface next to his pile of stuff.

Some six or so minutes later, teeth brushed, hands and face washed, and a light covering of fresh makeup applied, Elizabeth smoothed her palms over the fine wool slacks she'd put on for traveling, retucked the long-sleeved silk shirt into the waistband, and then, making a quick detour into the bedroom to collect the fruit basket, hurried down the stairs.

Family and friends were gathered, wassail cups in hand, waiting for De De and Elizabeth to join them.

The room was brightly lighted and festively

decorated. Christmas music blended with the animated conversation, and a magnificent tree stood ceiling tall between the two long front windows lit by electric candles. The tree was glittering with white lights and garlands, and was adorned with dark red velvet bows of various sizes.

"Mother must be in the kitchen," De De said when her searching gaze failed to spot Maryanne. "I'll go see if there's something I can do to help."

"I'll come too," Elizabeth offered at once, feeling awkward about entering the room alone.

De De shook her head. "Not necessary," she said. "Knowing Mother, I'm sure she has everything under control. You go on in and mingle, get to know everybody."

Elizabeth was beginning to feel silly holding the large basket, so she thrust it into De De's hands. "Please, take this with you and give it to your mother."

As she hesitantly stepped into the large, noisy room, a festive cup was thrust into her hand.

"Wassail, wassail," Jake drawled, his bold glance raking over her from the top of her head to her black leather boots.

Elizabeth smiled faintly, made uneasy by the blatant appraisal, the sardonic thread woven through his words, the I've-been-there-done-that-too-many-times-already expression in his eyes.

"You don't like Christmas?"

"It's a commercial circus." His eyes mocked her.

She took offense at that, and at his condescending attitude. "Then why do you celebrate?"

"I like my family."

She felt an immediate softening toward him. To Elizabeth, family was the number-one priority.

"So do I, at least those I've—"

De De's mother interrupted her. "Elizabeth, really, you didn't have to do this." Carrying the fruit basket like a trophy, Maryanne swept up to her guest with a rustle of her long forest green taffeta skirt. "Thank you. The basket is beautiful." Her face was a picture of admiration. "It looks so professional, and De De tells me you arranged it yourself."

"Yes, I did, but—"

"I do envy people with talent," Maryanne rushed on, interrupting Elizabeth once again. "She tells me you write as well." She flashed a smile at her brother. "It seems I'm blessed with a house full of talented people."

Flushed and flattered, Elizabeth didn't know quite how to respond to the lavish praise.

Jake suffered no such difficulty.

"Maryanne, every human being has talent," he said, with absolute authority. "And you possess more than most."

His sister opened her mouth to dissent, but he didn't allow her to speak.

"You could be a corporate CEO, if you desired," he went on in that same positive tone. "You have the patience of a saint, a mind for the most minute detail, and you're the best organizer I know."

The pink glow to Maryanne's cheeks, the sparkle in her blue eyes—a shade lighter than his—gave her the look of a much younger woman. She actually giggled. Dipping her head, she bestowed a kiss on Jake's taut-skinned cheek.

"You are the nicest baby brother a woman could possibly have."

Her compliment drew a chuckle from Elizabeth and a scowl from Jake.

"Knock off the baby brother stuff, will you?" While he growled the protest, his eyes reflected amusement. "I'm closing in on forty, as you well know."

"Jacob Ruttenburg, behave yourself." The soft command came from his mother, who had silently come up beside him. "You know better than to remind a lady of her age."

"Yes, Mother," he said contritely. His lips twitching with laughter, he glanced at Elizabeth. "She will be forty-seven in late January," he informed her in a stage whisper.

"Mo-ther!" Maryanne cried, the sparkle in her eyes growing brighter. "You rat," She directed the last words accusingly at Jake.

Laughing all the while, Elizabeth shifted her gaze from one to another of the family. Finally it landed on Jake. Her breath caught as she saw the deviltry dancing in his eyes.

"You see the abuse I take?" He shook his head and heaved a sigh. "Between my sister, my mother, and that imp De De, I'm surrounded by nagging women."

Elizabeth opened her mouth to reply, but before she could form the words, De De and her father joined them.

"Every one of whom," George drawled in response, "pampers you, babies you, and rushes to fulfill your every whim, wish, and request."

"Yeah." De De jumped into the fray. "And I wish you'd wish for dinner. I'm starving." She shot a sly glance at her mother. "And so are the kids."

"Oh, yes," Maryanne exclaimed. "Poor angels. How thoughtless of me."

A swish of her skirt, and Maryanne set about proving her organizational skill.

Elizabeth meanwhile determined to learn the names of her fellow guests. She sipped from the cup; the wine was warm, and spiced, and delicious. "Hmmm, good."

"An old family recipe," Jake said, his dark eyes seeming to drink her in as she sipped the wine. "I'll share the secret with you," he murmured in a lowered, conspiratorial tone of voice. "If you like?"

Elizabeth pitched her voice to match his. "I'd rather you repeat the names of the children and their parents. I missed them the first time around."

He chuckled.

She was forced to repress a responsive shiver.

"Come with me, hesitant one." Cupping her elbow, he steered her to the couple seated on the couch to one side of the fireplace, conversing with Margaret and George who sat on wing-backed chairs opposite them.

"In the confusion of arrival, Elizabeth lost track of your names," Jake said, his tone urbane, his smile charming. "Elizabeth, say hello to Alan and Judith Patterson, and, oh, yeah"—he grinned at the kids—"Mason and Allissa . . . who aren't at all excited about Christmas."

The children chorused a protest.

The adults laughed, which made Elizabeth feel more relaxed.

Having finessed what could have been an uncomfortable situation, Jake raised his cup. "Peace, ladies and gentlemen, and good will."

"Dinner," De De called from the dining room. "Bring your drinks . . . and let's eat!"

Eleven

It was Christmas . . . just.

Elizabeth was tired. She was also a little nervous.

Her spine stiff, she mounted the stairs to the third floor. The echoing footsteps behind her caused a fluttering sensation in the pit of her stomach.

Attaining the landing, she quickly moved to the door to her room. Grasping the doorknob, she turned, surprised to find Jake standing less than a foot away from her.

"Good night, Jake, and Merry Chris—"

"Wait a minute." His voice, though soft, held command. "What's the hurry?"

"Hurry?" Elizabeth swallowed to moisten her suddenly parched throat. The house was silent. The others had gone to their rooms. She was alone. On the third floor. With Jake.

He made a show of frowning and glancing around the narrow hallway. "Is there an echo up here?"

Elizabeth gave him a quelling look.

Jake appeared serenely unquelled.

"It's after one." She had stated the obvious;

he knew what time it was. Hadn't they heard the bells peal out the arrival of Christmas as they were entering the church for midnight services? "I'm tired; it's been a long day, and a long night."

It had been after ten-thirty when, dinner over, the Pattersons had bundled up their sleepy-eyed children and had headed for home to await a visit from Santa Claus. On the heels of their departure, the family members had passed around coats, scarves, and gloves, and had swept Elizabeth along with them to their cars.

"A few minutes more, that's all." Reaching out, Jake curled his fingers around her free hand.

The facets on the old-fashioned glass knob dug into the palm of her other hand.

"Maryanne told me you're a widow."

"Yes. My husband died from a coronary early last spring."

"I'm sorry."

Elizabeth swallowed again. "Thank you."

"Maryanne also mentioned your daughters." He arched his dark brows. "They're skiing?"

If there had been so much as a hint of censure in his tone, Elizabeth would have sprung to their defense. But there wasn't; his tone was curious but polite.

"Yes, with their grandmother . . . my mother-in-law. My husband was an only child." She didn't know why she was defending the elder Ella. Possibly out of a sense of duty.

Jake didn't pursue the subject; he tactfully changed it. "You have two daughters?"

Relieved, Elizabeth nodded. "Ella and Sally."

"And they're missing their father."

Beginning to feel pressured, Elizabeth said only, "Yes."

"And you're missing them like hell, aren't you?"

Elizabeth's composure slipped. "Of course. This is the first . . ." She broke off; the faceted glass scored her palm.

His long fingers stroked the inside of her wrist. "I'm sorry. I didn't mean to upset you."

She felt the effects of his stroking from her wrist to the base of her skull. The short hairs at her nape quivered. The glass doorknob grew slippery against her suddenly damp palm.

"I . . . I . . ." She wet her lips as his gaze fastened on her mouth.

"Good night, Elizabeth, and Merry Christmas to you." Releasing her hand, he turned away.

"Good night." Her hand felt cold; her throat ached. "Merry Christmas," she whispered.

"By the way." Jake paused, slanting a look at her over his shoulder. "Does anyone ever call you Liz?"

She shook her head. "No." At least not anymore, she reflected.

"May I?"

"If . . . you like," she answered, wondering why she didn't mind, why she rather liked it when she had hated Richard's calling her Liz.

His smile was slow, almost frightening in its attractiveness.

"I like."

"Good night." Her voice a bare whisper, Elizabeth twisted the knob, pushed open the door, and stepped inside the dark room.

"Good night, Liz." Jake's low voice crept under the door, curled around her ankles, and flowed through her veins.

She felt lightheaded . . . and stupid for it.

Turn on the lights, you fool, a reasoning remnant of her mind ordered; Elizabeth jerked reflexively, swinging up her hand to hit the wall switch.

Her gaze swept the room, settling on the open suitcase on the bed. She groaned. She was so tired, but she had to unpack, put her things away.

Clearing her mind, Elizabeth dispatched the chore with her usual efficiency, stashing foldables in dresser drawers and hangables in the closet.

She had to use the bathroom.

The realization hit as she slipped a nightgown over her head. Her lips set in determination; she could wait until morning. And go to bed without washing her face or brushing her teeth?

Yuck.

Idiot. The reasoning remnant surfaced again. Put on your robe and cross the hallway.

Following the edict, Elizabeth shrugged into her robe, opened the door, and peered at the bathroom. The door was closed. Not so much as a sliver of light could be seen along the floor beneath it.

Heaving a sigh, Elizabeth dashed across the hall and into the bathroom.

He had been there, and very recently. Beads of condensed moisture from a steaming shower trickled down the mirror. Elizabeth's suddenly acute senses caught a whiff of the scent of masculine soap.

She liked the fragrance. Too much.

Collecting what remained of her wits, she rushed through her nightly ritual. She was back inside her room, the door closed, the light off, in ten minutes flat. Tossing her robe aside, she slid between the cold sheets.

It was Christmas.

The thought wiped her mind free of male scents, and of one male in particular.

Ella and Sally were in Colorado.

Her parents were in Florida.

Richard was gone.

She was alone. Elizabeth shivered, not only from the cold. For the first time in her life she would not be spending the holiday with family, but would be amongst virtual strangers, friendly strangers but strangers nonetheless.

A rush of tears stung her eyes. A spark of resentment reared its ugly head.

They had deserted her. The beloved daughters—she would willingly have laid down her life for them—had skipped away without a care, leaving her alone on this most special of holidays. Alone, cold, and lonely in an unfamiliar bed, she finally admitted to herself that it hurt like hell.

Feeling sorry for herself and ashamed of that, Elizabeth cried herself to sleep.

Liz.

Heat gathered and pooled around Jake's loins.

He smiled into the darkness.

A widow of less than a year, and with two children in the bargain.

The smile dissolved into a frown.

Had Elizabeth loved him, this unnamed husband? he wondered. Was she still in mourning, grieving for him?

The question was important to Jake, because the answer would dictate his actions.

He wanted her. Here. Now. Badly.

Dream on, Ruttenburg, Jake told himself, shifting in the hope of easing his physical discomfort. It didn't help, no more than the scalding hot shower had helped. The ache remained, a constant reminder of how long it had been since he had enjoyed a release from sexual tension.

Was it really almost six months? Incredible. He, Jake Ruttenburg, the notorious seducer, celibate for half a year? Whatever would the tongue waggers say, if they knew?

Jake gave a harsh-sounding snort of mocking

laughter, aimed at the gossipmongers, as well as himself.

The cause of his celibacy certainly could not be attributed to lack of opportunity.

A series of willing females flashed through his mind, beginning with a nubile young sales rep for his publishing house and zipping right through to the barracuda reporter in Philadelphia and the suntanned beach-bunny impersonator in Arizona.

Ahhh, yes, the luscious hot-to-trot Cassie.

A vision of her presented itself for Jake's mental examination. In living color, he saw Cassie, her flame blue eyes devouring him, her glistening mouth open, her nipples tightly pouting on her jutting implanted breasts, her sleek thighs parted, her hips arched and undulating in wanton and abandoned invitation.

His loins throbbed in atavistic demand for physical surcease.

But his mind rejected the image of the arousing wanton, and conjured up instead—as it had that night in Arizona—a vision for comparison.

Elizabeth.

Elizabeth as she had appeared on her arrival at the house, reticent, uncertain, her lovely hazel eyes shadowed by apprehension and sadness.

Elizabeth as she had slowly relaxed, her hesitant smiles turning to laughter in response to the excited anticipation of the children during supper.

Elizabeth as she had bent her head in worship in church, the candlelight shimmering in the auburn highlights in hair smoothed back close to her head into a neat and oh-so-proper-looking twist.

Elizabeth as she had looked, so lost and forlorn, when he had mentioned her daughters after offering his condolences for the demise of her husband.

Elizabeth.

Jake ground his teeth together. Damn him for the bastard he was. He ached for her, desired to see her, naked and every bit as wanton and abandoned as Cassie had been, opening her mouth, her arms, her body to him. He burned with a need to taste her mouth, her skin, her feminine honey; to suckle at her breasts, to bury himself in the sweet coolness of her, making her as wild, hot, and sweaty for him, as he was for her.

On the point of bursting from that need, Jake flung himself from the bed, to prowl the confines of the winter-chilled room.

God help him, he was losing his mind. Grimacing at the thought, Jake raked an unsteady hand through his hair, and continued to pace, unmindful of the chill until the frigid tendrils curling around him leached the heat of passion from his body.

When his teeth began to chatter, Jake dove into the bed, burrowing beneath the covers.

Maybe he should have written a letter to Santa Claus, he mused, with newly cooled detachment, requesting the gift of Elizabeth wrapped in warm satin.

"No question, Ruttenburg, you are definitely losing contact with the real world," Jake muttered to himself.

His chest heaved with a heavy exhalation. In the real world, a comparison could not be made between Cassie and Elizabeth; they were complete opposites.

Cassie probably had been had by just about anybody who wore pants and could lay claim to a smidgen of fame.

Elizabeth, on the other hand, was of a different caliber altogether, cool, contained, circumspect.

Gut instinct, and a lifetime of observing human nature, warned Jake against involvement with her.

He had opened himself to one woman, only to have his emotions mangled in the grinder of her selfishness. His emotions were now off limits. He took his pleasures where he pleased, with whom he pleased, ruthlessly adhering to a policy of no strings, no involvement, no commitment.

Yet, better judgment or no, he wanted Elizabeth, wanted her so badly his teeth ached.

And Jake very much feared—knew—that Elizabeth was a forever, an unto death, kind of woman.

Nevertheless, he wanted her.

Wonderful. Jake shivered and pulled the comforter closer around him. How clever of him. He, the no-strings, emotionally frozen cynic, the much vaunted writer of carefully plotted, ultimately logical intrigue novels, lay awake in the wee hours of Christmas morning, his supposedly fertile mind scrambling for a method to employ to lure this "forever" kind of woman into his bed—and life.

When was a self-proclaimed and dedicated loner not alone?

When his emotions were keeping company with another.

Damned if he wasn't a living, breathing conundrum.

It was a hell of a blow to his self-image.

Twelve

Elizabeth had decided that she was not *doing* Christmas morning . . . she could not.

Despite the lateness of the hour when they had all retired, everyone was up early.

The family gathered, as families do throughout the country, around the tree in the living room.

After wishing everyone a Merry Christmas, Elizabeth sought refuge in the kitchen, not wishing to intrude on family rituals. Overriding immediate protests from not only De De but every family member, excluding Jake who merely smiled in a rather cynical way, she managed a serene smile and offered to prepare the holiday breakfast.

When the meal was over, mindful of the time difference, and judging the girls had likely been up for at least an hour, Elizabeth requested to use the phone in George's study to place a call to Colorado.

Both girls sounded depressingly happy, although each in turn declared she was missing her mother.

It wasn't much, but it was something.

Elizabeth hugged their declarations close, salving her bruised feelings with the balm of the words of reassurance.

The study door opened as she was winding up her duty greetings to her mother-in-law.

"Oh, I'm sorry," De De whispered, beginning to back away. "I thought you were finished."

Grateful for the interruption, Elizabeth held up her hand and mouthed Don't go before saying aloud: "I'm afraid I have to hang up now, Ella, someone else wants to use the phone." Then, reflecting the insincerity in the older woman's tone, replied, "Thank you, and a Merry Christmas to you, too."

"I'm in no hurry," De De said, frowning as she came into the room. "You didn't have to hang up."

"Oh, but I did." Elizabeth grimaced. "My blood sugar level was getting dangerously high—from my mother-in-law's cloyingly sweet crowing."

"The nasty bitch."

De De's gritty tone brought a twisted smile to Elizabeth's lips. "Precisely," she agreed. Indicating the desk phone, she headed for the door. "It's all yours."

"Are you okay?" De De asked with obvious concern.

"Yes." Elizabeth paused in the doorway, her expression revealing self-knowledge. "Battered but bloodless."

"Oh, well, that's comforting."

"Don't worry about me, De De." She managed a credible shrug. "I appreciate it . . . but it's unnecessary. I'll survive and maybe even learn something from the experience, painful as it is."

De De appeared stricken. "Wow, thanks. That makes me feel a lot better."

"I'm sorry." Elizabeth sighed. "Look, De De, I'm fine, hurting but fine. There is nothing more you can do. We live, and sometimes even learn." The smile she offered her friend was a soft one. "I truly feel like one of the lucky ones, because I have you on my side."

"Oh, Elizabeth, I . . ." De De's face crumbled.

Elizabeth shook her head. "Don't you dare fall apart on me. I'm going to have another cup of coffee. And you are going to make your call to . . . whomever." She flicked a hand toward the phone. "Get on with it."

Whomever.

De De's hand shook as she punched in the long-distance number to "whomever."

"Hello?" His low voice made her shake all over.

"Hi, Beau, Merry Christmas." De De cringed at the too bright, too chipper sound of her own voice. Oh, God, why had she done this? she asked herself, all the while knowing she had had to hear his voice.

You're a sick chick, she told herself, barely aware of his return greeting.

"Is something wrong, De De?" Concern tinged his normally mild tone. "Is Jake okay?"

Jake. De De felt crushed. Beau's concern was, always had been, for Jake. As much as De De loved and admired her uncle, at that moment she almost hated him.

"No, no, everything's fine," she quickly assured him, fighting a tightness in her throat, the sting of tears in her eyes. "I . . . just wanted to wish you and your mother a Merry Christmas."

"That was thoughtful, De De. Thank you."

Had she heard a tiny catch in his voice, a slight thickening in his softened tone? De De now fought against an impossible hope.

To him, she was thoughtful. De De swallowed; it hurt. So did the truth. She wasn't thoughtful at all. She was lustful, needful, consumed with wanting him.

Dear God, growing up was tough. Her life, her outlook had been so much simpler before, when she had loved Beau with the purity of hero worship. He was so beautiful. So gentle. So kind to the giddy teenager she had been.

The problem was, Beau still saw her as that teenager. He did not see—did not recognize— the passion and hunger in the woman she had become.

Thoughtful? Sure. She was thoughtful all right. And every one of her thoughts centered on him.

"De De?" The concern deepened in his voice; that concern was her undoing.

"I love you, Beau."

Ringing silence followed her blurted confession.

De De crunched her eyes shut, and bit her lip to keep from crying out in condemnation of her own weakness.

"I love you, too, De De."

Pain lanced through her, the intensity of it ripping a sharp gasp from her throat. Of course he loved her, wasn't she the cherished niece of Beau's hero?

De De didn't want to be loved by him simply because she happened to be related to the one man Beau idolized and admired above all others. She wanted him to love her for herself, for the woman she was, for the gifts she offered to him—freely, joyously, unconditionally.

"You don't understand," she cried, unable to hold the pain inside any longer. "I don't need or want your avuncular affection, offered because I'm Jake Ruttenburg's niece." A sob tore free of her guard. "Damn you, Beauregard Kantner, you don't understand."

Appalled at herself, her lack of control, her emotional outburst, De De slapped her palm over the mouthpiece, while groping with her other hand for the disconnect button. The sound of his harsh laughter vibrating along the line froze her hand, her body.

"Oh, I understand." Beau's voice was as strained as his brief burst of laughter. "I know what it's like to lie awake nights, my body writhing and slick with the sweat of hopeless passion. I know too well the agony of wanting—of aching for—the sweet healing touch of you."

Her? Her! Oh, sweet Lord. A terrible combination of sheer joy and abject despair struck De De like a physical blow. Tears streaming down her face, she swayed, rocked by the force of the emotional jolt. Beau shared her feelings; yet he had never said a word, never given her so much as a hint.

"Beau . . . why?" Her whisper rang out, a dry, strangled cry from the heart.

"Because I'm nearly old enough to be your father," Beau's cry echoed hers. "Because I respect your parents, and know they wouldn't approve." His voice had grown faint, pleading. "But, my love, mostly because you *are* Jake Ruttenburg's niece. And I will deny myself, and you, before I would do anything to hurt him."

"Why?" De De demanded, certain, as she had always been that the ugly rumors about the relationship between the two men were untrue.

"Because I owe him my sanity," Beau answered, "and very likely my life."

The calm finality in his voice filled De De with dread; even as he admitted the depth of his feelings for her, he rejected them—and her.

De De couldn't bear it, or accept it.

"But I love you," she sobbed.

"And I love you." His soft sigh of defeat pierced her to the quick. "There, I've said it, made myself—my feelings—clear. But that doesn't change a thing."

"But how do you know Jake wouldn't understand?" she demanded, clutching at the straw of her uncle's sophistication, his compassion.

"De De, you're his pet, his little girl, the child he never had and now never expects to have." He sounded tired . . . no, weary. "You know that, or at least you should."

"But I'm twenty-five years old!" she exclaimed in protest, and self-defense. "I'm a woman, not a little girl."

"You know that. I know that. And intellectually Jake knows that."

"But, then—"

"But, then, nothing," he gently cut in. "Think, De De. Jake was a young man when you were born . . . the beautiful baby girl of his beloved older sister. He immediately fell in love. Then, when his own marriage produced no children, he lavished his affection on you. So, in effect, to Jake you represent not only his adored niece, but the child his self-centered ex-wife viciously denied him."

De De was quiet for a few seconds, assimilating his theory, reluctantly concluding it was valid.

"If you're right, and I have a nasty suspicion you are," De De said with bitter acceptance, "Jake will never see me as a mature woman. Will he, Beau?"

"Not unless something occurs to cause some major change in his outlook."

"But he loves me!" De De cried in protest. "Why won't he let me grow up?"

"Because he loves you."

"It's so unfair," De De whimpered, unaware that she sounded like the child Jake still considered her to be.

"You expected fair?" Beau made an uncharacteristic, rude noise. "Who promised you fair?"

Startled by the bitterness tainting his normally pleasant voice, she tried to reach him. "Beau—"

He again cut her off. "This is all pointless and painful. I'm going to hang up now, De De."

"Beau, please, no!"

"Merry Christmas, love."

There came a soft click, the buzz of the dial tone, and then the soft sound of weeping.

So close, and yet so far away.

Staring at the phone, despair a weight on his soul, Beau smiled sadly at the reality of the truism.

Mere miles separated him from the woman who held the key to his heart, and yet, De De might as well be on a strange planet in a different solar system rather than in a state not far removed from his home in North Jersey.

She loved him.

Beau shut his eyes against the mingled thrill of pleasure and pain.

"Who called, Beau honey?"

Beau collected his composure and managed

a creditable smile before turning away from the phone to face his mother.

"That was Jake's niece, De De," he said, his voice only cracking a trifle over her name. "She called to wish us a Merry Christmas."

"That was nice of her." Camellia Kantner's smile was gentle; a reflection of her true personality. "De De is such a lovely child."

She is not a child. She's a woman.

Beau clenched his teeth to keep from shouting the words at her. Drawing a careful breath, he hung on to his patience, and his smile. "Yes, she is," he agreed, his despondency deepening.

The last person on earth he would deliberately hurt was his mother. She even took precedence over Jake.

Camellia Kantner had not had an easy life. Born in Atlanta, Georgia, she came from a genteel, if poor, family of impeccable lineage that could be traced back to long before the Civil War. Always fragile, she had an innocence and a sweet nature that had drawn young men to her as the sweetest flower draws bees.

Beau knew that several of those young men had had much in the way of material possessions to offer Camellia; yet she had chosen to entrust her future to his father, a handsome, gentle giant of a man who, unfortunately, had had very little, other than his fidelity and his undying devotion.

Beau had been witness to the fact that his mother had struggled to maintain a serene and stable home while balancing a budget that never seemed to reach from one payday to the next.

Yet Camellia had always appeared content and quite happy caring for her husband and her son.

Having been educated in the North, and having subsequently worked at two other jobs before accepting Jake's offer of the position as his assistant, Beau had settled permanently in the house he'd purchased in upstate New Jersey.

When his father retired, Beau had suggested his parents give up their struggle of maintaining the house that was eating up their income and come live with him.

They had politely, but firmly, refused.

Only after his father was fatally injured in a hit-and-run accident, leaving his mother devastated by grief and rudderless in a sea of debt, did Beau take command of the situation—and Camellia.

While retaining her gentility and her loving nature, Camellia had worked unceasingly, during her marriage for her beloved husband and her adored son.

She had taught Beau the true meaning of love and gentleness, of the sanctity of life.

Having at last relieved her of financial worries, Beau strove to make her life as balanced and serene as she had made his. He told himself the very least he could do was offer her a smile, even when his heart, his mind, and his soul cried out in anguish.

"Are you ready for lunch, dear?"

Camella's soft voice jolted Beau out of his introspection. "I'm sorry, Mother, what did you say?" he asked, shaking his head and forcing yet another smile.

"Beauregard Kantner," she gently scolded, "were you thinking you should be working on the pages Jacob faxed to you three days ago?"

Beau had never deliberately lied to his mother; instead, he occasionally committed the sin of omission. He did so now, letting a sheepish expression answer for him. "I'm sorry," he repeated. "What was your question?"

"I asked if you were ready for lunch?"

Lunch? Beau's stomach roiled. After hearing De De confess her love for him, and being painfully aware that their love could never be consummated, he felt certain he would never want to eat again.

"Yes," he answered, infusing a false note of enthusiasm into his voice. "I'm ready to have our Christmas lunch."

Thirteen

Christmas was over.

Replete from the array of food Maryanne had served buffet-style for lunch and tired from entertaining a continuous stream of visitors throughout the day and into the early evening, the family members and Elizabeth sat around the fireplace, nightcaps in hand, in a round-robin discussion of the events of the day.

"It was a lovely holiday," Maryanne murmured dreamily. "Wasn't it, George?"

"Lovely," he repeated, his lips quirking at the corners as he raised his glass, and his eyebrows, at his brother-in-law. "As it always is."

"It was a zoo." Jake grinned and lifted his drink in a return salute. "As it always is."

"Bahh, humbug, Mr. Scrooge," De De chided, making a sour face at Jake, not for the first time that day.

"You said last night that it was a circus," Elizabeth jumped into the fray, casting a glance at De De and wondering what could have caused this strange, nearly belligerent attitude toward her uncle.

Jake shrugged. "Same difference. Zoo. Circus. Everybody acts like a clown. Hail fellow, well met. A perfect excuse for all that hugging, kissing, laughing too much, eating too much, drinking too much—all that crap."

"Jacob." Margaret Ruttenburg's voice was soft, gentle, yet laced with steel. "Watch your language."

Maryanne, George, and De De managed to keep their expressions straight.

Elizabeth hid her smile inside her wineglass. It hadn't taken her long to decide she liked the older woman, who was at once gentle and forceful.

"Yes, Mother." Though Jake sounded contrite, the effect was ruined by the devilish gleam in his eyes. "I do offer my abject apologies to the ladies."

"The tree is beautiful," Maryanne said, in an obvious attempt to change the subject.

"Yeah." De De sighed. "Reminds me of the trees we had when I was a kid."

"I've always loved the scent of live trees," Elizabeth said, her eyes misty as she glanced at the majestic blue spruce standing tall between the two front windows.

"And I," Margaret agreed, smiling softly. "For all the improvements they've made to artificial trees, they are still just . . . artificial."

Jake groaned aloud. "It must be time to wax nostalgic." He heaved himself out of the chair. "I'll have another drink. Anyone else?"

His query was answered with rejection by everybody, save one.

"Not I," Elizabeth said, shaking her head. "I'm off to bed."

"Me, too," De De echoed. "I'm beat."

"It's way past my bedtime," Margaret murmured, smothering a yawn behind her hand.

"And we've got a full day tomorrow, don't forget," Maryanne put in. "Company coming for lunch and dinner."

"I'll have one with you, Jake." George was the only holdout. "The ladies need their beauty rest."

"The ladies are wusses," Jake declared, his beguiling smile robbing the insult of its sting.

"And the gentlemen—at least one of them— is not a gentleman," Elizabeth retorted.

She was rewarded for her temerity by a female chorus of praise and agreement.

George merely chuckled.

Jake leveled a superior look on her. "My dear Ms. Leninger," he drawled, "if the criteria for being a gentleman is to forever avoid voicing one's beliefs, then I fear I must forever more remain a philistine."

"Whoa! Hey, Elizabeth," De De said sarcastically. "Are you impressed with the verbal posturing of the great author . . . or what?"

Already on her feet, and on her way to the door, Elizabeth turned, her smile serene. "Or what?" she replied, flicking a glance of dismissal at Jake before sailing out of the room.

The sound of appreciative laughter followed her up the stairs to the second-floor landing.

"I'll get you for that, Liz," Jake's amused

voice, rising above the laughter, trailed her all the way up the third-floor staircase and into her bedroom.

Mulling over the method Jake might employ to *get* her, Elizabeth performed her nightly ritual, slipped out of her clothes, and got into bed. She fell asleep within moments, an anticipatory smile curving her lips.

She woke early to a gray morning light and a familiar hushed stillness.

Snow?

Deserting the warmth of the covers, Elizabeth padded to the window. Beyond the frost-rimmed pane, the ground, trees, and bushes lay quiescent under a mantle of white.

It was snowing fitfully, but the inch or so coating of white gave proof of a heavier fall during the night.

The first snowfall of the season.

Like a child, full of wonder and delight, she quickly and efficiently made her bed, showered, and dressed. Descending the stairs, she caught the mouth-watering aroma of freshly brewed coffee and warming cranberry muffins. Stomach grumbling, Elizabeth tracked the scent into the kitchen.

Margaret was standing by the counter, pouring coffee into two cups. Maryanne was removing a plate of muffins from the microwave.

Elizabeth greeted them as she entered the room. "Good morning. It's snowing," she went on, aware that she was stating the obvious.

Both women returned her greeting, Maryanne adding, "Isn't it pretty?"

"Yes, it is." Elizabeth inhaled. "The coffee and muffins smell wonderful."

"So, have a seat," Margaret invited, reaching into the cabinet for another cup. "Would you like something else first . . . eggs, cereal?"

"No, thank you, the muffins will be enough." She arched her eyebrows. "Can I do anything to help?"

"Nothing to do," Maryanne said, setting the plate of steaming muffins on the table. "Except help yourself." Turning away, she went to the fridge to remove a carton of orange juice and collected a small glass from a cabinet and a knife from the cutlery drawer on her way back.

Margaret served the coffee before seating herself.

"Are the others still asleep?" Elizabeth asked as she raised the juice glass to her lips.

"Hmmm." Maryanne nodded and swallowed the bite of muffin in her mouth. "And I hope they stay asleep for a while longer." She smiled. "Mother and I can get a lot more done without them cluttering up the kitchen."

"You and Margaret and I can get a lot more done," Elizabeth corrected her, feeling decadent as she slathered butter on half of a muffin.

"But you're a guest," Margaret protested.

"Really, Elizabeth, you don't have—"

"I want to help," she told Maryanne. "So, what needs doing?"

* * *

They had finished breakfast and were busy cutting and arranging vegetables on two trays, one for lunch, the other for dinner, when George put in an appearance.

"Morning," he mumbled, grinning sheepishly as he made a beeline for the coffee carafe, warming on the hot plate of the automatic coffeemaker.

While Elizabeth and Margaret returned his greeting, Maryanne glanced up from the vegetable dip she was mixing, her expression cool, reserved.

"And what time did you stumble into bed, Mr. Davidson?"

George winced at her tone of voice, which reflected the frigid conditions outside.

"Ah . . ." He eyed her warily.

Elizabeth and Margaret exchanged looks of amusement; then, as one, they returned their eyes and concentration to the business at hand.

"Yes?" Maryanne prodded her reluctant husband.

"Somewhere around two . . . I think."

"Uh-huh."

Silence followed her dry-voiced response. Elizabeth shot a glance at Margaret and repressed a chuckle at seeing the laughter in the older woman's eyes.

"Ah, honey, give me a break," George pleaded. "Family gatherings are the only times Jake and I get to talk in private."

"And drink."

He sighed. "Well, yeah."

"I see," Maryanne said, her tone one of sweet reason. "It's a guy thing."

"Yeah," George said, assertively.

"Hmmm," Maryanne hummed. "You'll pay, you know?"

"How?" George asked, less assertive than wary.

"By driving me into town to the supermarket to pick up a few things I forgot."

George met her stated punishment with a groan.

She transferred her gaze to Elizabeth. "Like most men," she said sweetly, "George hates to shop, most especially for groceries."

Margaret lost it; the inner laughter erupted, flowing into the room like benign lava. "I think I'd better go with them," she said to Elizabeth. "If only to insure my daughter's safety from the beast."

"Ah, Margaret," George groused.

Maryanne laughed.

Elizabeth soaked up the verbal sparring like a dried sponge. Family. Though she missed her daughters, she was thoroughly enjoying the interaction between the members of this closely knit family.

Being an only child, and married to a man who had been an only child, she had never had occasion to witness this particular kind of loving byplay.

Elizabeth only wished her Ella and Sally

could witness it, too. With no aunts, uncles, or cousins to gather for holiday or birthday, the girls had never experienced this family warmth or the good-natured bickering.

Basking in the glow for the first time in her life, Elizabeth happily chopped away at the vegetables, while the friendly altercations continued around her.

"What's the bone of contention?"

Elizabeth turned to the new voice on the scene, a greeting on her lips. "Good morning, De De. It's snowing."

"I know, but is it a good morning?" she asked, her frowning look skimming the others and settling on Margaret. "What's up, Gramma?"

"Well, I'd say you are," Margaret scolded. "Finally."

"Wrong." Shaking her head, De De crossed to the coffee pot. She frowned when she saw it was empty, then proceeded to brew a fresh pot. "I've been up for hours."

"Doing what?" Maryanne arched her brows. "Cleaning your room?"

"Get real," De De retorted, in a pleasant tone. "I've been slaving over my notebook, working on my novel."

"You're working now—over the holidays?"

"Mother," the girl said patiently. "I'm a writer, and writers work when inspiration strikes." Her pixie face became animated with excitement. "I had this great idea for a scene when I woke up. I just had to get it down. I'd still be at it, except I'm starving."

"What would you like to eat?" Maryanne asked, suddenly all mother, concerned for her child's nutrition.

"Just juice and toast—raisin bread, if there is any, and this," the coffee ready, she poured a cup for herself. "Lots of this."

Elizabeth got a glass of juice while Maryanne popped two pieces of raisin bread into the toaster.

"I'm glad to hear the work's going so well for you," Elizabeth said as she carried the glass to the table and set it before De De.

"Thanks," De De murmured. "I don't know what it is about this place, but I'm always inspired here. Jake, too. I'll bet he's in his room working like mad."

George rolled his eyes.

Maryanne laughed.

Margaret snorted. "If your Uncle Jake is working, it's at sleeping off his indulgences of last night in the company of your father," she said acerbically, bringing the conversation full circle.

De De grinned at George. "Tied one on, did you?"

"Good grief," George exploded. "Jake and I had a couple of drinks after the rest of you went to bed. And that's all, so give it a rest."

Four pairs of female eyes made contact. There ensued a brief pause. Then laughter again filled the room.

Grumbling about being outnumbered in a kitchen full of women, he shoved back his chair. "So, if we're going grocery shopping, let's get a move on," he ordered, scowling at his wife. "Before I change my mind."

Teasing him with unrelenting glee, Mary-anne and Margaret nevertheless got ready to go.

Elizabeth sat down at the table to have a cup of coffee while De De ate breakfast.

It was nearly eleven when Jake, looking sleep-tousled and much too attractive, made an appearance in the kitchen.

De De had returned to her bedroom to work.

Having finished with the vegetables, and the clearing away of the breakfast dishes, Elizabeth was taking a break, enjoying a mid-morning snack of a tangerine.

"Smells good," he said, eyeing the fruit.

"Tastes good, too," she replied, popping another tangy section into her mouth. "Coffee?"

"Hmmm." Jake nodded. "Funny, but no matter what month of the year it happens to be, the smell of tangerines reminds me of Christmas and home."

"Really?" Coffee carafe held in midair, Elizabeth turned to look at him, startled by an odd sensation of connectedness. She shrugged off the feeling with a laugh. "With me, it's fruit-cake."

"Fruitcake?" Jake's lips twitched.

"Yes." Appreciating his attempt not to laugh at her, she poured and served his coffee, then elaborated. "I know that many claim to detest fruitcake, but I must confess, I love it."

Jake motioned with his index finger. "Come closer," he said, making a show of glancing around furtively. "I've got a confession."

Feeling excitement way out of proportion to his antics, she leaned forward and whispered, "What is it?"

Eyes narrowed, he looked to the right, then to the left, and then directly into her laughter-sparkled eyes.

"I love it, too." With a quick move of his head, Jake stole a kiss, and her breath, from her surprise-parted lips. "But you have to promise not to tell anybody."

Bemused and beguiled, Elizabeth stared into his midnight blue eyes, her senses whirling, her pulses thrumming, and her heart pounding.

"Hey, Liz," Jake whispered, rattling her even more with the feather-light brush of his breath across her lips. "That tastes even better than tangerines. Tastes like more." Maintaining eye contact, he moved toward her again.

Elizabeth's vision blurred, and somehow the blurring jarred her common sense into overriding her rioting senses. She pulled back just as his mouth touched hers.

"Ah . . . Liz, why—" he began.

She silenced him by stuffing a tangerine slice between his parted lips.

"You'll have to settle for the fruit," she said, slightly amazed at the even tone she had managed.

Jake cocked an eyebrow at her, but chewed and swallowed the tangerine slice before responding.

"The other is forbidden fruit, is it?"

Presenting a cool front that conflicted with the heat building inside her, Elizabeth retreated, out of harm's way. "I . . . I don't know how to play these games, Jake," she admitted honestly. "I never did."

"Can be fun," he said in soft enticement. "A lot more fun than Monopoly or card games."

Elizabeth didn't doubt his claim; how could she, when simply watching him devour what was left of the tangerine gave her a hollow, shivery feeling inside? In an effort to negate the squishy sensation, she raked her mushy mind for something—anything—to say.

"Did you see? It's snowing!" She despaired at the feeble attempt.

"You like snow?"

"Well, it's the first of the winter," she answered defensively. "Don't you like it?" she asked, a glimmer of an idea for escape niggling at her brain.

"Sure." He gave her a wry smile. "I wouldn't have a place in the mountains if I didn't like it. We get a fair amount of snow in the Poconos."

"Yet De De told me you don't ski."

"De De talks too much." He released a blatantly exaggerated sigh. "But it's true. I don't. I prefer my bones in one piece. Do you ski?"

"No." Elizabeth shook her head, then

quickly voiced the idea forming in her mind.
"But I do enjoy walking in snow. So, I think I'll
leave you to your coffee, get my coat, and go
for a walk." Edging around him, she bolted
through the doorway.

As it had the night before, his roar of laughter chased her all the way up to her third-floor
room.

Gasping, her heart racing, Elizabeth told herself her breathlessness was due to the dash up
two flights of stairs, not the result of his effect
on her.

Still, she couldn't deny the excitement simmering in her trembling body, the sense of expectation dancing inside her.

Ridiculous. Elizabeth chastised herself, kicking off her comfortable flats, then pulling on
her boots. She was a mature woman, a mother,
a widow, nearly middle aged.

She winced at the thought. Middle aged. She
didn't feel middle aged. She felt . . . she
felt . . .

How did she feel?

Standing stock-still by the bed, Elizabeth examined her fluttery feelings.

She felt young. Yes. And eager.

Eager?

About what? For what?

Life.

The answer came too swiftly to be deflected.

Life—and new, exciting experiences.

Exciting.

Jake.

Elizabeth groaned, suddenly very much afraid that by pursuing life and experiences she would be courting trouble, most especially if Jake had set his sights on her, as he had indicated.

If only half of what was said and written about him, about his exploits with women, was true, she was way out of her league, and she would be playing with fire if she allowed him to draw her into his games.

And yet . . . yet . . . Her mouth still tingled with the imprint of his, and she could still taste the alluring, masculine flavor of him.

Shaking herself free of these thrilling, yet troubling thoughts, she smoothed her trembling hands over the neat French twist confining her hair, straightened her shoulders, and, drawing a deep, calming breath, made her way down the stairs.

Jake was waiting for her at the front door.

Fourteen

Elizabeth's heartbeat did a little skip-jump at the sight of him, the sheer masculine impact of him on her senses.

Jake's hair was still unbrushed, tousled from sleep, but his eyes were alert, glittering with inner laughter. He had pulled on a buff-colored, sheepskin-lined jacket, which gave him more the look of an outdoorsman than a creative writer bound to a desk and computer. He had removed her coat from the hall closet and held it draped over one arm. The hem of the mid-calf-length garment brushed against the black denim encasing his muscular thigh.

Elizabeth entertained the errant thought that there was something intimate and vaguely possessive about her favorite coat seeming to curl around and caress his leg.

His leg. What did his leg look like beneath that black denim . . . long muscles covered by smooth, dark-hair sprinkled, warm skin?

Elizabeth shivered at the vision that filled her mind, inflamed her senses.

What in heaven's name was wrong with her? She had never, ever wondered what a man, any man, not even Richard when she was young, looked like unclothed.

The naked truth was, she wondered what Jake, all of Jake—every inch of Jake—looked like naked.

Unnerved by the thought, Elizabeth wavered on the bottom step, torn between turning and retreating back to her room or taking that final step to the foyer—and to him.

"I like to walk in the snow, too."

His low voice contained an invitation, and a challenge. Or was she simply imagining things, reading meanings that weren't there into the glitter in his eyes, the blue velvet tenor of his voice, the overall aggressive look of him?

Lifting the coat from his arm, Jake held it aloft, ready for her to slip into.

Reflecting on how childish she would appear, should she suddenly turn tail and run up the stairs, Elizabeth took that last step into the foyer. Crossing to him, she slid her arms into the sleeves.

"Thank you."

"You're welcome." Opening the door, he made a sweeping motion with his arm. "After you."

But was he after her?

The query caused a ripple of trepidation and uncertainty along her spine. Elizabeth reacted to the sensation as she always responded to apprehension. She stiffened her spine against the quivery feeling, squared her shoulders, lifted her head, and went sailing by him and out onto the porch as if she hadn't a doubt about what she was doing—or about him.

Fortunately, from behind her, he couldn't see the frown of indecisiveness that scored her brow, and she had smoothed it away before he stepped onto the walkway beside her at the bottom of the porch steps.

The low, whitish-gray cloud cover still spit bursts of fine flakes of snow into the swirling wind. The wet stuff clung to every surface it touched. Within moments, Elizabeth's hair and eyelashes were dusted with the tiny flakes.

"It's cold," she said, delving into her pockets for her gloves. "A lot colder than yesterday," she went on, brushing her leather-protected fingers over her eyelashes, while cringing inwardly at her inane prattle.

When bereft of conversation, fall back on the weather, she thought, somewhat irrationally.

"Hmmm . . ." Jake murmured agreement—at least she assumed it was. "Wanna have a snowball fight?"

Startled out of her self-doubt by the casual way he tossed out the question, as well as by the question itself, Elizabeth stopped in her tracks to look at him in wide-eyed surprise.

"But you're not even wearing gloves," she pointed out rationally.

"I like feeling what I touch." He arched one eyebrow. "So, are you game?"

Since nothing could have compelled her to comment on this explanation of his, she went straight to his taunting question. "Are you serious?"

"Sure." He slanted a wicked smile at her. "Why not?"

Breathless from the impact of his smile, she sputtered, "Why, why because . . ." She broke off, because he wasn't listening. He had turned away and had bent over, intent on scooping up a mound of snow with his bare hands.

"Jaaake," she said, in her tone equal parts of warning and amusement. She took a step back, and then another. "Behave yourself."

"C'mon, Liz, lighten up, have some fun." His devil-bright eyes tracked her retreat, while he loosely packed the snow in his hands.

"You wouldn't dare." Watching him warily, she took another step back.

"No?" He hefted the white ball in one hand.

"No."

He tossed it.

She ducked.

The wet missile skimmed over her head, missing her by barely an inch.

"Arm yourself, Liz." He called, bending to gather more ammunition. "This is war."

A rush of excitement brought a gurgling laugh from her throat. It sounded young; she felt young. Carefree, playful. Elizabeth hadn't been in a snowball battle since her girls were little. An anticipatory thrill shot adrenaline into her system.

"Okay, you asked for it." With the warning,

she feinted sideways, just as another ball skimmed past.

Crouching, she raked snow into her gloved hands, molded it, then sent it flying.

"First hit!" she crowed when the ball caught him on the shoulder.

The battle was joined.

Laughing like children, calling out whenever they scored a hit, they ran around the front lawn, circling each other, firing shots from behind the cover of trees and bushes, churning up the pristine snow.

Elizabeth couldn't remember the last time she had laughed so hard or had so much fun.

But it was a short war.

"Time out," she cried, gasping for breath after about fifteen minutes of sustained laughter and intense activity. "My fingers are numb, I've got a side stitch, and I have to catch my breath."

His breathing every bit as labored as hers, Jake tossed aside the ball he was in the process of forming, then strolled to where she stood beneath a tree along the side of the road at the end of the driveway.

"I guess we're not as young as we used to be." Coming to a stop less than a foot from her, Jake drew in a deep breath, and exhaled noisily. "It was fun though, wasn't it, Liz?"

"Yes," she admitted, her reedy breath catching as her gaze got tangled in the blue velvet of his eyes.

"And the exercise was good for you," he said,

his voice low, seductive. "Your eyes are bright and sparkling, and your cheeks are flushed, glowing from exertion."

"And . . ." Elizabeth swallowed. "And yours," she murmured, her gaze sketching the ruddy swath highlighting his cheekbones, the gleam of laughter in his eyes.

Considering the rugged look of him and his cynical, world weary attitude, who would have believed that Jake could laugh and play and look so young and carefree?

"You're beautiful."

Although his voice had dropped to a ragged whisper, Elizabeth heard him, heard him with every fiber of her being, every racing beat of her heart. That beat went crazy when he raised his cold-reddened hands and cradled her over-heated face in his palms.

"Jake?" Her voice was barely audible.

"Liz." His voice was little more then a groan.

She felt his hands move, felt his fingers tug at the pins anchoring the twist in her hair. Tendrils fell free, tickling her nape.

"What . . . what are you doing?"

"I want to see it loose, feel it."

The last pin fell to the snow; the auburn mass fell to her shoulders; his fingers curled into, around the unbound tresses, as slowly, excruciatingly slowly, he lowered his head to capture her mouth with his.

His lips were cold, yet Elizabeth felt their fire from her mouth to her toes, and she wouldn't have been at all surprised if the snow melted beneath her boots.

But that was just the beginning.

Making a sound, half groan, half growl, deep in his throat, Jake raked his fingers down the length of her hair, then lowered his hands, enfolding her trembling body within the warmth of his strong arms.

His lips, no longer cold, were a searing brand against her mouth. With a muted whimper, she parted her lips. Like a leaping flame, his tongue speared into her mouth.

The kiss went on forever . . . and ended much too soon.

Tearing his mouth from hers, Jake muttered, "Damn coats." Freeing one arm, he slid his hand between them and with unsteady fingers unfastened the buttons on their garments.

Feeling she should, Elizabeth opened her mouth to protest; Jake stifled it with his lips. His mouth moving on hers, he separated their coats, then pulled her tightly to him, molding her soft curves to the hard angles of his body.

Richard had never kissed her quite like that.

Elizabeth began to shiver, not from fear, but from the surge of wanting that forged through her. Drowning in the flood of rampant desire, she curled her arms around his waist, needing him closer, closer.

Jake's response was immediate and devastating. While insinuating one hand between them to cup her breast, he slid the other down to the base of her spine, lifting her into the hard, rigid heat of his arousal.

Elizabeth was sinking deeper into the swirling sensuality, arching her body into his heat, when a distant sound got through the sensuous haze clouding her mind, piercing that barrier as the sound drew nearer.

A car was moving slowly along the road.

Oh, God! Sanity returned with consciousness. Sanity and the realization of where she was, who she was with, and what she was doing.

The car had slowed, almost to a stop, as if to make the turn into the driveway.

Elizabeth's eyes flew open, and she began to struggle. Raising her unfettered arm, she pushed against his shoulder as she pulled her mouth from his.

Jake released her at once.

"What the hell!" Stepping back, he shook his head, as if to clear his thoughts and sight. His face was flushed; his frown fierce. "Elizabeth . . . what?"

"Listen, there's a car," she said in a strangled whisper, fragile, nearly shattered by the enormity of her uninhibited response to him.

She shuddered. Never before in her life had she become so aroused so swiftly, nor had she ever responded so ardently to a kiss. But then, Richard had never controlled and ravished her mouth as Jake had done. Feeling lost, confused, panicky, yet at the same time, oddly free, she stared at him, her body still simmering with desire, her mind hiding from that truth.

"So, there's a car." Jake shrugged, and flung his arm out. "There's a road. So what?"

"Your sister? Her lunch guests?"

He shot a glance at the driveway, the road beyond, then back to her, shaking his head. "No, not Maryanne or her guests. The car went by, I caught the tail end of it." He smiled lazily and reached for her again. "So, you can relax."

"Relax?" Elizabeth skipped back, avoiding his arms, the lure of his embrace, the aching demand of her treacherous body. "Are you out of your mind? They'll be here any minute. Maryanne, George . . ." Her breath caught, and her eyes widened. "Your *mother!*"

He gave her a bemused, confused, and slightly amused look. "What about my mother?"

"What about her!" Elizabeth's laugh held a note of hysteria. "Jake, suppose that had been George's car. They would—your mother would have *seen* us."

"So?"

She stared at him in horror. "We were kissing . . . passionately. What would she have thought?" She shivered, appalled at the very idea of having anyone, most especially his mother, see them in such an intimate embrace.

"That we were kissing—passionately?" He chuckled. "My mother is in her sixties, Liz, and the mother of two. I think she knows all about kissing, and passion."

"It's not funny, Jake," she said, annoyed by his teasing tone, the smile quirking his lips. "I feel certain she, and your sister, would disapprove, because as a mother, I would not be amused."

"Understandably," he agreed. "But then, your daughters are still teenagers." He followed as she continued to back away, toward the house. "However," he went on reasonably, "you and I are adults. There is a difference."

She shook her head. "But that makes it even worse!"

"How so?" He had nearly closed the distance between them; she could see the spark of laughter in his eyes.

"Teenagers have not yet learned how to control these impulses." Elizabeth winced inwardly at the edge to her lecturing; still, she prattled on "Adults should have. I've always felt rather embarrassed by undisciplined public displays of affection."

"Oh, Elizabeth." Jake laughed. "You are one uptight, buttoned-down, circumspect lady. Aren't you?"

Possibly because she knew his accusation was true, she bristled. "I do know the difference between decent and indecent behavior."

"Well, no harm done. You came to your senses in time." While now solemn, his voice trembled with contained laughter. Coming to a stop in front of her, Jake took her hand, then had the audacity to run his index finger over her wrist above the edge of her glove. "You saved both our reputations." His eyes danced caressingly over her face. "Of course, I didn't have much of a one to save."

The responsive tingles radiating up her arm from her wrist, along with his admission of a shadowy reputation with women, sounded an alarm inside her head. She tugged against his hold. "Please, let go," she said, when he held firm. "I want to go inside."

"I'll let go on one condition," he murmured, the rhythm of his finger setting her skin on fire.

Weakening, the warmth from her wrist invading her being and deactivating the alarm in her mind, Elizabeth felt pressured enough to agree to anything, just to get him to stop. She wet her lips. "What . . . condition?"

"Have dinner with me tonight."

She wasn't sure what she'd been expecting, but it certainly wasn't an invitation to dinner. Knowing she should refuse, she said, "Where?"

"There are several excellent restaurants in the area, any one of them will do."

"But Maryanne has guests coming, and I—"

"That's exactly why I want to get out of here," he said, overriding her protest. "It'll be a zoo again."

"Yes." She conceded his point, simply because, in all honesty and against her better judgment, she wanted to go with him.

"Ah, c'mon, Liz," Jake's voice was soft, a siren song to the senses. "I know Maryanne won't mind, and besides, it'll be a lot more relaxing than spending the evening with a houseful of strangers."

"Well . . ." Elizabeth hesitated.

Jake didn't. "I'll call one of the restaurants and make a reservation." Yanking on her hand, he strode toward the house, pulling her along with him.

"If Maryanne says it's all right," Elizabeth hedged, appeasing her disapproving conscience.

"She will." Jake slanted a conscience-blanking smile at her. "Or I'll sic George on her."

Despite her reservations, Elizabeth laughed, recalling how Maryanne had handled her husband that morning.

They left their snow-caked boots on the porch. Jake caught her arm, halting her as she turned the doorknob. Elizabeth raised an eyebrow questioningly.

"Your hair is so beautiful. Why not do me a favor and leave it loose tonight?"

Standing at her bedroom window overlooking the front lawn, from which she saw the antics and the embrace of her uncle and her friend, De De resented the blatant sensuality of the kiss they shared.

Her breath caught painfully in her throat when Jake quickly dispatched the buttons on their coats, then pulled Elizabeth into a deeper kiss and an arching embrace.

For an instant, her imagination projected two different images onto the couple, and she saw her own small form locked within the strong arms of a beautiful blond giant.

Sensations, wild and hungry, coursed through her. Her mouth yearned for the knowledge of Beau's kiss, her body ached for the fulfillment of his possession.

It isn't fair, she railed in silent frustration. Why should I be denied the love Beau confessed to feeling, while the reason for that denial indulges himself—out in the open, for the world to witness?

It just isn't fair.

A sob tore free of the tightness in her throat. *You expected fair?*

The echo of Beau's voice, soft, tender, brought a mist of tears to De De's eyes. She blinked to clear her vision, and when she refocused on the couple, she saw that they were no longer entwined.

Elizabeth was moving away from Jake. The stark and uncertain expression on her face dissolved the resentment burning inside De De. In its wake shame rushed through her.

Would she deny her friend, simply because she herself had been denied? A sad smile touched De De's lips at seeing the conflicting emotions revealed on Elizabeth's unguarded face.

From the look of her, Elizabeth was having her own problems in dealing with what De De guessed were feelings she wasn't yet ready to experience.

Poor Elizabeth, De De mused, watching her

friend retreat from the man, and the situation. She was such a self-contained, moral, and proper person. And Jake was a rather overpowering, determined man.

De De switched her attention to her uncle. Even from her position behind the curtained window on the second floor, she could see the sheen of laughter in his eyes, the purpose in the set of his squared jaw.

Jake's look convinced De De that, fight against it though she might, it would not be long before Elizabeth succumbed to him.

A deep sigh broke the silence of De De's room. Her chest ached from the knowledge that, while her uncle and her friend were free to explore their feelings, she and Beau were left on the sidelines, separated by possible objections to the difference in their ages.

In all honesty, De De could not fault her friend. It certainly wasn't Elizabeth's fault that Beau would not chance alienating Jake.

Tears trickled unnoticed down her face. Could she fault Jake for loving her?

What a mess, De De thought, swiping at the tears as she turned away from the window. Sniffling, she sat down at her desk and stared at the small screen of her notebook computer. Then with another, softer sigh, she switched off the machine.

How could she infuse a sense of reality into her fictional love scene after seeing the power and intensity of the real thing enacted by Elizabeth and Jake?

* * *

"A holiday romance. How charming." Cassie Metcalf smiled at catching her sarcastic tone. She glanced in the rearview mirror. Her gaze saw the bend in the road just beyond the Davidsons' driveway. But her mind's eye still witnessed the embracing couple on the Davidsons' front lawn.

"That bastard," she snarled, continuing to speak aloud, as she often did when alone. "I'll bet he's not leaving *her* hurting and hungry. Oh, no. Since she's there, she's obviously been accepted by the family. And he's probably banging her brains out. Night and day." She snorted. "Christ, it looked like he was shoving it to her standing there, right out in the open, in broad daylight."

The idea shot heat into her; it pooled between her thighs. Recalling the feel and the taste of Jake's tongue—a famous author's tongue, no less—in her mouth, Cassie wriggled on the plush seat. The car veered toward the edge of the road. Laughing, she smoothly steered the vehicle back into line. Then, flicking another glance at the mirror, she queried her own reflection.

"Who is she, I wonder?"

Her reflection smiled back at her. Cassie laughed again. She'd know soon enough. Oh, yes, she'd know everything worth knowing about the woman. A smirk twisted her lips. She was very good at ferreting out information.

When one had nothing to do, no clock to punch, no employer to answer to, one was forced to do something to fill the days. Of course, the nights—and she herself—were usually filled with exciting forms of entertainment.

It hadn't taken her long to find out where Jake-the-famous-author-Ruttenberg would be spending the holidays.

While doing so during the days, she had used her nights to have her voracious appetites appeased. Cassie's self-satisfied laughter reverberated inside the car as she reflected on the vehicle of her satisfaction.

His name was Mark, which was apt, since he'd been such a willing and eager "mark" for Cassie.

A self-styled stud, Mark worked in the mailroom of Jake's publishing house.

Delicately pulling on some highly placed strings, Cassie had arranged to be given a tour of the place. Along the way, she had earmarked several likely possibilities, including a young assistant editor and a green copy editor. But, at seeing and making eye contact with, Mark, she had known she had hit pay dirt.

The man was a bold-eyed pushover.

Cassie laughed and flicked her tongue over her lips, savoring the memory of her encounters with the pliable, easily manipulated Mark.

Young, good-looking, and with a superb body, he was so infatuated with himself, he took it as natural, his due, when Cassie evidenced interest in him.

She chuckled again, amused by her recollection of the way he had preened. Poor jerk. The size of his ego outweighed any common sense he might possess.

All she'd had to do was fix a wide-eyed stare on his crotch, then direct a sidelong look at him. Her silent, if blatant, message apparently went directly to his primary thinking apparatus, evidenced by the sudden bulge in his pants. He had responded minutes later by slipping her, on the sly, a piece of paper on which he'd scribbled his home address. Then, raising his eyebrows, he had mouthed the word "tonight"? She had answered with a quick nod.

Cassie had spent several nights partying with Mark, and had used him shamelessly. She had blown his mind—along with other parts of his anatomy—and Mark had reveled in every wild and decadent minute of it. By the end of that week, Cassie was privy to every bit of information the publishing house had on Jake Ruttenburg.

She had walked away from Mark without a care or a backward look. He had served his usefulness. Even so, she figured he had no cause for complaint. Besides enjoying utter satiation, he had received an invaluable tutoring in the fine art of bacchanalia.

Cassie figured she had performed a service for Mark's future lovers.

Now Cassie hummed along with the music blaring from the car radio as she headed for the simple, but acceptable motel room she had taken for an unspecified period. She had some planning to do, a modus operandi to formulate.

A tiny frown line marred the surgically smoothed perfection of Cassie's brow. It would help if she knew the woman's name.

Oh, well, she'd think of something . . . she always did. A confident smile banished the frown.

Cassie Metcalf was supremely confident in her ability to learn everything and anything she needed to know about Jake's latest conquest.

Fifteen

Lunch was over. The guests, four adults and six children ranging in age from three to twelve, had departed. The cleaning up had been done.

"Whew!" Maryanne exclaimed, collapsing onto the sofa next to George. "We have one hour to rest before the arrival of our dinner guests."

"A whole hour?" George rolled his eyes, before casting a wry look at his brother-in-law. "Whatever will we do with all that time?"

"Now, George," Margaret said in a mild scolding tone. "You enjoy the holidays, and you know it."

"Yes, I do," George readily admitted. "But do we really have to entertain the entire community?"

"The community you're referring to just happens to include a lot of your business associates," his wife reminded him. "As well as our neighbors."

"I know. I know," he muttered, heaving a sigh. "Was it my imagination, or were a few of those neighbors hitting the booze a little heavily."

"It wasn't your imagination," Jake drawled, in a position to know, as he had taken on the chore of tending bar. "And two of them weren't hitting the sauce a little heavily—they were knocking drinks back almost as fast as I could pour them."

"Carol and Tony." Maryanne nodded. "They're going through a rough time at present."

"Financial?" Margaret asked sympathetically.

"No." Maryanne shook her head, looked uncertain for an instant, then elaborated. "It's no secret; in fact it's been the main topic of gossip for several months now. It appears that Tony has been . . . er . . ."

"Screwing around?" Jake inserted bluntly.

"Jacob!" Margaret sharply reprimanded him.

Amused by the older woman's censoring of her son's language, Elizabeth had to suppress a smile.

Whereas De De, sitting quietly a bit away from Elizabeth and the circle of family members, gazed narrow-eyed at her uncle, her normally soft lips drawn into a thin tight line.

"I'm sorry if I shocked you, Mother," Jake dutifully apologized, not sounding as if he were.

Margaret reproved him. "Well, you did."

"I don't know why you should be shocked," De De observed, dry voiced. "You read his books, and he uses a lot worse language in them. A whole lot. I've even heard them referred to as filthy."

Seeing her own feelings of consternation and surprise reflected on the look Jake shot at the girl, Elizabeth wondered what could be bothering De De; she had been sniping at her uncle on and off for the past two days.

Jake didn't so much as open his mouth to defend himself or his work. But then, he didn't have to, his mother was as quick to defend him as she was to chastise him.

"Your uncle Jake does not write filthy books, De De, and you know it," Margaret said with utter conviction. "He writes . . ."—she paused, as if searching for a definitive description, then continued—"realistically."

"I stand corrected," De De said sardonically.

"You're sitting down," Jake retorted, teasingly.

De De grimaced and leaped from her chair. "No, I'm outta here. I'm going back to work."

Her brow mirroring the frown of every family member, Elizabeth stared in astonishment as De De stormed out of the room and up the stairs.

Jake gazed pensively at the empty doorway.

"What in the world . . . ?" Maryanne directed a confused look at her husband.

George gave a helpless shrug. "Beats me. PMS, maybe?"

"Or too much holiday," Margaret opined.

"It has been a little hectic," Maryanne admitted.

"And it's not over yet," George groaned, glancing at his wristwatch. "The second installment of the day will be descending on us in a little over half an hour."

"Not on me, friend," Jake said, pushing himself out of his chair. "Or on Elizabeth," he added, stealing the initiative from her.

"What are you talking about?" Maryanne demanded, glancing from Jake to Elizabeth and then back to him.

Jake smiled at his sister. "I've invited Elizabeth out for dinner," he explained. "If you have no objections?"

"Why, of course I don't," Maryanne protested good-naturedly. "Why would I object?"

Why indeed? Elizabeth mused, thinking Maryanne's response held a note of relief.

"Hmmm, delicious," Elizabeth murmured, licking her lips to remove traces of foam from the Irish coffee.

Jake chuckled. "That's what you said about the clam chowder, and the Caesar salad and the bread sticks and the shrimp scampi."

"Hmmm," she murmured again, her dreamy smile denoting repletion. "And everything was delicious." She raised her eyebrows. "Wasn't your meal?"

"Uh-huh." His lips twitched. "Delicious." He raised his own frothy cup. "To the chef."

Elizabeth startled herself by giggling. Must be

the wine, before and during dinner, she mused, because she never giggled; teenagers giggled.

Jake lost control of the twitch. He grinned. "Can I take it you've enjoyed the night out?"

"Oh, yes." She grinned back at him, and looked around the dining room. The decor was early American. The Christmas decorations were live greens, holly, and real candles. The tables were draped in dark green cloths accented by crisp white napkins. "What's not to enjoy? The restaurant's charming, the atmosphere congenial, the food . . ."

"Delicious?" he broke in.

She managed a haughty expression. "I was going to say excellent." Haughtiness gave way to another giggle.

"You're a hoot with a half a buzz, Liz."

"I am not half drunk!" she objected. Then she frowned. "Am I?" she asked anxiously.

He gave a quick shake of his head. "No, you're relaxed, and mellow." His smile was so gentle, so tender, it caused a pang in her heart. "And completely captivating."

Richard had never looked at her or complimented her quite like that.

"Ah . . . I . . ." Flustered and flattered, Elizabeth didn't know how to respond. She settled for a simple, if inadequate sounding, "Thank you—for everything."

"Thank you . . . for your company," he responded. "But, was it as good for you as it was for me?"

Elizabeth ignored the teasing double meaning, and queried the return, "The company?"

"Yes." He shrugged. "The company, the conversation, the entire evening."

"Better than the zoo back at the house?" she asked lightly, feeling certain she had chattered away like a magpie all evening out of sheer nervousness. But then, it had been years, over twenty years, since she had been out on a dinner date. And she never had been adept at small talk.

He didn't answer aloud, but his droll expression spoke for him. "Didn't I tell you Maryanne wouldn't mind?"

"Mind?" Elizabeth laughed. "I think she was relieved to see us go."

He nodded, and grinned. "Yeah, but who knew she was expecting all those people?"

Elizabeth laughed again. "How many were there, anyway? Do you have any idea?"

Jake laughed with her. "At last count, and that was just before we left, there were around twenty-five or thirty. It was already a zoo."

"Or a circus," she teased.

"That, too." He grimaced. "I only hope most of them are gone by the time we return."

"Which will be very soon," she said, her spirits sinking at the thought of the evening ending. She had had a wonderful time. In retrospect, it was rather surprising, considering how nervous she had been at the outset.

Jake had unsettled her from the beginning, throwing her off balance when she had come down the stairs by thanking her for leaving her hair loose, as he had asked her to do. And, although being made to feel attractive was pleasant, being so openly admired was an altogether new and rather exciting experience for her.

Elizabeth was not blind or dense. She knew she was a reasonably attractive woman . . . in a conservative way. Considering the genetics, it was hardly surprising; her parents were attractive people.

But she had never remotely thought of herself as beautiful, never mind sensuous.

Jake had called her beautiful, and had competently demonstrated to her how sensuous she could be.

While it was admittedly thrilling to be so complimented, it was also unnerving, which had made the initial part of the evening a little awkward for her.

Fortunately Jake had persevered, and he had finally managed to draw her out. In retrospect, now that the evening was almost over, it occurred to Elizabeth that he was as easy to talk to as De De.

"Hey, Liz, are you with me?" Jake's teasing nudge penetrated her reverie.

"Yes." She smiled. "Sorry if I seemed to be drifting. I was thinking about what a lovely evening it was."

"Yes, it has been." His blue velvet gaze caressed her face; she felt its impact like a soft physical stroke. "We've covered a lot of conversational territory."

"Yes." Her voice had a breathy sound. Realizing she was staring at his mouth as he raised the coffee cup to his lips, she quickly averted her eyes.

"And we've made a few discoveries," he went on, his own voice low, a little rough-edged.

"Yes," she repeated, silently acknowledging that some of the discoveries she was making about herself, her vulnerability to him, were a bit frightening.

"We have many similar interests," he reminded her, unnecessarily, since she herself had been startled to learn how very similar their interests and tastes were.

"We both love Irish coffee," Elizabeth declared, then took another sip of the frothy brew.

"Among other things." Jake agreed with her. "We have the same food preferences—light on the red meat, heavy on the sea food and vegetables—and we lean toward the basic colors." His pointed glance went from his chocolate brown sport jacket and true yellow shirt to her hunter green knit dress. "We even enjoy the same music . . . easy listening, some jazz, some classical. As for our dislikes, they're in accord too—skiing, excessive violence on TV and in movies"—he grimaced—"And in real life. But, most importantly," he concluded, "we both love mystery stories, written and filmed."

"We do." Elizabeth set down her empty cup. "And now it's over." A soft sighed escaped her.

"We could have another coffee," he suggested, inferring that he was as reluctant as she to see the evening end.

"I'd burst." She said regretfully.

He gave an answering nod. "Then I suppose we'd better leave." He motioned to the hovering waiter for the check, and added in a murmur, "Before they throw us out."

Elizabeth was forced to suppress another giggle.

The night had turned bitter cold, and the snow, which had sporadically come down in flurries throughout the day, had begun falling in earnest.

"This looks like it could mean business," Jake muttered, while keeping his attention riveted on the curving back road. "It's slick in spots."

Strangely, though Elizabeth didn't like driving in snow, even with someone else handling the car, including Richard, she didn't feel at all uneasy with Jake behind the wheel. She couldn't help wondering if this sense of security came from the four-wheel drive of his all-terrain Land Rover, or from Jake himself.

Suddenly aware that she was staring at his hands, at his long fingers confidently curled around the leather-covered steering wheel, Elizabeth strongly suspected it was the man, rather than the machine. Perhaps he was enjoying the feel of the smooth leather.

Elizabeth shivered, recalling his hands on her face, his fingers in her hair.

The quick and arousing response was disquieting.

She reluctantly admitted to herself that she liked Jake Ruttenburg, the man. Merely liking him would have been acceptable. But liking him, compounded by the exciting and sensual feelings he aroused in her, was in opposition to her sense of propriety.

She had been widowed less than a year. To be interested in, attracted emotionally and physically to, another man, any other man, went against every standard of behavior she had been taught and had previously adhered to.

She felt a betrayer . . . and yet, and yet . . . her gaze was drawn to his sharply defined profile. A warm strand of excitement uncurled inside her.

"Something?" Jake asked, slanting a quick, probing glance at her.

"Ummm . . . no. Why?" Elizabeth winced inwardly at the inanity of her reply.

"You were staring, Liz." Jake speared another glance at her. "Like what you see?"

"Are you fishing?"

"Are you evading the question?"

"Yes," Elizabeth confessed.

"For God's sake, why?" He laughed; the sound of it drew a smile from her.

"Maybe I'm evasive because I'm an uptight, buttoned-down, circumspect lady," she gently reminded him.

"Then again, maybe you're evasive because you're afraid of the consequences," he taunted.

Challenged, she unwisely tossed a taunt back at him. "What possible consequences could there be?"

"Oh, Lizzy, you already know the answer to that one," he softly chided. "You had just a taste of the consequences this morning, in the snow."

"Lizzy?" Inexperienced in the game of male-female banter, Elizabeth pounced on the name in the hope of distracting him. In vain.

"Don't change the subject." He sliced another quick, glittering look at her. "Did you, or did you not have a taste this morning?"

"Jake . . . really, I don't . . ." Elizabeth broke off, relief washing over her as the glare of the Land Rover's headlights swept over the turn into the Davidsons' driveway. "Oh, look, we've arrived."

"And not a moment too soon for your comfort," Jake muttered wryly. "Right?"

Elizabeth remained silent, choosing not to rise to his baited barb.

Except for the lantern-style porch light, and the dimmed light in the foyer, the house was dark.

"Everyone must be in bed," Elizabeth said as they mounted the steps onto the porch.

"I'd say that's a pretty safe assumption," he drawled, keys jingling as he dug in his pants pocket. "Maybe the circus exhausted them."

Unlocking the door, he swung it open. "Or the zoo animals."

"You're awful," Elizabeth whispered, scraping the snow from her shoes on the porch mat before stepping into the foyer, one hand clamped over her mouth to muffle a choking burst of laughter.

"Yeah, I know." Jake frowned. "De De has taken great pain since yesterday to point out how awful I am."

"I noticed," Elizabeth murmured, her laughter giving way to a frown.

Moving to the closet, she slipped out of her coat, hung it inside, then held out her hand for his topcoat, a beautifully tailored, dove gray cashmere.

He gave her a puzzled look as he handed the coat to her, then lifted his hand to brush the snow from his hair. "Have you any idea what's bugging her?"

Elizabeth sighed. "No . . . But I had wondered if, since her attitude seemed to change at some point after all of you had opened your gifts yesterday morning, perhaps you and De De had had some sort of disagreement."

He was shaking his head before she had finished. "Not a word. Nothing. Zilch. De De appeared happy, excited as a kid, but . . ." He narrowed his eyes, frowning in thought. "It strikes me that the change in her came right after she made a phone call to . . . somebody." His gaze pinned her. "I recall that you also made a call, to your daughters. Did you happen to hear who it was she talked to?"

"No. Sorry, but I can't help you." She moved her shoulders in a helpless shrug. "I left the room before she placed her call."

He nodded. "Well, whatever is troubling her, I figure it must be related to that conversation, and in some way directly related to me."

A sudden idea, a probability, sprang to mind, but Elizabeth hesitated to mention it. Apparently something gave her concern away, for Jake moved closer to her and peered into her face.

"What are you thinking?"

"Oh, it's nothing." She shook her head, unwilling to chance offending him and thereby ending their lovely evening on a sour note. She edged toward the stairs. "Really, it's nothing."

"Why do I have the sneaky suspicion that it's a very big something?" he said, reaching out to clasp her hand and keep her from bolting up the stairs. "Elizabeth, I want you to tell me what is on your mind."

She sighed. She was tired, and not up to a show of resistance. Besides, even if he didn't like what he heard, there just might be some benefit for De De in his knowing.

"I know that De De submitted a proposal to a house for consideration, and I was wondering if she dialed her answering machine for messages and received bad news," she finally replied.

"Maybe," he conceded, frowning. "But if that's the case, why take it out on me?"

That was the sticky part. She silently berated herself for voicing her opinion.

"Well . . ." Elizabeth vacillated.

"Spit it out." Jake pushed the issue.

"It's pure speculation," she insisted.

"Get on with it," he ordered.

She sighed again.

He scowled.

"All right," she snapped. "But please remember that you asked for it." She drew a breath, then plunged into an explanation. "Supposing she had called her machine, and received bad news in the form of a rejection . . . Perhaps De De might be resenting the position you've taken regarding helping her to get published."

For an instant, Jake's expression was unreadable.

Elizabeth held her breath, waiting for, fearing, his response. Would he be furious? Insulted?

"So, she's told you about that, has she?" The very mildness of his tone came as a shock.

"Yes . . . but only because I asked her," Elizabeth answered. "I thought it odd that she was unpublished, after I learned that you, the famous writer, were related to her."

"Uh-huh." He nodded, and a faint smile shadowed his lips. "You think I should use my influence"—his smile turned wry—"to get her published?"

"Well . . ." Elizabeth broke off and let a light shrug be her answer.

"Yeah." He exhaled. "I could do that. I have enough pull in the business to get her published—at least once." His gaze bored into her. "Matter of fact, I could do the same for you. De De tells me you have nearly four chapters completed. That's enough for a proposal." He arched his dark eyebrows. "Would you like me to send it to my editor with a recommendation that she buy it?"

"No!" Elizabeth's voice was as sharp as the quick movement of her head.

"Why not? She would probably make you an offer." His voice was as hard as the look in his eyes.

"Because then I'd never know whether it was my work she wanted or your—"

"Ex-act-ly," he said succinctly, cutting her off. "You would never know—and neither would De De. Why the hell would I want to rob her of the thrill of that first call from an editor who genuinely likes her work?"

Elizabeth's feathers were ruffled, so was her temper. "I knew that was your reasoning," she snapped. "I was merely suggesting that De De might not get it." Pulling her hand free, she turned and started up the stairs.

"Liz, wait." He followed her.

She kept going, to the top, across the landing, and then up the third-floor staircase.

Jake was right behind her. He caught her

arm, halting her once more when she reached for the knob on the door to her room.

She stiffened at his touch.

He sighed. "You're mad at me."

"No. I'm not. I'm tired, and I want to go to bed."

"So do I." His low voice reflected the blue velvet quality of his eyes. "The damn thing is, Liz," he murmured, moving closer to her. "I want to go to bed with you."

Elizabeth's lips parted on a shocked gasp at his bluntness.

Jake seized the moment—and her mouth.

With an unnerving immediacy, she was caught up in the sensuous web he had spun around her that morning. His arms encircled her, drawing her trembling body to the hard reality of his chest, his thighs, his . . .

Feeling the stabbing, raking sweep of his tongue in her mouth, the rigid, probing proof of his desire for her, Elizabeth's pulse danced to the drumming rhythm of her heartbeat, to his need for her, her need for him.

Surrendering to erotic sensations, she raised her hands to his head, holding him to her with the fingers that speared through his hair.

He was devouring her with his mouth.

She couldn't breathe.

Sexual tension, like a live wire, sang along the connecting paths of her nervous system, bringing her to vibrant, glorious awareness.

It was exciting, thrilling—and terrifying.

Grasping his hair, she pulled his head back,

tearing his mouth from hers. Drawing in a breath, she stared into the blue depths of his seductive eyes.

"Liz." Jake's voice was a ragged plea.

"No." It was a whispered cry. "I can't. Jake . . . please. Try to understand. It's too soon. Too soon." She closed her eyes, shielding herself from the allure of his, of him. "I . . . I can't."

"I know." Expelling a harsh breath, he released her and stepped back. His stark, tight expression revealed his inner struggle for control. "I know."

"I'm sorry." Her voice was barely audible, almost lost to her own inner struggle.

From somewhere, he found a trace of a smile and a hint of humor. "Not nearly as sorry as I am." He took another step back. "Good night, Elizabeth Leninger. Sleep well." His lips quirked again. "At least one of us should."

Sixteen

It snowed through the night.

Elizabeth knew it; she had been awake, watching the steady fall. The encounter with Jake had left her too keyed up to sleep. Every atom and molecule of her body ached, punishing her for denying herself, and him, the mutual release and ultimate satisfaction of the physical desire they felt for one another.

But Elizabeth had taken that route before, had given in to the pleas of another, younger man and had reaped the benefit not of satisfaction but shame.

Telling herself there was no comparison between then and now didn't appease her body or her mind. For most of the night, while staring out the window, she was looking inside, at the memories swirling around in her mind, memories more forceful than the strong wind sweeping the snow before it.

In those memories, she was young again, a lonely University of Pennsylvania freshman, away from home for the first time. And that lonely young girl had gratefully accepted an invitation to accompany a new acquaintance to a private party at the home of a senior, one of the most popular men on campus.

Upon arrival at the impressive colonial-style house, Elizabeth had felt out of place, and she had become even more uneasy on learning that the parents of the young man were away for the weekend.

Nevertheless, at the urging of her new acquaintance, Elizabeth had remained at the party instead of heeding her common sense that urged her to abandon the scene.

As the evening progressed, and the party grew more wild, Elizabeth didn't join in but remained on the fringes, both alarmed and shocked by the crudeness and the wanton behavior of the young men and women.

While hanging back, trying to blend into the wallpaper, she had noticed a good-looking, serious-seeming young man also hanging back and frowning as he observed the high jinks of his friends and contemporaries. During one his contemptuous perusals of the room, he noticed Elizabeth and subsequently made his way to her.

"Are you as disgusted with this stupidity as I am?" he asked, his voice raised to pierce the din.

Rather than shout, Elizabeth nodded agreement.

"I'm cutting out of here," he practically bellowed. "You want a ride?"

She hesitated a moment, wondering if she would be jumping from the frying pan into the fire. But he looked decent and nice, and she had had enough. She answered with another nod.

Once they were outside, away from the racket, Elizabeth quickly learned that his name was Richard Leninger and he was a senior at the Wharton School of Business. He was quiet, kind of shy, but comfortable to be with. He drove her directly home, never suggesting anything else. But he did ask to see her again. Flattered, she had agreed.

Within a month, Elizabeth was head over heels in infatuation with Richard. The throes of first love. The outcome of the association was almost inevitable.

She surrendered her virginity to him on the back seat of his ten-year-old Chevrolet. She did not find the act either pleasurable or satisfying.

Two weeks later, she did not have her period. After missing the second period, and suffering bouts of morning sickness, she knew she had to tell her parents.

The outcome of her confession was predictable.

Elizabeth's father summoned Richard to the house, to inform him he was going to become a father—and a bridegroom. On being told of the situation, Richard's parents likewise insisted on marriage; to both sets of parents, appearances mattered.

Appearances had always mattered to Elizabeth, as well.

And a strong sense of right and wrong had been instilled in her from day one.

So, despite the physical and emotional attraction she felt for Jake, her conscience insisted it would be wrong to succumb to him, especially while she was a guest in his sister's home.

The inner conflict kept sleep at bay until sheer exhaustion caught up with her in the wee hours of the snowy morning.

Elizabeth jerked awake with a start, and a headache, a little after seven-thirty, less than four hours after she'd finally fallen into a shallow, dream-troubled sleep.

Overall she felt lethargic, with scratchy eyes and dulled mental processes. The condition was familiar, if infrequent, the price paid for the occasional meander down memory lane. She had become accustomed to these side effects since Richard's death, for she, like many another in a similar circumstance, revisited her past, their past.

It had been months since Elizabeth's last debilitating memory jaunt. She had almost forgotten how devastating one could be, leaving her feeling drained physically and psychologically.

And what purpose had it served, that inner conflict?

Staring at the weak morning light playing over the white surface of the ceiling, Elizabeth acknowledged that this one served to keep her

from making a fool of herself over Jake Ruttenburg.

It certainly hadn't succeeded in quenching
the fire of desire burning in her; the blaze
roared unabated. But it had instilled a caution-
ary sense of self-protection.

Elizabeth admitted to herself that she wanted
Jake, wanted to know him in the most intimate
of ways.

But there were considerations other than
self, and self-indulgence. The most important
of those were in Colorado with their grandmother. Her daughters' happiness, their expectations and sense of stability, held sway over her
decisions and her actions.

Even as she accepted the sentence of self-
denial, Elizabeth knew she was laying a guilt
trip on herself; but then, it would appear that
most mothers, at least most of the mothers
she knew, had a tendency to take on guilt without questioning.

Was the acceptance of guilt, earned and un-
earned, a malady of the majority of females,
she ruminated muzzily, inserted inside of them
along with the necessary reproductive organs?

Oh, the agony of self-recrimination, Elizabeth mockingly protested.

Woe, woe. Oh, woe is me.

Grimacing, sick of her fruitless thoughts, and
even more sick of herself, she pushed back the
covers and dragged her reluctant body from
the bed.

Deciding it would be to her advantage to

avoid Jake as much as possible, she decided a shopping excursion with De De was in order, if the girl was willing. Elizabeth stretched her tight muscles by walking to the window to check current weather conditions.

The sight that met her gaze through the frost-rimmed pane was less than encouraging.

It was still snowing, and obviously had been throughout the night, as evidenced by the apparent depth of the snow on the ground. The churned-up results of her snowball battle with Jake were gone.

Had it been only yesterday morning that they had laughingly romped, then passionately kissed there in the snow?

Enough thoughts of passion and kisses, Elizabeth silently chastised, swallowing a sigh of regret. She had a life to live, children to nurture, and, hopefully, a career in writing to actively pursue.

Who needed a man around, cluttering up her life, her emotions, her mental stability?

Dumb question.

She swallowed hard, hurting her throat.

Despairing her lack of moral fiber and integrity, she turned from the window, shrugged into her robe, and headed for the door, praying she would not run into Jake in the hallway.

Her prayer was answered; the hallway and the bathroom were blessedly empty.

The house was quiet, as houses are when cloaked by a sound-muffling blanket of snow.

Unfortunately, after taking her morning

shower and brushing her teeth, Elizabeth stepped out of the bathroom, and into the path of Jake.

"Good morning." His fantastic blue eyes were shadowed, his voice low and rough.

"Good morning." She returned the greeting, her voice every bit as low and rough as his.

"Sleep well?" His hooded gaze probed her eyes.

"Not very," she admitted, aware of the dark puffiness beneath her eyes.

"But you did manage to get some sleep?" he persisted.

She sighed, noisily. "Yes, some."

He smiled, grimly. "Then you're better off than I am. I didn't sleep at all."

"I'm sorry." She lowered her eyes.

"That makes two of us."

He took a step toward her.

She took a step back.

"Liz, this is nuts." His chest expanded and contracted on a deep, harsh breath. "We've got to talk about this."

"This what?" she demanded, suddenly angry and impatient, with him, with herself, with the untenable situation. "I told you last night, Jake. I can't give you what you want."

"You don't have a clue as to what I want," he retorted. "How could you, when I'm not even certain what it is . . . other than sex." He paused for a breath, then raked a hand through his recently brushed hair. "And hell, I can get that anywhere."

Quashing an impulse to reach out, smooth those disheveled dark strands, Elizabeth took refuge in offense. "Then I advise you to do so, because you're not getting it from me." Her tone had a bite, and was colder than the wind driving the snow outside.

Jake winced, but forged on. "Elizabeth, you know as well as I that the attraction between us is more than physical. We can't ignore it or wish it away. We need to explore the . . ." He broke off, frowning when she moved. "Damnit, Liz, where the hell are you going?"

"I'm not adventuresome, not keen on explorations," she flung over her shoulder, continuing on to the bedroom door. "And what I *need* is a cup of coffee."

He caught her arm, turning her to face him.

She jerked free, glaring at him. "If you don't mind, I want to get dressed."

"Okay, okay." His voice was tinged with regret. "But don't reject the possibilities . . . or me . . ." His voice dropped on the last words, and he loosened his grip, trailing his hand caressingly down her arm before releasing her.

Elizabeth steeled herself against the shiver activated by her skin's reaction to his fingers on the soft wool sleeve of her robe. "Jake, I—"

"No," he interrupted, shaking his head. "Don't say it—not anything now." He offered her a wry smile. "Maybe you'll be more inclined toward adventure and exploration after you've had one, or several, reviving cups of coffee."

She frowned. Couldn't he take no for an answer? Evidently not, she concluded, noting his expectant expression.

"I doubt it," she said, softening her tone, in the hope of softening the blow. Still, he persevered.

"Look, Liz, all I'm asking for is some communication." He looked baffled. "Hell, how can talking to me do any harm? A private conversation. Is that too much to ask?"

Too tired to argue any longer, Elizabeth gave in. "All right, Jake, we'll talk"—she even managed a wisp of a smile—"*after* I've had my coffee."

"Deal." He flashed her a quick grin as he turned toward the stairway. "I'll have a fresh pot ready and waiting by the time you're dressed."

Jake was true to his promise.

The distinct aroma of freshly brewed coffee wafted to Elizabeth as she descended the stairs to the first floor. Following the scent, she hurried along the hallway to the kitchen. Jake was pouring her a cup as she entered.

"Are we the first ones up?"

"Appears so." He shrugged. "Would you like something solid to go with this?" he asked, setting two steaming cups on the table. "Eggs, cereal, Danish, a warm muffin?"

"Muffin," she murmured, crossing to the breadkeeper. "I'll warm it. Want one?"

"Yes, please." He moved to the fridge, stepping sideways when their paths intersected. "You want some juice?"

"Ummm." She nodded and set two cranberry muffins onto the glass microwave tray.

They held an in-depth discussion of the weather while they ate their muffins. Jake put an end to the banality after pouring them second cups of coffee.

"I hear movement upstairs, so we can't talk now, or in here." He paused, as if pondering, then went on, "We could go into the den while the rest of the family have breakfast." He quirked one eyebrow. "Okay?"

Elizabeth heard footsteps on the stairs and several muted voices. Feeling cornered and pressured and nervous, she responded with a quick, sharp nod.

"Well, good morning," Maryanne said as she swept into the room. "Any coffee left?"

"Sure. I'll get it for you," Jake offered, crossing to where the coffeemaker sat on the countertop next to the sink.

"Make that two," George said, trailing in Maryanne's wake into the kitchen.

"You got it." Jake tossed a look at his sister. "Mother not up yet?"

"Not yet." She grinned at him. "She's awake, but informed me she's trying her best to go back to sleep."

"Is she feeling all right?" he asked, concern scoring his expression.

"Yes, yes. Relax. Mother's fine, a little achy,

but fine," she hastened to assure him. "She claims the weather is playing hell with her arthritis. *I* think she probably was a little too active yesterday."

Jake didn't look convinced. "Maybe I'll just go up and see if there's anything she needs."

"Jake, really," Maryanne protested in exasperation. "All mother needs is some rest. Sit down and have another cup of coffee."

"You're going to have to make another pot first," George said, settling into a chair. "I just emptied it."

"While I'm at it," Jake said sarcastically, "Would you like me to heat you a muffin, cook some eggs?"

"Would you?" George laughed.

"No." Jake's refusal was instantaneous.

"I will," Elizabeth pushed her chair back. "Which will it be? Muffins or eggs? '

"Both." George shrugged. "Snowy mornings always make me hungry."

"Mornings make you hungry," Maryanne taunted, "regardless of the weather."

Enjoying their banter, Elizabeth went to the fridge to collect the eggs. "What about you, Maryanne?"

"Oh, I may as well have the same," she replied. "I always enjoy my food more when somebody else does the cooking."

"Make that for three, Elizabeth," De De instructed, ambling into the room. "Better count yourself in too, we'll likely need the fortification."

"Fortification?" Elizabeth straightened to stare at De De over top of the open fridge door. "For what?"

"The long drive ahead of us."

"Drive?" Jake rapped out, turning from the sink where he was rinsing the glass coffee carafe. "Drive to where?"

"Home." De De looked toward the window. "I just heard the weather report on the radio in my room. Seems this snow we're having is only the front-runner of a massive Canadian clipper moving Southeast. The National Weather Service is predicting a major snowstorm for the entire Northeast." She looked apologetically to Elizabeth. "If you don't mind, I'd like to leave for home as soon after breakfast as possible."

"Oh, honey, you just got here!" Maryanne was obviously disappointed.

"I know, and I was looking forward to a long visit." De De sighed her regret. "But, with a weather forecast of a big storm, I really think I should leave while the roads are still passable. I can't afford to be snowed in up here past the New Year. You can't either, can you Elizabeth?"

"No, and of course I don't mind heading back," Elizabeth said at once. From the corner of her eye, she saw the annoyance that fleetingly tightened Jake's features. Then quickly, his expression eased, and he turned to finish making coffee. "I'll scramble enough eggs for all of us, that is . . ." She glanced over her shoulder at Jake. "Do you want eggs?"

"Might as well."

Had she detected a hint of resignation in his voice? Elizabeth wondered, shutting the fridge door with a sideways bump of her hip. Or was it her imagination? But she wasn't given time for speculation, for at that moment the last member of the group walked stiffly into the room.

"Make it unanimous, Elizabeth," Margaret said, smiling at her granddaughter when De De rushed to her side to assist her into a chair. "May as well make this a breakfast going-away party."

"Right!" Maryanne cried, jumping up and crossing to the fridge. "That's a wonderful idea, Mother. Now, how many for sausage or bacon?"

"Don't forget the fruit salad left over from lunch yesterday," George said. "I'll set the table."

Laughing, De De headed for the bread-keeper. "I'll make toast and warm the muffins."

Gripping the edge of the table, Margaret started to get up. "And I'll—"

"Stay where you are." Jake cut her off with the gently voiced command. "We'll take care of breakfast."

Margaret grimaced, but subsided, grumbling, "You'd think I was completely disabled or something."

"No, just loved, Mother," Jake soothed, giving her a smile so soft and caring it caused a pang in Elizabeth's heart. "So, relax, and let us baby you."

Pleased color brushed Margaret's cheeks, and she perked up considerably. "Well, I can still help sitting here. De De, bring the toast over here, I'll butter."

With all of them working in concert, they turned the everyday breakfast into a festive occasion.

But too soon it was over, the remains of the meal cleared away, the kitchen restored to order. With evident reluctance, Elizabeth and De De went to their rooms to pack.

Less than fifteen minutes were required for Elizabeth to ready her things. After closing her cases and setting them next to the door, she stood and stared in consternation at the bed she had made earlier, debating whether or not to pull off the sheets and remake it with fresh bedding.

"Ready?"

Elizabeth started and spun around to the doorway at the sudden and unexpected sound of Jake's voice.

"Oh . . . ah, yes," she said, filling her memory and her senses with the sight of him. "I was wondering if I should change the bedding before I go. What do you think?"

"I think you worry too much about unimportant things." He walked to her. "Leave it."

"But that will make more work for Maryanne," she said. "And I hardly consider that unimportant."

He raised his eyes, as if beseeching help from above. "I came up here to lug your bags down," he went on, in a tone of controlled patience. "You're leaving. We didn't get a chance to have our talk, and you're angsting about the bedding." He shook his head. "Your thoughtfulness is commendable, Liz, but at times it's also a pain."

"I'm sorry if the way I am—my concern for doing what I believe is the right thing—bothers you." Her shaky voice was in conflict with her cool tone.

Hurt way out of proportion to his mild rebuke, she drew that protective barrier of composure around herself and started to go around him.

Jake moved faster, sidestepping to bar her way. "No, *I'm* sorry." His smile was rueful. "I'm disappointed that you're leaving. Mother would say I'm behaving like a spanked ass."

Elizabeth didn't want to laugh, didn't feel like laughing, and yet she had no choice, simply because it sounded exactly like something Margaret would say.

"You have the most enchanting laugh."

The look that flashed over Jake's face was one of such intense longing, it stifled the laughter in her throat, replacing it with an achy tightness.

"Jake . . ." she began, only to break off with a gasped "Oh" when he raised his hands to cradle her face.

"May I call you . . . after you get home?" he

asked in a near whisper, as he slowly lowered his face to hers. "I still want that talk with you."

"Yes. Yes," she breathed the words, shaken to her core by the effect of his nearness on her. "I . . . I'll write my number down for you before—"

"Liz . . . shut up," he murmured, then proceeded to cover her mouth with his.

The effect of his bold action was immediate and fiery. Heat sizzled through Elizabeth, searing her senses, cauterizing her resistance. And, at that moment the willing captive of his searing mouth, she didn't care if she burned to a crisp.

"I'm finished and ready to go, Elizabeth," De De called from the foot of the stairs, her voice dousing the inferno melding Elizabeth to Jake.

She tried to tear her mouth from his, but he held her head firm, drawing the kiss out to a shattering conclusion before releasing her.

"I'll call you in a day or so," he murmured, then raised his voice to call out, "Elizabeth's checking to make sure she hasn't forgotten anything, De De. I'll be bringing her bags down in a couple of minutes."

Elizabeth used those precious minutes to gather her scattered thoughts and emotions; then, both grateful and regretful that he allowed her to do so, she preceded him down the two flights of stairs.

Jake stood back, watchful but silent, as Elizabeth and De De exchanged hugs with the oth-

ers. At the last, when they were about to get
into the car after he and George stowed their
bags, he pulled De De into his arms with a muttered, "Take care, brat." Gazing at Elizabeth
over the top of De De's head, he softly added,
"You, too, Liz." Then he mouthed a promised,
"I'll call."

Getting into the car, closing the door, smiling
as she returned his wave, were about the most
difficult things Elizabeth had ever had to do.

Distracted, Elizabeth by the feelings churning inside her, De De by the need to concentrate on her driving, neither woman noticed
the car that suddenly seemed to appear from
nowhere to follow at a discreet distance behind
them.

Seventeen

Incredible!

Driving sedately as befitted the increasingly bad road conditions, one car removed from the vehicle driven by Jake Ruttenburg's niece, Cassie Metcalf laughed aloud in astonishment at her amazing stroke of luck.

On awakening earlier that morning to find the snow still falling, and piling up on the ground, Cassie had briefly considered her position, then quickly had decided to decamp to warmer climes, like Palm Springs or Mexico, and leave her vendetta against Jake for another day. Hell, there was no hurry, she had figured. Besides, anticipation would make her revenge all the sweeter.

After trudging to the motel coffee shop for breakfast and back again—God, she hated staying in motels without room service—she had set about packing the two large suitcases and the small jewelry/makeup case she'd been living out of since right after Thanksgiving.

Of course, there had been no bellhops—another inconvenience Cassie hated—which meant she'd had to wheel the heavy bags to the car and load them herself.

Having worked up a thirst, she'd needed another cup of coffee, which had made her late getting started.

It was pure impulse that had directed Cassie to cruise past the home of Jake's sister one last time, and unbelievably sheer luck that she had caught sight of the group—Jake, his new woman, his niece, and another man—stowing luggage into the back of a compact car, just as she was inching past the driveway to the house.

Mulling over the probabilities of the scene she had witnessed, Cassie stopped, and then backed into a neighboring driveway a little farther down the road.

A short time later, surprise and excitement flared to life inside her, as the compact containing Jake's niece and the other woman slowly passed by.

Giving an incredulous hoot, and advising herself to follow her nose, Cassie scuttled her plan to seek warmer weather in favor of trailing the two women.

Feeling certain the Fates were smiling on her, she turned on the radio, full blast, and settled in for the duration of the drive to wherever Jake's niece might be heading.

Cassie didn't care what that destination might be; she had all the time in the world, and if not all the money, a comfortable chunk of it.

Humming along with the pop tune on the

radio, she carefully tooled her car through the snow in single-minded pursuit of her quarry.

"I guess I'd better get my ass in gear, too."

"You're leaving?" Maryanne exclaimed. "But why? I mean, you have four-wheel drive and all."

"I also live on a mountain," Jake reminded her. "In case you've forgotten."

"But you don't even know if it's snowing in Pennsylvania," she argued.

"It's snowing," George said, strolling into the kitchen from the living room. "I was watching the Weather Channel. It's snowing all along the Eastern Seaboard."

Jake frowned and glanced at Margaret. "You want me to run you home, Mother?"

"Why?" she asked wryly. "So you can get snowed in there instead of here?"

Thinking he'd be a lot closer to Elizabeth in Lancaster than in Connecticut, and liking the idea, Jake persisted. "But, if you don't leave with me, and this storm proves to be as bad as the weather service predicted, who knows when you'll be able to get a flight home or how long you'd be snowed in here."

"So?" Maryanne demanded indignantly. "Why should she go home to be snowed in alone, when here we can be snowed in together?"

"Uh-huh." Jake glanced at his brother-in-law,

in an eloquent if silent comment on the logic of the females of the species.

George grinned and shrugged.

"You're outnumbered," Margaret said, her eyes gleaming with inner laughter. "If you're going, you'd better get a move on, while the getting's good."

"Right." Shaking his head, Jake turned and walked out of the kitchen.

He pulled out of his sister's driveway a half hour or so later, less than two hours after De De's departure, his mother's familiar parting command ringing in his ears and bringing a smile to his lips.

"Drive carefully and call when you're home safe."

Driving was a nightmare.

Sitting tense and quiet, Elizabeth stared in mesmerized fear at the fury raging beyond the windshield.

She and De De hadn't been on the road long enough to be a quarter of the way home when the storm had escalated into a terrifying example of the power of nature unleashed.

Fortunately, though De De's car was small and compact, it had come equipped with front-wheel drive, otherwise, they very likely would have found themselves stuck and helpless along the side of the highway, in the same straits as many other cars they had crawled past.

"Lord, this is definitely not my idea of a fun

holiday," De De muttered, intently peering at the car creeping along in front of her.

"You must be exhausted," Elizabeth commiserated.

"And hungry." De De gave a strained laugh. "Why didn't we bring along some of the goodies from Mother's? They had enough to feed a small, starving country."

"We could get off the interstate at the next exit," Elizabeth suggested, "then search out a motel with a restaurant."

"And get stuck there for who knows how long?" De De gave a quick shake of her head. "No motel, but . . . there," she said, removing one hand from the steering wheel an instant to indicate a sign at the side of the road some yards before them. "Thank the gods for the snow-capped golden arches." She heaved a sigh. "Can you see well enough through this blinding mess to read how many miles it is to the exit?"

"Not through the window," Elizabeth answered, reaching for the button to lower the pane. "Brace yourself for a blast of the frosty stuff."

"Braced." De De chuckled. "Lower away."

Smiling despite the tension rippling through her, Elizabeth activated the electronically controlled window, and gasped as the wind-driven snow smacked her in the face. Narrowing her eyes, she peered at the familiar sign.

"Next exit," she read aloud. "A mile and a

half." She paused a beat, then went on, "There's also a motel."

"Good to know," De De muttered. "Just in case."

"Just in case." Elizabeth was almost afraid to ask. "Of . . . what?"

"Of not being able to get back onto the interstate." Her friend snorted. "Hell, of not being able to *see* the interstate by the time we've finished eating."

"What a cheerful thought," Elizabeth commented with all the aplomb she could muster.

De De grimaced. "Yeah, well, that's . . ." Her voice faded away; then she said, "Hello, there's an unexpected bonus. The car in front of us is also heading for the exit. It'll be a lot easier following its tracks."

"You could follow them right into a ditch," Elizabeth pointed out, with a dry wit she had forced. "Or a bank of drifted snow."

De De shot a grin at her. "Gee, you're a fount of optimism, aren't you?"

"You want optimism, rent *Mary Poppins,*" Elizabeth retorted, grinning back at her. "Me, here and now, I'd settle for a cranky kid serving me a hot cup of coffee."

"Well, friend, lookie there," De De motioned forward with a nod of her head, indicating the fuzzy lights beaming through the swirling snow. "Hot coffee coming up."

"You know," Elizabeth mused aloud, sighing in relief as De De brought the car to a stop in the parking lot. "I have never been crazy about fast food of any kind. But now I can hardly wait to sink my teeth into a quarter-pounder with cheese—cholesterol and calories be damned."

"Way to go, Elizabeth!" De De repeated her praise of a few days ago.

Could Christmas Eve have been only a few days ago? Elizabeth marveled, trudging through the deepening snow after De De to the beckoning restaurant. And could it have been only last night that she had come to the very edge of succumbing to the desire induced by Jake's heated kisses?

The shudder that tore through her was unrelated to the frigid temperature, the icy sting of the windblown snow.

Even so, the warmth that enveloped Elizabeth when she stepped into the restaurant behind De De seemed heavenly. As the aromas of burgers and fries struck her, they drove thoughts of seduction from her mind.

It was at once evident that Elizabeth and De De were not the only travelers who had sought shelter and sustenance. The restaurant was doing a brisk business, thanks to the weather-weary, dull-eyed, and disgruntled drivers within.

The only reason Elizabeth noticed the woman who had entered after De De and herself was, when turning away from the counter, she nearly slammed her food-laden tray into her.

"Oh! I beg your pardon," Elizabeth said, quickly shifting the tray to one side and missing the woman's midsection by a hair.

"No harm done." The woman flashed a smile, revealing teeth almost too white and perfect to be real.

Returning the smile, Elizabeth skirted around her and wove a path to the table De De had claimed by the wide window at one side of the spacious room.

"Do you know that woman?" De De asked, glancing up from the tray she was unloading.

"No." Elizabeth shook her head as she slid into the molded plastic seat. "I spoke to her to apologize." She grimaced. "I came close to knocking her over with my tray."

"Sleek . . ." De De mumbled around the French fry she was nibbling. "Did you notice?"

"Umm." Elizabeth nodded, finished chewing a bite of burger, then swallowed. "All blond and golden tan."

"Yeah. She looks like she made a major wrong turn somewhere, wound up here in snow country instead of Florida or California."

Elizabeth nearly choked on the sip of coffee she had in her mouth, but she couldn't help it, she had to laugh; De De's assessment was so on target.

"Yes, she does," Elizabeth agreed, glancing through the window.

The sight of wind-whipped snow outside chased all thoughts of the tanned woman from her mind. Munching her burger, and wondering why she had never before noticed how good they tasted, she shivered at the mere idea of going back outside and onto the highway in that storm.

Through the heavy curtain of white, she could discern a red neon motel sign across the way from the restaurant. A sudden longing for a hot shower swept through Elizabeth, and she debated again raising the subject with De De of taking a room for the night.

"I'm ready whenever you are." De De's voice intruded into her thoughts, ending her inner debate.

Suppressing a sigh, Elizabeth nodded and finished the last of her coffee. But her trepidation must have been visible.

"Cheer up, Elizabeth, I can handle it," De De assured her, with commendable confidence under the circumstances. "Don't forget, we're over three-quarters of the way home."

Home. Trudging through the snow in De De's wake as they plodded back to the car, Elizabeth repeated the word. It filled her with yearning.

The confounding thing was, each time the word home came to mind, a vision rose alongside it. A vision both attractive and disturbing.

It was Jake—in living color.

This vision teased her mind and senses all the way home.

To Elizabeth's astonishment, they made it back without once sliding off the road or into another vehicle.

* * *

"So that's where Jake's new paramour lives," Cassie murmured, peering through the windshield and the whiteness beyond. "Not bad . . . if one's into colonial."

Cassie was not; she wasn't into the parking space too well along the curb at the end of the block, either. She didn't care; she wasn't planning on taking up residence, only on checking out the address of the big house once the two women were done carting stuff into it.

When the door to the place closed and light began to blaze from the windows, Cassie fired the engine, switched on the headlights, then slowly drove back onto the street and along it until the car was parallel to a snow-capped mailbox attached to a post at the curb.

" 'Elizabeth Leninger,' " she read aloud, noting and memorizing the address printed below the name.

"Prissy name. E-liz-a-beth," Cassie enunciated, setting the car into motion again. "Like the queen . . . staid, responsible, and oh, so proper." Her mouth twisted with disdain. "Probably wouldn't dream of getting undressed in front of her lover, never mind having sex with the light on."

The evaluation of Elizabeth Leninger brought a gleefully nasty smile to Cassie's lips.

"Poor Jake. I suppose I must, in good conscience, rescue the man." Laughing aloud, she maneuvered the car back into the tracks previous vehicles had made in the snow. "But first, I need a place to stay."

Fortune continued to smile on Cassie.

Some four or so miles after winding her way through the subdivision and onto the state highway, she spotted a sign indicating an exit ramp leading to an interstate. Directly behind that sign was another one, advertising food, fuel, and—glory be!—a motel.

Cassie headed for it like a homing pigeon.

The place was packed with other travelers. All of them had sought refuge from the storm.

Still, Lady Luck was with Cassie.

The harried-looking desk clerk appeared both grateful and relieved when she requested a suite—Cassie was not into self-denial.

Confiding that every room was taken, but there were still two suites available, the desk clerk slid a registration card across the desk and, with a flourish, offered her a pen.

Cassie had just one question for him; it had nothing whatever to do with the price of the suite.

"Is there an on-site restaurant?"

He looked offended. "Of course!"

Cassie filled out the card. Then, with a flourish, she offered *him* her gold credit card.

Due to the intensifying storm and the steadily worsening road conditions, Jake didn't reach his mountain retreat until well after midnight, and approximately half an hour after the storm abated. The primarily wood and glass, three-level structure nestled snugly on the side of a mountain had never looked so good to him.

The first thing he did on entering the house was turn up the thermostat, which he had set lower before leaving two days before Christmas.

The place was as cold as a tomb.

Damnit, if he had to be snowed in and cold, why couldn't it have been with Elizabeth?

The thought brought a smile to his lips. If he were snowed in with her, he wouldn't mind the cold. He'd generate his own heat.

At the reassuring sound of the heater humming along, he shrugged out of his jacket and tossed it onto a chair as he went to the phone on the end table next to the couch. Dropping onto a thick cushion, he grasped the receiver, then hesitated for a moment, a finger hovering over the buttons as he weighed the advisability of punching in the number Elizabeth had written down for him—and which he had committed to memory.

Jake felt compelled to call, hear her voice, know she had made it home safely. But it was very late, and she might be asleep, whereas he knew his mother would be awake, waiting to hear from him.

After long moments of indecision, he placed a call to his mother. The receiver was picked up on the first ring.

"Jake?" Margaret's voice betrayed her anxiety.

"Yes, Mother," he answered soothingly. "I'm

home, and I'm in one piece—but driving was a bitch."

"I know," she said, for once not chastising him for his language. "De De called when they got back a couple of hours ago. She said basically the same thing."

The relief that washed over Jake was startling in its intensity.

Elizabeth was home . . . and she was safe.

Thank God.

Suddenly, weariness claimed him. Telling his mother he'd call her again in a couple of days, he hung up, turned off the lights, and went to bed.

He was dead to the world within seconds of crawling between the cold sheets.

Eighteen

The holidays were over.

All the Christmas presents had been put away in various closets and drawers. The decorations had been boxed and stored. Ella and Sally were back in school.

Once again, Elizabeth was alone in the house.

After enjoying the company of De De, who had given in to Elizabeth's coaxing to stay at the house until the storm was over and the roads were passable, and Ella and Sally's return from Colorado, Elizabeth had dreaded facing an empty house again, a dull and bare one, stripped of the bright holiday ornaments, the candles, and the shimmering tree.

But, to her amazement, instead of feeling abandoned and lonely, left deserted and wandering in a desolate-looking house, she found herself savoring the solitude.

Of course, Jake's telephone calls accounted in large part for Elizabeth's frame of mind.

His initial call had come early in the morning of the day after she and De De had completed that awful drive home from Connecticut.

Elizabeth had been in the kitchen, having her first cup of coffee. De De still slept.

"Oh, Jake, I'm glad you made it home safely," she had immediately exclaimed upon hearing his voice, unwittingly revealing her anxiety about him. "Your mother told De De you left soon after we did."

"And she assured me you and De De were home safe," he'd responded, his own relief evident.

"Well, at least it has finally stopped snowing," she'd observed, glancing out the kitchen window.

"Yeah. It stopped before I got home." He'd chuckled. "The house was as cold as a witches'—"

"So was mine," Elizabeth had broken in, cutting him off. "But it's nice and warm now." She'd winced at the sheer banality of the remark.

"Mine, too."

There had ensued a moment of silence, while she had groped for something else to say, something of value and import—like how much she was already missing him.

But she had been unable to say that, too out of practice in confiding her feelings to a man other than her husband; besides, she hadn't even communicated her feelings to Richard for some time before his death.

Better to wait for Jake to speak of feelings, she had decided, silently wondering if he might be groping, as well.

Then, as if neither could maintain the silence, they had spoken simultaneously.

"Did you have any trouble getting home?"

"Did I wake you?"

They had both laughed, considerably easing the long-distance tension.

Jake had answered first. "No, I had no trouble, other than avoiding the drivers who were having difficulty staying on the road . . . or what could be seen of it."

"I know what you mean," Elizabeth had said before replying to his query. "And, no, you didn't wake me. I've been up for all of fifteen or so minutes. De De's still asleep, though."

"She's there?"

"Yes. She wanted to forge on home, but she was so tired I insisted she at least wait until today."

"Good for you. And thanks."

"For what?" She'd frowned.

Jake's chuckle had let her know he heard the confusion in her voice. "For caring about, and looking out for, my niece. She tends to be a little strong willed, in case you haven't noticed."

Elizabeth had laughed. "I noticed."

"When will your daughters get home?"

"The day after New Year's."

"Then it's back to school?"

"Yes. Actually, Sally is going to miss a day; her classes resume on the second. And, even though Ella is on break until the end of January, I'll be driving her back to Easton on the third."

"How come?"

"She took a job to earn extra spending money, tutoring a ninth grader who's having difficulty with algebra."

"Oh." He'd paused, as if again searching for something to say, then asked, "Ella's good with algebra?"

"Yes, straight *A,*" she'd answered, even though she had felt certain he couldn't seriously be interested.

"Great." He'd laughed. "I was always lousy at it."

"So was I!" Her laughter had echoed his.

Again there had been a long moment of silence.

Tension had crawled through Elizabeth once more, tightening her grip on the receiver. Then she'd heard the unmistakable sounds of movement upstairs.

"I think I hear De De now," she'd said. "Would you like to talk to her?"

"Yes, but,"—he'd sighed—"from her attitude the last few days, I doubt she wants to talk to me."

"I could ask her."

"No, don't bother. It's enough that I know you're both safe and sound." He had cleared his throat. "I'm gonna hang up now. I'll call you again . . . after the second."

The line had gone dead. Elizabeth had gone blank, the dial tone buzzing in her ear.

De De had stayed at the house three days; they were the most work-intensive days Elizabeth had ever lived through.

She had loved every minute of them. She had completed an entire chapter of her story, while De De was close to finishing the manuscript she had been laboring over for months.

But, although they had worked hard, Elizabeth in the second-floor office, De De on her notebook computer at the kitchen table, they had also laughed a lot together when they weren't working.

They were lingering over dinner on the evening before De De's planned departure for home, when Elizabeth finally brought herself to the point of delving into matters that were, she admitted, none of her business.

"Ah . . . De De, I was wondering if I might ask you a personal question," she had hesitantly said, already sorry she'd decided to broach the subject.

"How personal?" her friend had responded, grinning.

"It's about your uncle, Jake."

De De's grin had immediately vanished, to be replaced by a rueful expression. "I behaved badly toward him, I know. Mother raked me over the coals about it before we left."

"But why? I don't mean to pry, but . . ."— Elizabeth had shaken her head in utter bafflement—"I couldn't imagine what he had done to make you so hostile to him, when his affection for you is so very obvious."

"He didn't do anything." De De had said, then she'd muttered, "I was just feeling sorry for myself."

"About what?" Elizabeth hadn't been able to keep herself from asking.

De De had looked uncertain for a moment; then, in a rush, she had blurted out the content of her conversation with Beau the day after Christmas.

"He loves me, Elizabeth, but he is resigned to denying himself, and me, because of his devotion to the man he claims saved his life and sanity."

"Odd." Elizabeth had frowned. "Do you know the story behind his claim?"

De De had shaken her head. "No, and so," she'd concluded, "I suppose I was punishing Uncle Jake for loving me too much."

"Are you as certain as Beau that Jake would object to the two of you being together?" Elizabeth had ventured to inquire, against her better judgment.

"Oh, I don't know." De De had answered dejectedly. "I know Mother and Dad wouldn't be wild about the idea at first, but I feel certain they would come around when they realize how much I love him." She'd sounded defeated. "The problem is, I won't get a chance to find out, because Beau won't allow me to talk to Uncle Jake about our feelings for each other."

Although Elizabeth had wanted to argue against Beau's right to impose his will on her, she had remained silent, not wishing to exacerbate the young woman's obvious unhappiness.

After De De left for her apartment in the city, Elizabeth barely had time to get lonely; she was too busy getting the house in order for Ella and Sally's return, and complying with De De's parting instructions to finish another chapter in the few days remaining until then.

As driving conditions were still not completely back to normal, Elizabeth was up before daybreak on the second to give herself plenty of time to get to Philadelphia International to meet the early flight booked by the elder Ella for herself and the girls.

It wasn't until she caught sight of Ella and Sally as they deplaned that Elizabeth realized how very badly she had missed them, and how intensely hurt she had been by their willingness to desert her over the holidays.

Shrugging off the lingering traces of pain, she met them with a smile and open arms.

They were home again. Her precious girls.

Her precious girls.

The thought sustained Elizabeth, arming her against the veiled barbs her mother-in-law sweetly fired at her about how much fun they had all had, how wonderful the holidays had been, and on and on ad nauseam.

Elizabeth smiled pleasantly, but she was relieved when at last she dropped the older woman off.

Then it was just her and her girls.

Ella and Sally were near to bursting with the

need to impart to their mother every minute of their trip. Taking turns, at times talking over each other, they filled her in on their exciting holiday experiences.

At times, Elizabeth had trouble keeping up.

"The slopes were fast and neat!" Sally enthused.

"But we didn't fall once," Ella was quick to reassure Elizabeth.

"Yeah! And we can't wait till we can go again."

"To Colorado?" Elizabeth inserted, frowning.

"No." Ella shook her head. "We'd love to go back there, but there are plenty of places to ski right here in Pennsylvania."

Elizabeth breathed a sigh of relief.

The girls chattered on, enraptured.

"The lodge we stayed at was awesome."

"The food was delicious."

"The guys were radical."

"The Christmas decorations were spectacular."

Interspersed with laughter, their chatter went on throughout the rest of the day, filling the house with the kind of noise only children can provide.

While striving to maintain a cheerful facade, Elizabeth was filled with a growing despair until, over the dinner table, her daughters stared at her with somber, luminous eyes.

"We missed you," Ella said, reaching across the table to give Elizabeth's hand a squeeze.

"Like crazy," Sally seconded, jumping out of her chair to give her mother a bear hug.

With those two brief but heartfelt admissions and displays, the lonely days and empty house were forgotten, and all was suddenly right with Elizabeth's world.

Ella and Sally went to bed rather early, tired out from their early morning flight, the excitement of homecoming, and their nonstop chatter.

Elizabeth had had their company for a whole ten hours. She counted herself lucky.

In the morning, everything was back to normal—which meant, utter chaos.

Ella ate her breakfast of dry wheat toast and orange juice standing at the kitchen counter. As usual, Sally ate nothing at all; she was not a breakfast person.

Comfortable with the routine, Elizabeth sat at the table, calmly sipping her coffee, unfazed by the girls exchanging of affectionate insults while dashing around and collecting their things.

Ella made several trips to the car to stash the mound of laundry she had brought home from Colorado for Elizabeth to do.

Elizabeth hadn't minded; that was par for the course. In fact, there was a measure of security and rightness in the everyday attitude of both the girls.

Then it was time to leave.

" 'Bye, Mom," Sally called, shrugging into her green and white Philadelphia Eagles jacket as she loped to the door. "See ya, El," she yelled, slamming the door behind her.

Elizabeth shot a resigned glance at the clock. Things were definitely back to normal; Sally had forty seconds to make it to the corner for the school bus.

"I'll be ready as soon as I brush my teeth, Mother," Ella said, making tracks for the stairs, oblivious to the glass, plate, crumpled napkin, and toast crumbs littering the otherwise spotless countertop.

A wry smile curved Elizabeth's lips as she rose to do the cleaning up; Ella was almost fanatical about her perfectly gorgeous white teeth.

Once mother and daughter were in the car and heading north to the college Ella attended in Easton, their conversation suddenly took a more personal trend.

"Were you pretty lonely, Mother? I mean with Sally and me away over Christmas?"

Elizabeth spared a glance from the highway to give her a reassuring smile. "Of course, and I missed you both very much," she admitted. "But besides going with De De to her parents' home, I kept busy and that helped."

Since Ella believed she had heard all the details about Elizabeth's weather-shortened trip to Connecticut, she homed in on the last part of that statement.

"Busy doing what?"

"Your laundry, for one thing," Elizabeth replied. "And the usual stuff."

Detecting her mother's evasion, Ella turned within the seat belt to level a skeptical look at her. "That wouldn't have kept you busy for long. So what else did you do?"

"Well . . ." Elizabeth paused, fighting an inner battle.

"Mother?" Ella's maturing voice suddenly cracked with uncertainty. "What are you keeping from me?"

The note of anxiety in Ella's voice broke down the reserve Elizabeth had maintained for over two months. Although she certainly wasn't going to tell her daughter about Jake, since it was too soon and the relationship was much too nebulous, she thought it time to confess to her writing ambitions.

"I . . . er . . . I kept busy trying to write," she blurted out, her fingers curling tightly around the steering wheel.

Ella gave her a blank stare. "Write what?"

"A book." Elizabeth's knuckles showed white through taut skin. "A mystery novel."

When there was no response for several very long seconds, she managed a sideways look at her daughter. Ella was staring at her with an expression that could only be described as wide-eyed wonder.

"You want to be an author?" she finally asked, excited and amazed. "A mystery writer . . . like John Grisham and Mary Higgins Clark and Jake Ruttenburg?"

The mere mention of Jake's name stirred a response deep inside Elizabeth, a response so strong, so startling, her mind went blank for an instant.

"Jake Ruttenburg writes suspense novels," she said without thinking. The sound of her own voice set her mental gears in motion. "But, yes, I want to write like those authors," she finally answered, hastily modifying the admission. "I'm a rank amateur in comparison to them, though."

"Well, so what? They were all amateurs at one time." Ella was gratifyingly quick to defend her mother. "I think it's just great! Did De De give you the idea?"

"No, honey." Elizabeth shook her head. "Although De De has been very supportive, and wonderfully encouraging, I have wanted to write for as long as I can remember. I even planned on majoring in journalism at college."

"But you never wrote anything?"

A tinge of color warmed Elizabeth's cheeks. "I wrote something in longhand the summer after I graduated from high school." She laughed. "I dug it out a couple of months ago and read it; it was rough, but salvageable . . . I think."

"High school!" Ella repeated in astonishment. "And you haven't written anything since then?"

Elizabeth answered with another shake of her head. "Not until recently."

"But . . . why not?"

"I've been a little busy, if you'll recall," Elizabeth reminded her in a dry voice. She didn't have to say more; both Ella and Sally knew their mother had left college in her freshman year to marry their father. They also knew that she was pregnant at the time.

"Yeah, busy taking care of us kids and Dad and the house." Ella made a whimsical face. "Does Sally know—about your writing, I mean?"

"No. I worked at it while she was in school and, of course, while you two were away." Her smile was sad. "The few evenings I wrote when Sally was home, I was in the office and . . ." Her voice faded and she shrugged.

"And Sally doesn't go in there because that's Daddy's room," Ella finished for her.

"Yes."

"Well, I think it's terrific. I'm proud of you for having the guts to do it," Ella said enthusiastically. "And I think Sally will feel the same."

"I hope so," Elizabeth murmured, "because I intend to stay with it."

Nineteen

Ella's conviction proved correct—initially.

Knowing her daughters talked by phone frequently, Elizabeth told Sally about her attempt at writing over the dinner table that evening.

"Are you going to be famous!" Sally screeched with excitement. "And rich?"

Elizabeth sighed in sheer relief, for she had worried about Sally's reaction; the teenager had been unpredictable at times, experiencing periods of moodiness since her father's death.

"First I have to be published," Elizabeth answered teasingly. "And you can keep famous, I'll take rich."

"Aw, Mom."

"Aw, Sally," Elizabeth echoed, laughing.

The exchange did wonders for her spirits. Sailing on a contentment high, she got to work the next morning right after Sally left for school.

Within minutes of starting, she was lost inside her story, her fingers flying over the computer keyboard.

***

Jan was running—running. She had to keep go-ing. She couldn't stop. She had to hide. Somewhere.

He was chasing her, getting closer.

Jan knew the man pursuing her. Oh, she knew him well.

He was handsome, intelligent, urbane, charming and rich. He had everything a man could possibly want.

And he had had her.

Jan's breath came in hard, sobbing gasps.

She had loved him . . . so much. And she had believed that he loved her. Wanted her.

A bubble of hysterical laughter lodged in her throat.

He wanted her all right.

He wanted her dead.

Sobbing aloud, Jan ran on, stumbling, falling, get-ting up again, going on.

She had to keep running.

If he caught her, he'd . . .

The phone rang.

Elizabeth's head jerked up, and she came out of her story.

"Hello?" She answered on the third ring, her voice sharp, edged with impatience.

"Liz?" Jake sounded puzzled, uncertain.

"Yes, it's me." She laughed and relaxed. "I'm sorry if I was abrupt. I was really into my story."

"I know the feeling."

"I'm sure you do."

"Hey, look, I don't want to cut off the flow," he said. "I can call back lat—"

"No," she interrupted him, clutching the receiver, as if that would keep him from hanging up. "That's not necessary. I'll be able to get back into it."

"Well, if you're sure."

"I'm positive."

There was a pause. Silence.

Elizabeth waited for him to say something.

Was he waiting for her to speak?

He had called her!

"Jake?"

"Yeah?"

"Did . . . did you call for a reason?"

"Yeah. I wanted to hear your voice," he admitted.

"Oh." Elizabeth experienced the same warm fuzzy feeling she'd felt at Christmas.

"Liz?"

"Yes?"

"That isn't all I want." His voice was low and intimate now.

Elizabeth suddenly had as much trouble breathing as her fictional heroine. "It . . . isn't?"

"No, it isn't." Jake's low voice caressed her, long distance. "I want to see you, to hold you. I want to kiss you and make love to you."

Oh, God, she thought.

"Oh, Jake," she whispered.

"I know. It's too soon for you." His voice revealed reluctant acceptance. "But knowing that doesn't seem to help—or stop the wanting."

Elizabeth wanted too. She ached with the

wanting. She ached so badly that she began to doubt the wisdom of her own self-imposed stricture.

"Are you still there?"

"Yes, Jake, I am."

"You were so quiet," he murmured.

"I didn't know how to respond."

"You could always change your mind," he suggested, his voice growing lighter, teasing. "Or the subject."

Elizabeth drew a settling breath, then frowned at the tremor in her fingers. "I think I'd better change the subject," she said, her tone now as light as his. "How is your work going?"

"All things considered, remarkably well." He chuckled. "I'm burning up the lines between here and there."

Elizabeth was at a loss as to what he meant, not in the first part of his reply—she understood that perfectly—but his last words left her baffled.

"Between where and where?"

Jake broke into a full-throated laugh. "That's right," he said as his laughter subsided. "You don't know my working procedure."

"It's different from anybody else's?" Elizabeth glanced from the phone to her computer. What could be different?

"Hell, I don't know," he admitted. "I don't know, or much care, how other writers work." He paused, but before she could respond, he went on, "At least I never have before. Now it seems I'm beginning to care very much about how one writer in particular works."

"Jake . . . I—"

"Never mind," he said softly, cutting off her stammering attempt. "You do know that Beau is my assistant."

It wasn't a question, but a statement. Elizabeth answered anyway. "Yes, I do."

"Uh-huh, but did you know he lives in New Jersey?"

"Yes." Elizabeth recalled De De mentioning it when she'd told her about a telephone conversation with Beau. "Northern New Jersey, isn't it?"

"Yeah, well, for a while he traveled back and forth each day from there to here. That got to be a drag. So, a couple of years ago, I updated my system and installed one in Beau's mother's place. Now I just fax stuff from my machine to his. He proofs, edits for spelling and grammatical errors, then prints it out. When the manuscript is complete, *fini*, he sends it off to my editor."

"And that's what you meant by burning up the lines from your place to his," Elizabeth concluded.

"Yes."

"Sounds like a good arrangement," Elizabeth said, envying him his gorgeous assistant.

"Whatever works," Jake drawled.

Elizabeth's roving glance collided with her blank screen, and she laughed. "Which reminds me, I'm not—working, I mean. And I left my heroine running for her life."

"Are you trying to tell me something?"

"I think I just did," she replied, traces of laughter lingering in her voice.

"I can take a hint." His response held laughter, too. "So, I'll let you get back to it. But, first, I suppose you wouldn't care to tell me why, and from whom, your female protagonist is running for her life?"

"You suppose correctly."

"That's what I thought." Jake heaved a dramatic sigh. "In that case, may I interrupt your story by calling tomorrow?"

An anticipatory thrill ran through Elizabeth, and she knew there was only one answer to give. "Yes."

"Same time, okay?"

She looked at the desk clock. Wondering how she could survive that long, she murmured another, "Yes."

For emotional and physical reasons, Elizabeth found it difficult to get back into her story after they had said their goodbyes and hung up.

Jake called her every morning at approximately the same time. Their conversations were lively, sprinkled with laughter, liberally peppered with sexual innuendo.

With each successive day, and barely noticed by Elizabeth, her confidence in herself as a woman blossomed in the warmth of his interest, the gentle rain of his stated desire for her.

Without pausing to think, consider, caution herself, she returned that interest and the implied, if unstated, desire.

In effect, they were engaging in a long-distance seduction—and enjoying every minute of it.

Before the end of that week, Elizabeth had not only revealed to him why and from whom her heroine was running, but her entire plot.

She was inordinately pleased by Jake's favorable response to her story concept.

Elizabeth was gratified as well by Sally's apparent interest in her endeavors. In fact, seemingly intrigued by the process of creative writing, Sally even managed to surmount her reluctance to enter her father's office, which had been commandeered by her mother, to get a closer look.

"Cool," she declared at the end of the week.

Elizabeth took Sally's comment as approval of her work. She considered the growing frequency of the girl's visits into the room as a milestone.

Sally spent the weekend with her grandmother Ella.

Left alone in the house, Elizabeth got a lot of work on her story accomplished, as there were no distracting calls from Jake. Assuming she would be devoting time to her daughter, he had said he'd call Monday morning.

He had given her his unlisted number, and she was sorely tempted throughout the weekend to place a call to him, just to hear his voice.

Instead, when her creative flow narrowed to a fine trickle late on Sunday afternoon, she called De De.

"Oh, I'm so glad you called." The younger woman sounded almost desperate.

"Why, is something wrong?" Elizabeth asked, suddenly anxious for her friend.

"Yes!" De De wailed. "I've got only three chapters to go and . . . Elizabeth," she cried out, "I don't know how to end this story."

Controlling the impulse to laugh from sheer relief, Elizabeth conveyed her compassionate understanding of her friend's dilemma. "Can I do anything to help?"

"Yeah, throw me a lifeline and pull me out of this quagmire."

"Put me in the picture."

Briefly and succinctly, De De outlined her plot, up to the quagmire part.

"Hmmm, I see what you mean," Elizabeth commiserated. "Well, you could . . ."

The following fifteen minutes were given over to brainstorming. Elizabeth and De De tossed ideas back and forth rapid-fire. Anyone save another writer would have thought the conversation strange indeed, if not perverted.

"He could kidnap her."

"It's been done . . . and done . . . and done."

"An accident?"

"Too contrived."

"Ravishment, maybe?"

"Or rape."

"Well . . . I don't know."

"Rape would do it, though, in this particular instance, don't you agree?"

"Possibly . . . Gentle rape."

"Isn't that an oxymoron?"

"Of course, but does it matter?"

"You're right. And it just could work."

When the discussion ended, Elizabeth didn't know if she had been of any help to De De; she did know she had thoroughly enjoyed the mental stimulation. And, strangely, she returned to her own story with a new perspective, completely unrelated to anything mentioned during the conversation.

"Hi."

Elizabeth started at hearing Sally's voice. Swinging around in her desk chair, she stared in surprise at the somber-faced girl standing in the office doorway. What, she wondered, had happened to Sally's yelling "Hi, Mom, I'm home!" the minute she stepped into the house?

"I didn't hear you come in, honey," she said on a half gasp. "Why so glum?"

Sally's only response was a dejected expression and drooping shoulders.

"Are you hungry?" Elizabeth asked, but went on before Sally could answer. "I'll shut down the machine and start dinner."

"It's seven-thirty, Mom. Grammom took me for dinner over an hour ago."

Elizabeth frowned, not at what Sally had said—she frequently had dinner with her grandmother before coming home—but at the thinly veiled note of disgust in her daughter's voice. That was new—and disconcerting.

"What's wrong, Sal?"

"Nothing." Sally turned away.

"Sally." Elizabeth's tone halted the girl, but she didn't turn around. "It's something. Give me a moment. I'll shut down the machine and we'll talk about it."

"Don't bother," the teenager said insolently. She took a step into the hallway.

"Don't you dare walk away from me, young lady." Elizabeth's sharply voiced command had the girl swinging around again as if pulled by strings. "Now, what is wrong with you?"

"It's just like Grammom said," she whined. "It's started already." Tears welled in her eyes. "Now that you've decided to be a career woman, you don't have time to think about dinner or even notice that I'm home."

Elizabeth's immediate reaction was anger at her meddling mother-in-law, but as the tears began trickling down her daughter's face, that was swept aside by a tide of remorse.

Intellectually, Elizabeth knew the time she had devoted to her writing had not been at the expense of her daughter, but emotionally she responded to the girl's teary-eyed vulnerability.

"That's simply not true, honey, and you know it," she said in a softer, placating tone. "I didn't notice you were home because you didn't announce yourself the minute you came into the house, as you usually do," she pointed out.

Sally opened her mouth; Elizabeth silenced her with a quickly raised hand.

"As to dinner," she went on, "I rarely start dinner before you get home from your grandmother's, because she usually takes you out for dinner before bringing you home." Rising, Elizabeth slowly walked to the girl. "Furthermore, I don't understand why you should be upset now about my having a career when just a few days ago you thought it was *cool.*"

"I know, but . . ." Sally's voice faded on a sigh.

"But what?"

"Well . . ." She hesitated, then blurted out, "Grammom said it wouldn't look right."

"Excuse me?" Elizabeth frowned. "What—in your grandmother's opinion—wouldn't look right?"

"She said people would think you had to do something to earn money, that it would give the appearance Daddy hadn't provided for us."

Appearance. Elizabeth nearly choked at hearing that word. Controlling an urge to curse, she gritted her teeth. As renewed anger vanquished guilt and remorse, she drew several deep breaths before attempting to respond.

"That may have been the case when your grandmother was a young woman, Sally," she said with hard-fought calm. "But it hardly applies today. Many women work, not because of financial necessity, but because they choose to do so. You should know that."

"Well, yeah, I do, but—"

"No buts," Elizabeth cut her off, warming to the subject. "My working at home, in this room, has not deprived you in any way, and you know it. Don't you?"

"Yes," Sally mumbled, lowering her eyes.

"All right, then. That's the end of this discussion," Though it galled Elizabeth to say it, she added, "You will respect your grandmother's opinion, of course, while keeping in mind that she is from another generation. Is that understood?"

Sally nodded, looking so forlorn that Elizabeth's anger melted in the warmth of mother love.

"Okay, honey. Now," she went on briskly, "give me a minute to shut down, then tell me all about your weekend while I have something to eat."

Though Sally seemed to accept Elizabeth's lecture, her enthusiasm for and interest in her mother's work waned, and her visits to the office dwindled over the weeks following their discussion.

Twenty

In truth, Elizabeth was so involved with her story, so distracted by Jake's daily phone calls, she gave only minimal thought to Sally's defection. Teenagers were unpredictable at best, and Sally had lost her adored father at a precarious point in her life.

On the other hand, Ella retained her interest and enthusiasm. She called home, collect of course, several times a week, and never failed to voice her support for her mother's aspirations—which made her mother certain that Sally had voiced her reservations to her sister.

Viewing the situation as one of the normal trials and tribulations of family life, Elizabeth sighed occasionally, but kept working on her quickly evolving story.

Her sighs while conversing long distance with Jake were of an altogether different sort. And he drew them from her with increasing regularity.

"You know, this is weird," he said, on Friday of the second week of January.

"What is?" Elizabeth asked, smiling although

she was feeling a bit down; he wouldn't call again until Monday.

"How much work I'm getting accomplished."

"I don't understand." She frowned, thoroughly baffled. "What's weird about that?"

There was a heartbeat of silence, then a grunt of exasperation sang along the wire to her receptive ear. "You're inside my head, all the time, right there alongside my story. I see your face superimposed on every female in the damn thing. I see it in my sleep, for God's sake. You're here, there, on the edges of my mind—teasing me, tantalizing me, making me hurt, making me sweat, making me . . . Dammit, Liz, I want to see you, I want to be with you, I want you!"

Elizabeth tensed.

"Liz?" Uncertainty colored his voice.

"Yes?" She was becoming more certain.

"Say something."

"I want you, too." There. She'd said it. She held her breath, waiting for his response; there was barely a pause in her breathing's rhythm.

"I'm coming down there, next weekend." His prior uncertainty had changed into hard conviction. "Now what do you have to say?"

"I'll try to arrange to have Sally go to her grandmother's."

His roar of exuberant laughter sparked a glow of anticipation in Elizabeth. Feeling light, free of restrictions and restraints, young again, she laughed along with him. Until his laughter abruptly ceased.

"What am I laughing about?" Jake asked on a rueful note. "It's going to be one hell of a long week."

Of course, his complaint only served to enhance the anticipatory thrill.

After saying a prolonged goodbye to Elizabeth, Jake sat unmoving at his desk, his hand still resting on the telephone receiver as if in some way retaining contact with her. When his gaze focused on his hand, he snatched it away. A fierce frown drew his dark brows together.

"You've got it bad, Ruttenburg," he told himself aloud. "And, as the old song goes, that ain't good."

Or was it? Jake mulled it over. It felt good. That should scare the hell out of him. Okay, he was going to spend next weekend with Elizabeth—in bed with Elizabeth—and that would do him a world of good. Other than that brief, aborted encounter with the California beach bunny, he had been without a woman for . . .

Almost three-quarters of a year!

The realization shocked Jake; he hadn't believed himself to be so physically strong willed, or so strong minded.

Yet he hadn't minded, he mused. At least, not too much.

Why hadn't he? Jake asked himself, knowing the answer.

Elizabeth.

When exactly *had* he decided that if he couldn't have her—until he could have her—he didn't want anyone?

Jake knew he had never made a conscious decision to abstain. His unconscious, subconscious—whatever—had decided for him.

And, what did that portend?

Oh, hell.

Jake groaned aloud.

He had vowed never again to allow a woman to touch him emotionally.

But how could he have known there was an Elizabeth out there, waiting to arouse his buried affections as well as his raging lust?

Lust.

Next weekend.

At the thought, shards of excitement shot through Jake, interfering with his breathing, making him hard.

Lord, how could he stand the wait?

Elizabeth wasn't much good at anything productive after talking to Jake.

Had she really asked him to spend the weekend, with the unstated but understood invitation to share her bed, herself, with him?

She had, and she wasn't sorry.

That was more than a little startling, not to mention shocking.

But there's no help for it, Elizabeth reasoned, shutting down her machine hours before her usual quitting time. What she had told Jake was the basic truth; She wanted him, in all the ways that implied.

While performing her habitual Friday routine of desk-straightening, dusting, and vacuuming in the office, Elizabeth honestly examined her feelings.

She admittedly had been attracted, almost violently so, to Jake from the outset, though she had attempted to paper over her interest with indignation over his reputation and to deny the depth of his attraction to her.

But being confined in the same house with Jake in Connecticut had blown to hell and gone that bit of self-deception.

Barely aware of the hum of the vacuum, or even of pushing the upright back and forth over the carpet, Elizabeth smiled wryly.

It was pretty hard to maintain lack of interest in a man while standing in the snow, uncaring of the cold, hungrily accepting his passionate kisses.

But her present mental and emotional condition could not be solely attributed to the few days they had spent together in his sister's home, to the few kisses they had shared, or even to the desire he had generated within her.

Against her better judgment, against her will, Elizabeth was forced to face an irrevocable fact. And it was that—via the telephone, for heaven's sake!—she had somehow managed to fall in love with Jake Ruttenburg.

Elizabeth feared that in the long run she

could be hurt—badly hurt—by her rash decision. Still, in the short term, she'd had no option. She wanted Jake, wanted whatever of himself and his time he was willing to give to her.

She wanted to be with him so much that next weekend seemed far away.

As it turned out, Elizabeth didn't have to try to arrange anything for Sally for the following weekend. Her daughter did that on her own.

On Wednesday evening, after Elizabeth had confirmed Angie Carmichael's permission, Sally went to her friend's house, so that they could study together for an upcoming math test.

Before she left, Sally was uncommunicative and moody due to a lingering residue from her grandmother's meddling. When Elizabeth picked her up at her friend's house a few hours later, Sally appeared enthralled.

"Mrs. Carmichael had a visit from a new friend tonight," she said, with more animation than she had shown all week. "And she is sooo cool!"

Praise indeed, Elizabeth thought, amused. Aloud, she merely murmured, "Really?"

"Yeah," Sally chirped. "She's been to so many places, done so many things . . . and she's so beautiful!"

Hmmm. How, Elizabeth pondered, did a fifteen-year-old girl define beauty? It being truly in the eye of the beholder, beauty was whatever each individual decided. In Elizabeth's opinion, Sally was a beauty, as was her sister Ella. But then, as their mother, she was slightly biased.

Sally prattled on. "And she's funny and so interesting, so . . . so with it!"

Sight unseen, Elizabeth was beginning to dislike the woman, which was unfair but for a mother, natural.

"And does this para—er, person have a name?" Elizabeth asked, compensating with an overpleasant tone for her unkind thoughts.

"Cassandra. Isn't that pretty?"

"Lovely."

On Friday afternoon, Sally came charging into the house, fairly bursting with excitement. "Hey, Mom, are you up there?" she called from the foyer.

"I'm on the phone, I'll be down in a minute," Elizabeth called back.

"Can you hurry?" Sally yelled. "I've got something to ask you."

"I've got to hang up now, Jake," she murmured into the receiver. "As I'm sure you heard, Sally's home."

"Are you finally going to talk to her about spending the weekend with her grandmother?" There was impatience in his voice; he had been after her all week about it.

"Yes, I told you I would." Not even to herself would Elizabeth admit that she was feeling some trepidation about the weekend.

"I'll be there no later than seven-thirty," he warned, holding her to the agreement.

"Jake . . . I—"

"Mom! Are you coming down?"

"Seven-thirty."

He hung up.

Swallowing against the tightness of incipient panic, she shouted, "I'm coming!"

She had to arrange something in a hurry, Elizabeth told herself, hearing his warning inside her head. Stealing a second to compose herself, she drew a deep breath, squared her shoulders, and went downstairs.

Sally was waiting for her, fairly dancing in place at the foot of the staircase, her coat still on.

"Okay, I'm here." Elizabeth noted the girl's eager expression. "What's this all about?"

"Janice told me in school that her mom said she could invite me over for the weekend," she said in a breathless rush. "May I go, Mom? Cassandra's going to be there, and it's gonna be so neat and fun."

It was a convenient answer to the problem, but . . . Elizabeth squelched a twinge of what she recognized as jealousy of the unknown woman. Telling herself to act like the mature woman she believed herself to be, she gave in to the girl's pleading with a smile.

"Yes, you may go, but are you certain Mrs. Carmichael meant the invitation for the entire weekend," she quickly added, before her daughter could dash away.

Sally appeared to hover on the brink of bolting for the kitchen—and the phone.

"Yeah," she answered, vigorously nodding her head. "I'm supposed to call Janice, to tell her if I can come, but you can call and talk to Mrs. Carmichael, if you want."

Elizabeth smiled again. "I want."

On the phone, Angie Carmichael sounded nearly as excited as Sally. "Oh, yes, Elizabeth, I did invite her for the entire weekend. Sally told you about Cassandra, my new acquaintance?"

"Yes, is she new to the area?"

"Oh, yes, from California. A charming woman. She's considering buying the house being built on the new extension to the subdivision. You know where I mean?"

"Of course." Elizabeth frowned. "She's relocating?"

"I don't know. She didn't say." Angie lowered her voice. "I think she's loaded." Her voice perked up again. "Anyway, she's been living in a motel for weeks, and I thought she might appreciate a break from it. Home cooking and all. And the girls had so much fun with her the other evening, I decided to include Sally in the house party. You can bring her over in time for dinner, if you like."

Thinking this Cassandra had to be some extraordinary person, Elizabeth gave permission for the sleepover, thanked Angie, and hung up the phone.

Having heard the exchange, since she had

practically been breathing down her mother's neck, Sally cried, "Thank you, Mom!" and flung herself into Elizabeth's arms.

Elizabeth dropped Sally off at the Carmichaels', at six, with orders to be on her best behavior.

On returning home, she fixed a light supper for herself, then immediately covered the untouched soup and salad and stashed both in the fridge.

Nervous, killing time, she proceeded to wipe every exposed surface; table, countertop, stove, microwave, and refrigerator saw the busy end of a dishcloth.

Finished, she wandered through the first-floor rooms, her restless gaze searching for something to do. The house was in order. It was her mind that was in disarray.

By seven-fifteen Elizabeth had showered, blow-dried her hair, applied her makeup, and dressed—in three different outfits—and was still dissatisfied with her appearance in the long flowing skirt and full-sleeved silk big shirt. Chewing the lipstick from her bottom lip, she clipped a gold-toned chain belt around her waist. It helped, but not much.

Heaving a sigh, she turned to collect the rejected clothing she'd tossed onto a chair. Moving back and forth from the bedroom to the spacious walk-in closet, she studiously avoided looking at the bed.

Clothes neatly hung away in the closet, she again braved the mirror. She reapplied lipstick, then scooped her hair into a loose knot, securing it, if somewhat precariously, with a velvet scrunchie. Finally, she stood staring in despair at her reflection.

Her eyes shifted, grazing over and then returning to settle on the mirrored image of the bed.

She couldn't do this, Elizabeth told herself in silent anguish, her wide-eyed stare fastened to the bed's reflection. It had been so long, over eighteen months, since she had made love with a man . . . and that man had been her husband, the act a familiar if uninspiring part of her married life.

Married life. Richard. She had shared the bed—and herself—with Richard!

I can't do this. The protest was repeated inside her head. Though not a skilled lover, Richard *had* been familiar. Whereas, Jake was still practically a stranger, a thrilling, arousing stranger, but a stranger nonetheless.

And that stranger would see her unadorned body, her imperfections. Her stretch marks!

Elizabeth moaned and drew her gaze away from the mirror. It landed on the bedside clock.

Seven twenty-three! She had forgotten to put the wine in the fridge to chill!

Tearing out of the room, Elizabeth dashed down the stairs and into the kitchen. Retrieving a bottle of white and one of red from a cabinet, just to be prepared, she shoved the white into the fridge, then, too keyed up to sit, paced from

the kitchen, through the dining room, and into
the living room. She was crossing to the foyer
to make another circle of the downstairs area
when the doorbell rang.

Elizabeth froze in place, one foot in the living room, the other in the foyer.

The bell rang again.

She felt foolish, excited, scared, and was just
about ready to run, throw up, fall apart.

She did none of those. Instead, moving stiffly,
carefully, she opened the door.

Jake looked cold and tired, and too mascu-
linely attractive to be believed.

"Hi." He smiled.

Elizabeth melted and swung open the door
in invitation.

Twenty-one

As the Fates continued to pour their blessings on Cassie, she was hard pressed to keep from smirking.

Her expression serene, she observed the friendly group gathered around her in the Carmichaels' living room.

How positively delicious, she thought, congratulating herself for having been in exactly the right place at precisely the right time.

And to think she'd been just about to throw in the towel!

Silent laughter lurked behind her benign smile.

But who would have thought, or believed, that the woman who had been standing in the entrance to the motel's coffee shop a week and a half ago would turn out to be Cassie's connection to her goal?

Laughing along with the group, adding a dry comment into the conversational mix here and there, Cassie mentally reviewed the events that occurred since the snowstorm had forced her to seek shelter in the motel over a month ago.

In truth, not much had happened, the time

having been utterly boring, Cassie ruminated. She had cruised the small local mall, which she'd immediately labeled as hicksville, with nothing of interest to offer a woman of taste. She had visited a nearby beauty shop, quaintly named The Ultimate Do. It wasn't. The manicurist savaged her cuticle.

Then, a week and a half ago, impatient and discerning an approaching ennui, Cassie had made her elegant way from her suite to the coffee shop for lunch, not from hunger, simply for something to do. So out of sorts was she, she had not even bothered to redo her makeup; and there really wasn't a way to repair the awful and inexpert French twist that idiot posing as a hair stylist had inflicted on her.

It was at the entrance to the coffee shop that providence beamed upon Cassie.

The coffee shop was full. One table remained free. And, bless her innocent heart, Angie Carmichael offered to share the table with Cassandra Metcalf.

Resigning herself to an endless stream of chatter from the suburban matron, Cassie had accepted the woman's offer. And, while the woman did talk too much once they were seated at a table, within her gushing stream, Cassie discovered nuggets of pure gold.

Angie Carmichael lived in the very same small, upscale subdivision as Elizabeth Leninger, their respective homes separated by a mere couple of blocks. What's more, Cassie learned that the widowed Elizabeth was a friend of

Angie's, that their daughters were nearly inseparable.

The daughter.

How better to get at a woman than through her child?

It was perfect.

Cassie scrapped every one of the elaborate machinations she had devised in favor of a simple plan to divide and conquer. Her first objective had been to cultivate Angie Carmichael. Open and friendly, Angie had been a piece of cake.

The only problem remaining was how to proceed. Cassie hit on the solution quite by accident. She had been poking around inside her makeup/jewelry case, searching for paler shades of makeup to lend her a less flamboyant and more quietly subdued appearance, when her gaze fell upon the moderate-size diamond solitaire in its plain gold setting. To all appearances, it looked like an engagement ring, not the kind Cassie would have ever accepted but perfect for the persona she had decided to portray.

As she slipped the ring onto the third finger of her left hand, a plan came to her.

"Isn't that right, Cassandra?"

Called from her reverie, Cassie gently smiled at Sally Leninger. "I'm sorry, darling, I'm afraid my mind was wandering." Her tone matched her smile for gentleness. "What were you saying, dear?" she asked, thinking, As if a teenage twit like you has anything important to say.

* * *

"Very nice," Jake said, shifting his glance back to Elizabeth after glancing at what he could see of the house from the foyer. Turning from hanging his coat inside the closet, she felt the impact of his gaze on her. "The house ain't bad, either."

His teasing tone drew a laugh from her and, strangely, drained away the tension coiling through her.

"Feel better? Less wired and frantic?"

"Yes," Elizabeth admitted. "But how did you know? Was my jangled state so obvious?"

Jake shook his head. "You looked as cool as a mountain spring," he said, his smile wry. "I knew because, despite appearances, I also felt frazzled."

"You did?" Her eyes went wide with disbelief.

"I did," he concurred.

"But you . . ." Elizabeth's voice failed as he closed in on her. "Wh-what are you doing."

"Isn't it obvious?" Halting inches from her, he drew her into his arms. "Never mind, I'll tell you," he murmured, lowering his head. "I'm going to kiss you senseless." His mouth brushed her lips. "And then, when you can no longer think, only feel"—he paused to brush her lips again—"I'm going to carry you up to bed."

"But . . . but . . ." she sputtered, trying, but not too hard, to avoid his mouth. "I'm chilling wine!"

"I don't need the stimulation." His mouth touched, tasted, moved away a fraction. "I'm overstimulated now." His tongue drew a moist outline of her mouth. "Liz, if you don't part your lips, let me in, I'm going to explode with stimulation."

What could she do? she asked herself. She certainly didn't want him exploding all over her foyer. She parted her lips, and Jake's mouth claimed hers.

A sigh of sheer bliss caressed his tongue as it slipped inside to explore her sweetness.

The heated, dedicated application of his mouth to hers immediately rendered her previous concerns unimportant, gently eroding away her anxieties about her sexual inadequacy, her less than perfect figure, her stretch marks.

Those things didn't matter; nothing mattered. Only the two of them, their mouths devouring, their bodies straining . . . needing, needing.

Elizabeth moaned a protest when he tore his mouth from her stinging lips.

"Shall I sweep you into my arms and carry you up the stairs in a reenactment of Rhett and Scarlett?" Jake whispered, his smiling lips teasing hers. "Or will my personal heroine deign to walk beside me up the stairs?"

Arching her head back, Elizabeth batted her eyelashes mockingly at him. "Is this your flowery way of telling me I am a tall lady and that is a long staircase?"

"Nnnn—yes," Jake confessed, winning her over with a grin worthy of a fictional hero.

She offered her hand.

His long fingers laced through hers.

Laughing together, they ran up the steps.

"I'm nervous," Elizabeth muttered tersely, her lowered eyes shying away from the clothing strewn around their bare feet on the carpet.

"Don't be." Jake cradled her chin in his palm, raising her head so he might stare into her anxiety-clouded eyes. With his free hand, he tugged the scrunchie from her hair, then ran his fingers through the tumbling tresses. Taking half a step back, he swept a darkened gaze over her trembling form. "Oh, Elizabeth, my Liz, you are so very beautiful."

His praise induced courage in her. Hesitantly, she lowered her gaze to examine the hard angles and flat planes of his muscular, magnificently aroused body. Quickly, she returned the compliment. "And you are . . . breathtaking."

He slid his palm from her face, to trail fingers down her neck and provoke shivers in her as they glided to the valley between her breasts.

She gasped in reaction to the sensations caused by the touch of his fingertip against the hardening crest of one breast, sighed as his hand cupped the soft flesh.

"Touch me, Liz." Jake's voice was little more than a raspy whisper. "I'm burning to feel your hands on me."

Emboldened by his plea, she tentatively placed her palm against his lightly haired chest. One finger touched, explored a hard flat nipple. His sharply indrawn breath thrilled her, gave her courage to explore at will. She moved her hand, testing the smooth texture of the taut skin of his midsection, his flat belly, and then . . . then, the silky skin encasing his rigid erection.

"Yes, yes," he groaned, shutting his eyes as if in pain. "More . . . please."

Elizabeth danced her fingers along the length of him before closing them around him possessively.

His breath harsh, ragged, Jake lowered his head to her breasts. Holding on to him, unconsciously working him, she arched her back, giving him access. His lips teased one nipple before taking it into his mouth. Her body jerked; her hand pulled at him.

Jake shuddered and began suckling her. His hands learned the contours of her body, skimming over her rib cage, her hips, her thighs, and then—then his fingers found her.

Elizabeth couldn't bear the tension crackling inside her, created by his suckling lips and deeply probing fingers. Her knees buckled; her grasp tightened around the throbbing solid extension of his body.

Suddenly her hand was torn away from him as she was swept up and then as swiftly set down, flat on her back, on the bed. Jake loomed over her. His hard, hair-roughened thighs parted her legs. His passion-fired gaze seared her surprise-widened eyes.

The time for talk was past. Reaching for him, Elizabeth grasped his waist and arched her hips in a silent offering of herself.

Jake accepted her offering with exquisite, heartrending reverence.

Which soon surrendered to unleashed passion.

Elizabeth's inhibitions became ashes in the flames of her desire. Crying his name aloud in a hoarse, needful voice, she clawed at him, begging him for more, and yet more of his tormenting pleasure.

Grasping her hips, lifting her into his powerful thrusts, laughing in exultant joy at her wild, unfettered response, Jake employed every bit of his control, of his strength, every inch of him answering her sobbed demands.

When she shattered around him, her pulsating release broke his endurance. Arching back, he gave one final deep thrust, then went still, calling her name as he attained his own earth-shaking climax.

"I'm hungry." Jake nibbled at her earlobe; it was fun, and arousing, but it didn't do much to appease the emptiness in his stomach. It was sometime Saturday. He didn't know exactly what time; he didn't much care, either.

"Again?" Elizabeth murmured sleepily, burrowing closer to his warmth.

"Food, Liz. I'm hungry for food."

"You're always hungry," she complained, peering at him through half-opened eyes. "For one thing or another."

Jake laughed and gave her a hard, tongue-lashing kiss. "And some of those things are more satisfying than others," he said, easing her arms from around his neck. "But right now, after spending so much time expending energy on the most satisfying of those things, I'm in dire need of refueling."

Heaving a sigh, Elizabeth pushed herself upright. The tangled covers pooled around her slender waist. The light slanting into the room through the loosely woven curtains bathed her naked torso, her tip-tilted breasts.

This feast for his eyes succeeded in overriding the growl in his stomach. Feeling a stirring of response, he lifted a hand to caress her creamy flesh.

Elizabeth arched an eyebrow. "I thought you were hungry for food?"

Propping himself up on an elbow, Jake sought a quickening nipple with his lips. "Ah, but Liz," he murmured, his body hardening in response to his lips's tasting, moving against, the tight bud. "This *is* food, ambrosia, a banquet for the gods."

"And are you one of those gods?"

The breathless sound of her reedy voice, the quiver that shook her at the quick touch of his tongue, caused a heated heaviness in his loins.

"Last night, this morning, a little while ago,

you made me feel like a god, my beautifully
sensual Liz. Your soft cries, your wildness, your
surrender to me—to wantonness—made me
feel like a legendary conqueror god."

"There speaks the writer," she said, spearing
her fingers into his hair to urge his mouth into
closer contact with her inviting flesh.

Excitement sizzled through Jake, leaping the
length of his expanding sex. Ignoring the yawn-
ing chasm in his stomach, he clasped her
around the waist, fell back, then, drawing her
over him, around him, eased her down, encasing himself within the moist heat of her sheath.

"No, Liz," he said, arching up and into her
as he pulled her down, over him. "Here speaks
a man caught in enthrallment, satisfied yet ever
hungry for his goddess of love."

It had happened again. Depleted, feeling
boneless, Elizabeth lay spent on Jake's chest,
stunned and amazed at the intensity of her release, or, more accurately, her multiple releases.

She had heard about this, read about it; yet
she had never really believed it possible.

With Richard, she had rarely attained one,
let alone the cataclysmic heights of recurring
spasms of ecstasy. And never before had she
experienced the nerve-twisting, body-clench-
ing, mind-divorcing sensations Jake had given
her with his greedy mouth and searching
tongue.

It was thrilling. Wonderful. Utterly exhausting.

"I'm hungry."

Jake's breath fluttered her hair; his growling voice tickled her funny bone.

"I can't get up," she said, laughing.

"Why not?"

"Your last godlike performance dissolved my bones."

"I'll starve." His chest shook with silent laughter.

"It'll serve you right."

"Maybe." His hand caught her chin, raising her head. The light of devilish laughter glowed in his dark eyes. "But then, there'll be no more godlike performances."

"I'll get up."

Their combined laughter filled the darkening room.

Jake woke Elizabeth at daybreak on Sunday morning.

Though they had agreed it would be best for him to leave early, as Sally had not given any indication of when she would be coming home, Elizabeth hadn't thought he would desert her quite so soon.

"I wish you didn't have to go," she said, curling her arms around him to hold him to her.

"I don't, not yet," he said, molding her body to his own. "But I want to love you, slowly, once more before it's time for me to head back."

Sighing her relief, her acceptance, she gave herself eagerly to his lovemaking, savoring each leisurely caress, each slow, arousing kiss; storing each sensation to warm her, console her, after he was gone.

When the laziness was lost to urgency, she reveled in the heat of his driving possession.

Descending from the rarified atmosphere of simultaneous inner explosions, they lay entwined, reluctant to move, disturb the shared intimacy.

Eventually, too quickly, reality intruded.

They showered together and, while they dressed, made small talk.

"Will you be stopping by to see De De before you head home?" Elizabeth asked, thinking it natural that he would.

"I considered it," he answered, glancing at her, his smile wry. "But, no." He sighed and shook his head. "I haven't heard a word from her since she left Connecticut, which leaves me to suspect she'd rather not see me."

"Oh, Jake, that's not true," Elizabeth said without thinking. "She told me she feels terrible about the way she behaved at Christmas."

"Did she happen to mention why?"

"Well . . ." She moistened suddenly dry lips.

His mouth thinned. "Spell it out, Liz," he ordered, looking as though he meant it.

Elizabeth hesitated, then told herself that Beau's forbidding De De to tell Jake in no way constrained her. Drawing a deep breath, she blurted out the explanation De De had confided to her.

When she had finished, Jake stared at her for a tension-fraught moment; then he began to swear.

"Of all the idiotic lunkheads," he concluded. "Beau has got to be the biggest—and I'm not referring to his size. Why, in the name of hell, didn't he trust me?"

"But he does," Elizabeth assured him, aware that he was hurt. "That's part of it, Jake. He told De De you had saved his life, his sanity; that he would do anything, even deny their love, rather than lose your trust."

"That big jerk." Jake expelled an exasperated laugh. "You know, I love that giant idiot like a brother."

"So I gathered." She smiled. "Then you don't object, you won't raise hell about it?"

"Oh, I'm going to raise all kinds of hell— with Beau—just as soon as I get home. Count on it." Before she could respond, he pulled her into his arms, crushed her mouth with his, and kissed her breathless.

"I'll be back next weekend, if you can make some arrangements for Sally," he promised as he lifted his mouth from hers. "You can count on that, too."

Twenty-two

Jake slammed into his house late Sunday afternoon and, without bothering to remove his jacket, strode directly to the telephone.

"Hello?" Beau answered on the second ring.

"I've got a question for you, buddy," Jake snarled, bypassing a greeting to get right to the point. "Are you or are you not in love with De De? I want a straight answer, yes or no, so help you God."

"Yes." Beau's voice was strong, certain.

"For how long?" Jake rapped out impatiently.

Beau's faint sigh whispered along the connecting wires. "Going on eight years."

"Eight years," Jake echoed, only much louder.

"Yes . . . Well, I've always loved De De, since she was a little girl, you know that."

"Yeah, I know. The first time I took you with me to Maryanne's, you fell under her pixie spell, as we all had; but I'm not talking about avuncular love, and you know it. So, the real stuff hit you eight years ago when"—he paused an instant to do some quick figuring—"De De was eighteen."

"Yes . . . at her eighteenth birthday party." Beau's voice was devoid of inflection. "I don't know how or why it happened, Jake, but I looked at her and, for the first time, saw a woman, a beautiful, enchanting woman, the only woman I—"

"I get the picture," Jake cut in ruthlessly. "And so, for over seven years now, you've been pining away for one—" He broke off as a consideration struck him, a consideration so unlikely, it defied belief. Still, he had to ask, "How long has it been since you've been with a woman?"

"That is none of your business, Mr. Ruttenburg." Beau's formal tone warned him off the subject.

It also told Jake all he wanted to know. The idea of self-imposed celibacy for the better part of a decade was a mindblower. But, as Beau had informed him, it was none of his business.

"Agreed," Jake conceded, deciding to get to the real purpose of the call. "But tell me this: don't you think it's time, past time, to slake this passion?"

There was a moment of utter silence. Then, quietly but succinctly, Beau asked, "You have no objections?"

Jake shook his head in wonder, raising his eyes to the open-beamed ceiling. "Would I have made this call to you if I did object?"

Again silence lay heavy. Finally the joyous

sound of Beau's laughter rang clear. "I'll call
De De at once."

"You will not," Jake shot back. "You, Beauregard Kantner, will haul your ass out to your car
the minute we hang up, then you will drive to
Philadelphia to tell De De in person. And that,
my muddle-headed friend, is an order."

"But . . . what about the work?" Beau said,
duty vying with anticipation.

"Screw the work!" Jake shouted, completely
out of patience. "Get cracking, Beau, and I
mean it. My niece is eating her heart out for
you."

Beau spared a moment to say "Thanks" and
then "Goodbye" before the clattering of a receiver being tossed onto the console assaulted
Jake's eardrum.

Grinning, he gently replaced his own receiver.

Elizabeth went to her office with a jaunty step
soon after Sally raced out the door on Monday
morning.

She felt good. No, great. Invigorated, young,
ready to meet head-on any challenge life and
living might mete out to her.

She was in love, and loving it.

Jake. Lord, he was wonderful.

Gone—banished—were all her doubts and
reservations about him, his reportedly cavalier
lifestyle, his numerous affairs.

Jake had fulfilled her completely, not only

her physical body but belief in herself as a
woman.

She was content, missing Jake, but content.
And Sally's return home a few hours after Jake
had left had only enhanced her contentment.

Her daughter had swept into the house with
her usual noisy entrance, happy and bubbling
over with news of how terrific her weekend had
been. And she had babbled on until bedtime
in praise of the apparently incomparable Cassandra.

The fact that Elizabeth had experienced only
a twinge of jealousy of the woman enthralling
Sally was an indicator of how very contented
and secure she felt.

Everything seemed to be coming together
for her, not only with her love life but with her
work as well.

Her story was rolling, unfurling in her mind,
and she was rolling with it.

The ring of the phone in midmorning broke
her concentration. Reading over the segment
she had just keyed onto the screen, she absently
reached for the receiver.

"Elizabeth," De De cried. "I'm in love."

Blanking the screen with her other hand, she
frowned and transferred her attention to her
friend. "I know."

"Ah, yes," De De fairly sang the reply. "But
did you know my love loves me back?"

"De De, you haven't been drinking this early
in the morning, have you?" Elizabeth asked in
concern.

"Drinking!" De De burst into laughter. "Heavens no! Who needs booze when you can get high on love?"

"High? The last time we talked you were morose."

"I was," De De concurred, happiness evident in her voice. "But that was before my wonderful Uncle Jake ticked off Beau—verbally—and sent him speeding here to me."

"Beau's there?" Elizabeth sent a silent, heartfelt thank you to her lover.

"Here, this very moment, his arms strong around me," De De said, dreamily. "He has asked me to marry him, Elizabeth. I, of course, said . . . not before lunch." A deep masculine chuckle followed her statement.

A sudden thought occurred to Elizabeth, dimming the happiness she felt for her friend. "De De, what about your parents?"

"Well, it may be a hard sell, but I believe they'll come around," she answered. "Beau and I are going to drive up to Connecticut this weekend and talk to them."

"I wish you luck," Elizabeth said. "And all the happiness there is. Congratulations."

After ringing off, she found it difficult to get back into her story; she was just so pleased for De De. Eventually, she did get back into the groove, and the story again began to unwind, scenes and dialogue flashing in and out of her mind, then onto the screen through her nimble fingers.

Elizabeth was writing the tense, final chase

scene that would set up the story's resolution when the phone rang again. She tried to ignore it, but couldn't. It might be Jake.

It was her mother, making her twice monthly contact.

"Well, hi." Elizabeth infused her greeting with enthusiasm. "How are you and Dad?"

"We're both fine," Sally replied. "The question is, how are you?"

"Me?" Elizabeth laughed. "I'm fine, too."

"Have you found a job yet?"

"Ah . . . that is . . ." Elizabeth winced, then, reminding herself she was a secure woman, rushed on, "I'm trying my hand at writing, Mother."

"Writing?" There was an instant's pause. "Writing what?"

"A book." Elizabeth held her breath and prayed her mother would remember, and approve.

"You mean fiction? Mystery stories, like the kind you tried your hand at while you were in high school?"

"Yes." She held her breath again.

"But that's wonderful, Elizabeth," Sally exclaimed, unaware that she'd saved her daughter from turning blue in the face. "But why on earth haven't you mentioned it before?"

"Oh, I don't know," she said, knowing she lied; she hadn't said anything before because she had been afraid of the reaction she'd receive, one on the same order of the elder Ella's. "I guess I wasn't sure I could do it."

"You always did have a tendency to hide your light," Sally chided. "Now you are sure?"

"Yes." Her voice was eager. "I'm almost finished, and I think it's pretty good."

"I'm sure it is," Sally decided. "I'm proud of you, and I know your father will be, too."

"Thank you, Mother, I appreciate your confidence." Briefly, Elizabeth considered telling her mother about Jake; then she shook her head. It was too soon for that sort of mother-daughter confidence sharing.

Elizabeth spoke to her father before saying goodbye, and went back to work with her spirits soaring.

When the phone rang for the third time a few hours later, Elizabeth felt certain she knew who it was, and she was right.

"Hi." The intimate warmth of Jake's soft voice sent shivers down her spine.

"Hi," she responded in kind. "Oh, Jake, if I had you here now I'd kiss you."

"Just because I'm a terrific guy?"

Elizabeth laughed. "No, even though you are. But I'd kiss you even if you weren't, maybe twice, for what you've done for De De and Beau. She's so happy."

"I know." He chuckled. "Boy, do I know! She called me up earlier this morning and gushed all over me."

"I'd love to gush all over you at this moment," Elizabeth said, never thinking about the connotations that could be derived from her remark.

But Jake thought about them and spoke them aloud, in an even softer, more intimate tone.

"Oh, Jake." Elizabeth sighed, and noted that she did so a lot when talking with him.

When, after a prolonged goodbye, she hung up the receiver, she didn't immediately go back to work. She sat, yearning for him, recalling every minute they had spent loving each other.

Elizabeth never did finish the chase scene that day.

She finished the scene Tuesday—before Jake called.

She was pulling the ends of her story together for resolution late Wednesday afternoon when he called. Since it was hours past his usual calling time, she had resigned herself to not hearing from him at all that day.

"I just got off the horn with Maryanne," he explained, his tone a purr of satisfaction. "I thought I'd defuse the parental landscape of mines, so to speak, smooth the way for De De and Beau."

"How did you make out?" she asked, hopefully.

"She wasn't thrilled at first, but . . ."—he broke off to laugh—"I have a hunch that by the time the lovebirds arrive on Friday, my sister will have convinced herself it was her idea to bring De De and Beau together." He gave another bark of laughter. "If I know Maryanne, and I do, she'll likely decide that Beau will be a stabilizing influence for De De."

"I think he will be," Elizabeth said.

"I *know* he will be," Jake returned.

They laughed together, and then the tone of the conversation changed. Lost to the world in his long-distance lovemaking, Elizabeth wasn't aware that Sally was home from school until her daughter interrupted from the office doorway.

"Mom, I've got to talk to you." The teenager's voice was rife with urgency.

Instantly concerned, Elizabeth murmured, "Jake, I've got to hang up now. Sally's home, and there seems to be a problem."

"Okay, I'll call tomorrow—earlier."

"Mom."

"Yes, good, tomorrow. Goodbye."

She turned to Sally as she cradled the receiver. A shock went through her at seeing the tight expression on her daughter's face, the intensity in Sally's eyes.

"What is it?" she demanded, crossing to her. "What's wrong?"

"Who was that on the phone?"

Elizabeth shook her head, confused by the girl's aggressive tone. "A writer friend," she answered vaguely, telling herself it was the truth, just not the complete truth.

"De De?" Sally asked, skeptically.

"No, not De De, another writer friend, one you haven't met," she answered, dismissing the subject while wondering why her daughter persisted. Sally had shown little interest before. "What did you want to talk to me about?"

Sally didn't respond at once, but just stood there, her shoulders slumped, as if in defeat, an odd look in her overbright, watery-looking eyes. Then she shrugged.

"Janice is sick, with a bad head cold," she said, turning away. "She wasn't in school today."

"And you were with her all weekend," Elizabeth said, following her along the hallway. "Do you feel like you're coming down with one, too?" she asked, halting when Sally stopped before the door to her bedroom and thinking the onslaught of a head cold would account for the girl's unusually high color, her apparent tiredness, the brightness in her eyes.

"I don't know, maybe." Sally shrugged again and opened her bedroom door. "I . . . I think I'll do my homework," she muttered. "Then go to bed."

"Without dinner?"

"I'm not hungry . . ." She stopped speaking as a shudder shook her slim frame. "I feel sick to my stomach."

"I'll call the doctor," Elizabeth said decisively.

"No!" Sally's spine went stiff. "It's only a cold, and a doctor can't do anything for that. Don't they always just tell you to get plenty of liquids and rest?"

"Yes, but . . ." Elizabeth gave up; Sally had never cared for her pediatrician. "I'll bring a cup of tea with honey and lemon up to you— they always tell you to drink that, too."

"Oh, okay," Sally muttered, stepping into the room and closing the door behind her.

Wondering if she would ever understand teenagers, most especially Sally, Elizabeth went to get the tea.

Perfect.

Cassie smiled with smug satisfaction as she watched Sally dash into the house.

It was simply too good to be true.

Oh, to be a fly on E-liz-a-beth's wall.

And all because of a kid's stupid head cold.

Laughing, Cassie set the car into motion, pulling away from the corner near the spot where the school bus stopped.

Cassie had been wracking her brain since the weekend, trying to come up with a subtle way of separating Sally from her friend so she could have a little talk in private with her. But, since the two girls seemed as securely fastened together as Siamese twins, she hadn't found a workable solution.

Then, that very morning, Cassie's break had come in the form of a phone call.

Over the weekend, she had made a date with Angie Carmichael for lunch on Wednesday. Angie had called around ten, sounding disappointed about having to break their appointment.

"Janice has come down with a terrible head cold, and I've kept her home from school," she had explained. "I hate to have to cancel lunch, but I won't leave her alone in the house when she's feeling so bad."

"No, of course not," Cassie had said, grimacing in her disgust for all overprotective mothers . . . like Elizabeth; not only was Sally not left alone, but from the bits and pieces Cassie had picked up, the kid rarely got out alone. Recalling herself at that same age, Cassie knew such supervision would have cramped her style. "We can have lunch together another time," she'd continued, soothingly.

"You're very thoughtful." Angie's appreciation was tiresome to Cassie. "Suppose I call you?"

"Anytime," Cassie had said, anxious to get the woman off the phone, and her back. "And give my love to Janice."

The minute she'd hung up, Cassie had rubbed her smooth, soft hands together and thrown back her head in exaltation.

She'd been parked at the curb, waiting, when Sally jumped from the bus. Leaning across the passenger seat, she'd rolled down the window to call to the girl.

"Hi, Sally, have a minute to talk?"

Her face brightening with a delighted smile, the kid had swung open the door and slid onto the seat.

"Hi, Cassandra," she'd piped—Cassie hated it when kids piped. "What's up?"

"It's a little personal," Cassie had murmured, in what she'd thought was a commendably woeful tone. "And more than a little embarrassing, I'm afraid."

"But . . . what would *you* have to be embarrassed about?" the "dear child" had protested, as if the concept of Cassie having to feel embarrassed about anything was beyond belief.

"Do you see this ring?" Cassie had thrust her left hand in front of Sally's eyes. "It's an engagement ring."

"I noticed it before and wondered about that." The girl's eyes nearly crossed from staring at the ring. "Are you engaged to some man from around here?"

"No." Cassie had given her head a quick shake. "For some complicated . . . er, work reasons, we haven't been able to see each other for some months. He's an author, you see, and he's been very busy, holed up in his place while finishing a book." She'd heaved a heartbreaking sigh. "At least I believed he was holed up and busy on his book. He's very famous. Perhaps you've heard of him. Jake Ruttenburg?"

Sally had made a face—denoting concentration, Cassie supposed. "I think I have, yeah." Her young, still blank countenance cleared. "You must feel pretty lucky."

"I did, until recently." Cassie was proud of the pathos she contrived. "But . . ."—she then contrived a sob—"I just learned that he's having an affair." She'd paused, letting the information sink in, waiting for the look of horror and disbelief to wash over Sally's expressive face; then she'd shot home her poisoned dart. "With your mother."

"That's not true!" Sally had shouted the denial. "It's not even a year since my father died—and anyway, my mother wouldn't do that!"

"Oh, dear. Oh, Sally, I'm so sorry." Cassie's tone dripped contrition. "I didn't know . . . or I wouldn't have dreamed of coming to you . . . but I was so distraught, so very unhappy," she'd managed another sob. "Because, you see, I'm very much afraid it is true."

"No. No. No." Sally had shaken her head in time with her denials. "Not my mother," she'd wailed, flinging open the door and stumbling out. "Not my mother!" Then, clutching her plaid schoolbag to her chest, she'd taken off at a run.

"A damn fine job of acting," Cassie applauded herself, neatly slotting the car into a space in the motel parking lot. "If I do say so myself."

Twenty-three

Despite Elizabeth's reservations, Sally insisted she felt well enough to go to school on Thursday. And, in fact, other than looking pale and wan, the girl didn't show the usual symptoms of a cold.

In the end, figuring Sally was of an age to know whether she felt up to attending a full day of classes, Elizabeth left the decision to her daughter.

Sally went to school.

Elizabeth went back to her work.

Resolution. It was unfolding rapid-fire within Elizabeth's mind. Not unlike a weaver of threads into cloth, she drew the strands of her plot together, braiding words into a complex pattern interweaving mystery and murder, suspense and sensuality.

It was incredible. It was exhilarating. And the truly amazing thing was, Elizabeth didn't have a clue as to where it all came from. As she worked, the words flowed into her mind, at times so rapidly they collided, tripping over one another. Quite often, sentences would appear on the screen, sentences she had keyed into the computer, and she would look at the words, the concept advanced, in bemusement, thinking, I didn't know that!

Then she would laugh to herself, and go on.

Caught up in the static realm of fictional time, and unaware of the progression of actual time, when the phone rang, she was startled to note that the morning had fled. As it had on Monday, the excitement in De De's voice jolted Elizabeth into the world of reality.

"Elizabeth! I'm joining the ranks of the published!"

"They bought it?" Elizabeth let out a screech worthy of any teenage girl.

"Yes!" De De shouted. "I just got off the phone with my agent. The advance they're offering isn't anything to brag about, but it's a start."

"Oh, De De, that's . . . that's . . . Congratulations!" Elizabeth was every bit as excited as her friend sounded.

"Not only that," De De ran on jubilantly. "The editor asked to see the manuscript I'm wrapping up now."

"Terrific!" Elizabeth laughed, thrilled for her friend. "You're on your way, De De, I just know it."

"Oh, God, I hope so! I'm so excited I can hardly stand it . . . Hell, I can hardly stand still!" She gave a trill of laughter. "But there's more. Gosh, I almost forgot. I told my agent, Lorette Diaz, about you, your story, and she was interested, very interested. She asked me to ask you to send her a partial—three chapters or so—for her to consider."

"Oh, De De, thank you," Elizabeth said emotionally, a sudden mist of tears stinging her eyes. "Thank you for everything."

"You're welcome," De De replied. "But I really didn't do anything to be thanked for."

"Oh," Elizabeth murmured through her clogged throat, "I can never thank you enough. You've done so much, so very much for me, not the least of which was becoming my friend in the first place." She was thinking that De De had introduced her to Jake.

"Oh, Elizabeth, now you've got me crying, so I'm going to end this tear fest." De De sniffled. "Besides, I've still got a bunch of people to call. Talk to you soon."

"You'd better," Elizabeth warned, swiping tears from her cheek. "I want to hear how you fare with your parents this weekend."

Too wound up after they finally said goodbye to get back to work, Elizabeth stared at the phone for some time, tempted but uncertain; she had never once placed a call to Jake.

A grim smile on his face, Jake ruthlessly, gorily killed off the villain of his story. Now, all that was left to do was the mopping up, he thought, elation soaring inside him.

The phone rang—again.

Jake made a rude noise, thought the hell with it, then, just in case it might be De De again, he snatched up the receiver and growled into it.

"Jake?"

Hearing Elizabeth's voice had an exciting, shocking effect on him. Not until that moment had he realized how very badly he'd needed to hear it.

"Hi, Liz," he murmured, fully aware his tone conveyed—betrayed—the depth of his feelings. "You've heard from De De, I presume?"

Her laughter strummed his senses, and played hell with his libido.

"Yes. Isn't it wonderful?"

"It is. Now, after hearing the delight and pride in her voice, do you understand why I refused to rob her of that thrill?"

"Yes, but I did understand before . . ." She hesitated, then admitted, "After I thought about it."

"You're incredible, Liz. One of a kind."

"Are you buttering me up?" she replied, teasingly. "For the weekend?"

"Ah, the weekend," he crooned. "Have you made arrangements for Sally?"

"Oh! Oh, Jake, I forgot," she said in despair. "Sally's not feeling too well. She thinks she's catching a cold. We may have to cancel this weekend."

"Cancel?" he repeated, startled by the sense of desolation her remark sent through him, desolation and desperation. "Look, Liz, why don't I come down anyway." He frowned at the urgency in his voice, but continued, "Sally must

be told about us sooner or later. I believe
sooner would be better, much better."

"Oh, Jake, I don't know." Uncertainty under-
scored her words. "It hasn't even been a year
yet since . . ." Her voice trailed away.

Suddenly afraid that she also might trail
away—from him—he said decisively, "I'm coming down, either way."

She argued.

He remained adamant.

She finally agreed.

He breathed normally again.

Jake had no sooner hung up the receiver
when the words he'd spoken aloud earlier echoed in his mind.

One of a kind.

Elizabeth embodied everything any sane man
could wish for in a woman, and gut instinct
assured him that she was his, probably for the
asking.

But, did he have the guts to ask?

He had been hurt, deeply hurt by one woman.
Did that mean every woman had to pay for the
injury? Jake asked himself. Come to that, did it
mean he had to continue paying, denying himself a normal life, perhaps a family, for one
woman's greed and selfishness?

The wound inflicted had not healed, Jake
knew, but he knew as well that in the guise of
self-protection, he had allowed it to fester all
these years.

All the hurting and hiding aside, Jake acknowledged that here and now the bottom line was:

Could he bear to lose Elizabeth?

Elizabeth fretted all afternoon about Jake's stated intention to come for the weekend, wondering whether Sally would stay with her grandmother or remain at home. Too frazzled and distracted to continue working, she shut down her machine, only to wander aimlessly around the house, looking for something to do to occupy her hands and mind.

Sally herself solved Elizabeth's emotional dilemma mere minutes after returning from school.

"I'm in the kitchen, honey," Elizabeth called when she heard her daughter come in. Taking refuge in cooking, she thought, in the hope of feeding the nerve beast.

"I'm going to my room," Sally called back listlessly. "I'll be down in a little while."

Elizabeth heard her mount the stairs . . . without bothering to wait for a response.

Some ten minutes or so later, just as Elizabeth was on the verge of following her to her room to ask if she was feeling any better, Sally walked into the kitchen.

The girl's appearance caused a sharp flare of concern to skitter through Elizabeth. Sally had an evasive, almost furtive look about her.

"May I spend the weekend with Grammom?" she asked abruptly, rather belligerently. "I just talked to her on the phone, and she said she'd take me to the plex, to see the movie I've been waiting for. It opens tonight." She paused to take a breath, then charged on before Elizabeth could get a word in. "Grammom said she'd take me shopping tomorrow, too."

"Do you feel up to it?" Elizabeth asked, feeling more than a little ashamed for her relief at not yet having to face the trauma of introducing Jake to her daughter.

Sally shrugged. "I'm all right. Maybe I just got a touch of Janice's cold." She smiled, almost.

It looked forced to Elizabeth. Nevertheless, an image of Jake filling her mind, warming her blood, stirring her senses, she grasped at the reprieve and gave her permission.

Jake rang the doorbell at exactly seven-thirty, precisely when he'd said he would. His greeting was the same.

"Hi."

Strangely, he seemed disappointed rather than relieved when Elizabeth told him that, after all, Sally had gone to spend the weekend with her grandmother.

This time, Jake didn't get the chance to immediately sweep her into his arms and then into bed.

"I spent hours preparing a meal, Mr. Ruttenburg," she informed him, holding him off when he moved to embrace her. "And you're going to help me eat it."

They had a slow, leisurely dinner, and then Jake swept Elizabeth off to bed for some slow, leisurely lovemaking, then more and more.

"After the feast for the palates," Jake murmured, sending thrills chasing through Elizabeth as he trailed his tongue up the inside of her thigh. "A feast for the senses," he promised, wrenching a gasp of pleasure from her with his shockingly exciting intimate kiss.

Divorced from the worries and concerns of everyday life, Elizabeth soared, free of constraints and inhibitions. Loving Jake with her heart and mind and soul, she gave of herself by ministering to him with her caresses, her kisses, her gliding tongue, her willing mouth.

"I'm hungry."

"Why am I not surprised?" Elizabeth asked, laughing. It was mid afternoon on Saturday, they had not eaten since Friday evening. "I'm hungry, too."

"Good, let's hustle." Jake tossed back the covers and stood up, grinning at her from the side of the bed. "Come on, Liz, I'll race you to the shower."

Showering required an inordinate amount of time.

Finally, with Jake attired in jeans and skin, and Elizabeth's nudity concealed beneath the folds of a velour robe, they worked together in the kitchen fixing scrambled eggs and toast. While devouring the food with their mouths, they devoured each other with their eyes.

The instant they finished cleaning up, Jake pulled Elizabeth into his arms.

"Dessert," he whispered against her lips. His hands moved down her back, flattening her breasts to his chest, molding her hips to his. And then, smiling at the feel of her responsive tremor, he fused his mouth to hers.

"Oh, God, it's true!"

Alarm shot through Elizabeth at hearing the anguished sound Sally made. She and Jake moved simultaneously, pulling apart, their eyes flying to the kitchen archway.

Sally stood just inside the room, her grandmother a half step behind her, their eyes wide, Sally's filled with pained disillusionment, Ella's with contempt.

"Sally . . ." Elizabeth took a step, her trembling hand outstretched.

The frantic-looking girl gave a sharp shake of the head, and cringed from Elizabeth's touch.

"It's true . . . I didn't believe her, didn't want to believe her. But I heard you say his name on the phone; that's why I asked Grammom to bring me home. To see if he was here, with you. And I didn't believe her!" Her voice was ragged, shattered.

Her? Elizabeth shot a furious look at her mother-in-law. The elder Ella returned it with

one of disdain, then shook her head in denial
of the silent accusation.

Elizabeth felt Jake's arm slide around her
waist, felt his hand press against her side in silent support. His gesture sent Sally into a
frenzy.

"She told me!" she shouted, tears streaming
down her pale face. "She told me my mother—
you—were having an affair with *him.*" Her lips
curled over the word. "Jake Ruttenburg, her
fiancé, the man she was going to marry."

"What?" Jake yelped. "Who told you that?"

"Yeah, right. Pretend you don't know," Sally
said insolently, giving him a look of such hatred
it should have curled his fingers and toes. It
didn't.

"A name, Sally," Jake said with soft intimida-
tion. "Her name. I want to hear it."

Sally thrust out her chin, glaring at him in
defiance.

"Sally, tell us who this person is," Elizabeth
ordered in her sternest I'm-not-kidding tone.

"Cassandra."

"Who?" Jake turned a perplexed look on
Elizabeth.

Recalling, too clearly, the praises Sally had
sung of the woman's beauty, her charm, and
remembering his reputation as a womanizer,
Elizabeth suddenly felt sick.

"Perhaps you'd better tell us . . . who," she
said, moving from his encircling arm.

Jake frowned, his expression one of utter bafflement, and then he swore. "Damnit, Eliza-

beth, I haven't a clue who in hell this woman might be."

"I told you," Sally shouted. "Her name's Cassandra—Cassandra Metcalf!"

"Metcalf?" Jake swung around like an enraged bull and fixed a hard stare on Sally. "Metcalf?" he repeated. At the girl's quick nod, he hissed, "Cassie."

"You do know her," Elizabeth whispered, raising a hand to her trembling lips as she backed away from him. "Are you engaged to be married to her?"

"Are you crazy?" Jake exploded. "I swore I'd never make that kind of commitment again, and especia—" He broke off, at that instant aware of what he was saying, of the expression now on Elizabeth's face. "Liz . . ." He held a hand out to her; she sidestepped. "Listen, let me—"

"You've said enough." She drew a breath and banished the expression revealing pain; she'd deal with the pain later. Now she had a vicious woman to deal with—and a man without morals to eject from her home and life. "I want you to go, Jake."

The coolness of her tone appeared to jolt him. "Go? Go where?"

She smiled.

He flinched.

"I really don't care." She hurt inside as she watched the color drain from his face. "You can go home. Or you can go to hell. It makes no difference to me."

"Liz, please, will you just listen?" Again, he held out a hand; she ignored it.

Brushing past him, she headed for the archway. "You will stay right here in the house," she said to Sally, in a hard, determined tone that had the girl quickly nodding in agreement. As Elizabeth drew alongside Ella, she paused to ask, "Will you stay with Sally until I return?" When the older woman also mutely nodded, she said, "And I'd appreciate it if you would see Mr. Ruttenburg out."

"With pleasure," Ella said triumphantly. "But may I ask where you're going?"

"To see a woman about a child," Elizabeth answered in a voice tight with anger. *"My* child."

Thirty-odd minutes later, Elizabeth strode to the motel reception desk. In a tone that carefully concealed the anger seething inside her, she requested that the clerk announce her to Ms. Cassandra Metcalf.

"You may go right up, Mrs. Leninger," he said a few seconds later, giving her the suite number as he replaced the house-phone receiver.

Cassandra met Elizabeth at the door to the suite and invited her inside. A satisfied smile curved her lips.

The woman was beautiful, Elizabeth acknowledged that, experiencing a sinking sensation.

"Well, we meet at last," Cassie said, her smile turning superior. "Sally has told me so much about you."

While dressing, Elizabeth had determined to retain the cool, calm self-containment De De had insisted she possessed. But Cassandra's snide remark ignited the explosion De De had also predicted.

Fury raced through Elizabeth, propelling her forward, slowly; and with each measured step, she whiplashed the retreating woman with sharp words of warning.

"I don't know what kind of twisted game you're playing, Cassandra—or Cassie or whoever you really are. And I don't want to know. But I'll tell you this, you're a pitiful excuse for a human being and your game is over, finished. If not, I will personally finish *you*. Do I make myself clear?"

Cassie glared at her, but took a step back. "How dare you! Are you threatening me?" Her tone was scathing; her eyes showed she was scared.

"Yes. Big time," Elizabeth gritted out, continuing to stalk the woman. "How well, I wonder, would you survive a child-harassment suit?"

"Don't be naive," Cassie retorted, retreating another step. "I can afford the best lawyers." Her laughter held the ring of fear. "You couldn't win."

Elizabeth smiled, in quite the same way she had recently smiled at Jake.

Cassie winced, exactly as Jake had.

"Ah, but you see, I wouldn't have to win the suit," Elizabeth said. "You would lose your reputation, in any case."

Cassie laughed, a little wildly. "Do you think that frightens me? After four husbands and countless lovers, I haven't got much of a reputation *to* lose."

Elizabeth was sickened by the woman's blatant admission, but she didn't let it show. She kept on, her voice low, menacing. "Perhaps, but could what is left of your reputation, your character, withstand the smear of a charge of harassing a teenage girl?" she asked, baring her teeth. "And all that unsavory sexual misconduct I would make certain went into the record?"

"I never—" Cassie's eyes went wide in horror.

"Perhaps," Elizabeth repeated, favoring her with a deadly smile. "But, you see, the bitch of it is, once accusations and charges are flung, they tend to stick . . . like shit."

Cassie Metcalf was completely vanquished.

Twenty-four

It was late February. It was sleeting. The weather matched Elizabeth's mood. Dreary. She was depressed, for a number of reasons. She had just rebuffed Jake's latest—the ump-teenth—attempt to talk to her. Sally, having accused her of betraying her father, was remote and resentful. And, as if she didn't have enough problems, after two weeks of morning sickness, she suspected she was pregnant.

Some women have all the luck, she mused, feeling sorry for herself. Yet, she couldn't deny the tiny thrill the suspicion of pregnancy gave her.

Jake's child. If not the father, at least the child.

So, miserable after closing her ears, and her heart, to Jake's plea to let him explain and then hanging up on him, the very last thing Elizabeth needed or wanted was another phone call . . . from anybody—except the agent to whom De De had told her to ship a chunk of her manuscript in January.

"I've got an offer for you, Elizabeth," Lorette

Diaz said. "The money's a pittance, almost an insult, but—"

"It's a beginning," Elizabeth finished for her, temporarily lifted out of her depression. "And I'll take it."

Under the circumstances, after telling Sally the news—thankfully she responded with warm congratulations—Elizabeth naturally forgot her aversion to the phone.

She called her parents in Florida. She called Ella at college. She called De De. The only person she didn't call was the one she wanted most to tell.

She sat staring at the phone, her eyes misty, when the thing suddenly rang, startling her.

"Congratulations, Liz, I knew you would do it." Jake's soft voice was a balm to her wounded spirits.

"De De called you?" She fought to keep the tremor from her voice; she lost the battle.

"Yes. She's so happy for you. We're both happy for you," he amended.

"Thank you." Elizabeth shrugged, even though he couldn't see her. "The advance isn't great."

"The amount doesn't matter. The money will get better, because you're good and you'll get better."

The mist in her eyes turned to rain; it poured down her face. "Oh, Jake," she moaned, a sob escaping her. "I . . . I'm sorry I hung up on you before."

"I'm coming down there," he said urgently.

"And I'm going to talk to you, and you're going to listen." He paused, waiting. When she didn't respond because she couldn't speak for crying, he said, "Do you hear me?"

"Yes . . . Yes, Jake, I hear . . . you." She was defeated by her need to see him, the emptiness inside her from missing him. "And . . . I'll listen . . . this time."

"Good." He exhaled, as if he'd been holding his breath. "You can expect me in a couple of hours."

"I'll be here."

Elizabeth suffered a few moments of doubt, of anxiety about how Sally might react to her having Jake in the house. Then her resolve hardened, and she set such upsetting thoughts aside.

I am the adult in the house, she reminded herself. Sally is the child.

As expected, Sally's recently voiced happiness reverted to resentment. Indignant, disapproving, she stormed up to her bedroom, making a production of slamming the door and locking it.

Elizabeth was getting pretty fed up with her daughter's moodiness. She considered following Sally and reading her the riot act, but decided to hold her peace. At least until after she had heard Jake's piece.

And then Jake was standing in her foyer, looking beat, hollow-eyed . . . and wonderful.

Elizabeth had missed him so badly. She loved

him so much, she was hard pressed not to fling
herself into his arms and beg *him* to forgive *her.*

She did no such thing, of course. Her facade
of composure intact, she invited him inside,
took his jacket, offered him coffee. He accepted.

When they were seated at the table, steaming
cups of the brew in front of them, Elizabeth
gazed into his velvet blue eyes, and waited for
him to begin.

Once he started, Jake talked rapidly, as if his
very life depended upon what he had to say.
He told her about his marriage; the agony he
had suffered on learning his wife had destroyed
their child, the bitterness he had carried with
him after ending their union, the vow he had
made to never again allow himself to be taken
in, to be used by a woman.

Elizabeth's stomach did a quick flip-flop
when he mentioned his baby, but she was too
caught up in his recitation to interrupt.

When he had finished, she maintained her
steady regard of him and asked him point-
blank about Cassandra/Cassie Metcalf.

"I met her while I was visiting friends in Arizona last fall, after the book tour."

Elizabeth had a swift recollection of De De
mentioning that he was headed for Arizona.

"My friends celebrated their wedding anniversary with a Halloween party. Cassie was
there. We danced." He sighed, and smiled in
self-derision. "I hadn't been with a woman in
about six months. She turned me on."

Elizabeth's composure slipped a tad; she bit her lip.

Jake reached across the table to grasp her hands; it was the first time he had dared to touch her. "Nothing happened, Liz." The urgency was back in his voice. "There were a few kisses. I was tempted. I admit that. I was hungry, and I *was* tempted. But I didn't take what was offered."

"Why?" Elizabeth was curious, then honest. "Forget I asked. I have no right. What you did or didn't do before we . . . were together is none of my business."

"You're right, it isn't." Jake smiled, a faint but genuine smile. "But I'll tell you why. At the last minute, an image formed in my mind, an image of a woman I'd recently met. A woman elegant, reserved, beautiful. The woman I really wanted."

"Oh, Jake," Elizabeth whispered, blinking against the hot tears welling in her eyes.

"I walked away from Cassie, left her lying there in her room, hot and ready for sex. She swore at me, swore that I'd be sorry. She was right. I am sorry." His hands tightened, crushing hers. "I'll be even sorrier if you turn me away." He swallowed, blinked, blurted out, "Don't turn me away, Liz. I love you. I need you in my life."

Elizabeth was crying openly, but there was something she had to say, quickly, before she lost her nerve. "But do you love me—need me—enough?" she asked. "Will you marry me, Jake?"

"Hey, Liz, that's my line," he said, releasing her hand to brush the tears from her face. "It was the closing line of my defense. Will *you* marry *me*?"

"Yes, Jake, I will."

Chairs scraped against the floor. The table was jostled. And then they were in each other's arms, laughing together, crying together, loving each other.

Later, when Elizabeth was curled up beside Jake on the sofa, supposedly watching TV, she dredged up the courage to confide her suspicion to him.

"Jake, I don't wish to spoil the moment," she said tentatively, "But . . . I think I may be . . . ah, pregnant."

He went stone-still, scaring the breath out of her, and then he laughed, a joyous, wonderful laugh.

Relief washed through Elizabeth. It would be all right. Everything would be all right. Even Sally. She was young. She'd come around. It would work. Elizabeth vowed she would make it work.

There might be difficult times, she thought, gazing misty-eyed at Jake, loving him. But it would be worth it. Happiness was worth the work it demanded.

Epilogue

Her labor was hard. The delivery difficult. But the long hours of work and strain had been worth the reward.

Elizabeth's son was beautiful and, thank God, perfectly formed and healthy.

Exhausted but elated, she lay propped up in the narrow hospital bed, unmindful of the late November rainstorm rattling the windows. Enchanted, she stared down in adoration at the tiny face of her hours-old son. Even in sleep, he was the image of his father.

The door to her room opened and Jake slipped inside. He looked as tired as Elizabeth felt. And why not? she thought. He had worked almost as hard as she, coaching her, telling her when and how to breathe, supporting her right through the delivery . . . and the necessary stitching up afterward.

He smiled, easing the tracks of strain on his face. Bending to her, he kissed her mouth and then his son's forehead.

"I spoke to your mother," he said softly, caressing the baby's tiny hand with a fingertip. "They're flying in tomorrow. De De and Beau will be bringing my mother tomorrow. Mary-anne and George will be here, also tomorrow." He smiled again. "But, tonight, for just a few minutes, I have a couple of visitors who insist on seeing you."

Turning, he walked to the door, opened it, and escorted her daughters into the room. Ella almost cried when she saw with her own eyes that her mother was all right. Rushing forward, she kissed Elizabeth's cheek.

Sally, still suffering pangs of guilt and re-morse for the trouble and upset she had caused Elizabeth and Jake until recently, hung back near to the door, as if thinking herself unfit to approach her mother and the infant.

As he had mere weeks before, when he'd fi-nally taken matters—and Sally—in hand, point-ing out a few home truths because he could no longer bear to witness Elizabeth's despair over the girl's attitude, Jake once again took command of the awkward situation.

Without uttering a word, he walked to the side of the bed and lifted his son from Eliza-beth's arms. He exchanged a quick, under-standing smile with Ella, then turned to cross the room to Sally. Her eyes widened in confu-sion, but before she could speak, he held the sleeping baby out, placing him in the arms she raised automatically.

"Hey, Adam," he said, loudly enough for all to hear, but softly enough not to wake the child. "don't you want to wake up and say hello to your sister?"

"Hello, Adam," Sally whispered, choking on her tears. "Your sister loves you. We all love you."

A few months later, on a Saturday afternoon in early March, content and happily listening to her husband and daughters laugh together as they fussed over the gurgling baby, Elizabeth stared out the window at the late winter snowfall. She smiled, serene with the knowledge that beneath the mantle of white, the promise of another spring stirred with renewing life deep within the bare branches of her favorite forsythia bushes.

About the Author

Joan Hohl is an award-winning multi-published author with over ten million copies of her romances in print. She lives with her family in eastern Pennsylvania and is currently working on her next mainstream contemporary romance, I DO, which will be published by Zebra Books in December 2001.

Joan loves hearing from her readers and you may write to her c/o Zebra Books. Please include a self-addressed stamped envelope if you wish a response.

Put a Little Romance in Your Life With
Joan Hohl

Put a Little Romance in Your Life With
Fern Michaels